It was as if she had conjured him . . .

Colonel Chattan stood in the door wearing his great coat. His eyes were two hard shards of light.

For a second, her heart quit beating.

He walked toward her. Portia wanted to take a step back. To run.

She couldn't move.

He moved into the circle of lamp light surrounding her, stopping when they were almost toe-to-toe. He placed his hands on her upper arms, lifting her until she stood on the tips of her toes. He stared into her eyes as if he could read her very soul.

She started shaking. He was too close, too powerful, too strong, too driven.

The air about them seemed to change, to grow warmer.

He was so close to her that she could see every line in his face and the color deep in his eyes. He was handsome. Noble. A man unlike any other.

A man who every woman wished to kiss.

A man who had captured her imagination in a way she'd not believed possible.

A man who brought his lips down on hers . . .

Cathy Maxwell

THE SCOTTISH WITCH

THE CHATTAN CURSE

AVON

An Imprint of HarperCollins*Publishers*

AVON BOOKS
An Imprint of HarperCollins*Publishers*
10 East 53rd Street
New York, New York 10022-5299

Copyright © 2012 by Catherine Maxwell, Inc.
Excerpt from *The Devil's Heart* copyright © 2013 by Catherine Maxwell, Inc.
ISBN 978-1-62090-592-0

For my agent, Robin Rue

The Curse

Macnachtan Keep
Scotland, 1632

The heart cannot lie, or so she had believed.

Day after day, Rose of the Macnachtan stood at the tower wall staring in the direction of England, believing with all her heart Charles Chattan would return to her. At any moment she expected to see him ride galloping at full speed to Loch Awe's shoreline to cross to the island on which Macnachtan Keep had been built and anxiously apologize.

He could not marry that Englishwoman. *He wouldn't.* She knew it to the marrow of her bones. Charlie loved her. They'd handfasted in a private ceremony of their own making. He would come for her.

Her brothers and sisters all warned her he was faithless. They had never liked him. His mother was Sassenach, and Charlie was too English for their tastes. Her brother Michael had sworn to her that the Chattans worshipped gold more than any other value on this earth, but Rose had argued Charles was different from his parents.

And so she waited, days turning into weeks . . . until, finally, it was the very hour of his marriage to the Englishwoman.

Rose stood at her lonely post, watching the road from the south, waiting—until the bell in the kirk's tower rang noon.

Only then did she realize her family had been right. Charles *had* chosen another over her.

The last clang of the bell reverberated in the air around her. The wind had picked up. It lifted her hair, swirled around her skirts, tickled her skin, mocked her.

For a long moment she stood mesmerized by the line of silent, brooding pines ringing the clearing. She knew every trail of that forest. There was no movement, no rider coming for her.

Her heart broke.

The world lost all meaning.

No one could live with the burden of such sharp, forlorn pain.

His name choked her throat. Shame of her own trusting loyalty filled her. They had all been right and she had been a fool.

Rose slowly turned. Below her was the stone courtyard. Her brother Michael was shoeing a horse. The blacksmith had died and his son was a poor substitute. Michael was determined to not give up on the boy, even if he had to shoe the horses a hundred times himself in teaching the lad what he wanted.

Across the way, in the house's solar, she knew her mother, sisters, and kinswomen would be plying their needles and enjoying a bit of gossip. How long had it been since she'd joined them? Not since that night she and Charles had secretly met and he'd told her he was leaving Scotland. His parents insisted he marry the Sassenach heiress. He had no choice in the matter.

"But what of us? What of the vows we made to each other?" she had asked.

Charles had not answered. Instead, he'd made love to her, and, trusting soul that she was, she had believed that *was* his answer. She was his mate, his chosen.

Her hand rose to her belly. His seed might already be growing within her. A son, a son whose father would deny his parentage.

Rose shared her mother's gift of the sight. The book of spells and recipes that had been handed down from mother to daughter, always going to those who shared the gift, would one day be hers—but she'd already used that book. In desperation, she'd attempted a spell to bring Charles to her and she had believed it would work . . .

Sometimes in life, there comes a point when the future holds no gain. When the darkness of reality triumphs over hopes and dreams. Love had betrayed her. It had humiliated her.

The pride of the Macnachtan of Loch Awe flowed through her veins. Rose could not face a life of shame, or let it be whispered her child was a bastard.

She climbed onto the tower wall. For one precious moment, she stood tall. March's fresh, chilled wind chafed her cheek. Below her, life went on as usual.

Rose glanced one more time toward the road that lay between herself and her love.

Her heart *had* lied—Charles *did not* love her. "Life come hither; Life is mine," she whispered feverishly. Her throat tightened. *He hadn't cared.* Tears filled her eyes. She took a step off the wall into thin air.

She fell.

There was no doubt Rose of Loch Awe had taken her life because of Charles Chattan's perfidy. There would be no saving her memory from the disgrace of suicide.

Her mother, Fenella, wished she had the magic to reverse time and bring her daughter back to life.

For the last three days she'd pored over her nain's book. Certainly in all these receipts and spells for healing, for fortune, for doubts and fears, there must be one to cast off death.

The handwriting on those yellowed pages was cramped and in many places faded. Fenella had signed the front of the book but not referred to it often, at least not once she'd memorized the cures for fevers and agues that plagued children and concerned mothers.

She'd been surprised to discover Rose had also been reading the book. She'd found where Rose had written the name "Charles" beside a spell to find true love. It called for a rose thorn to be embedded in the wax of a candle and burned on the night of a full moon.

They found a piece of the burned candle, the thorn still intact, its tip charred, beneath Rose's pillow.

Fenella held the wax in the palm of her hand. Slowly, she closed her fingers around it into a fist and set aside mourning.

Grief made her mad.

The Chattans were far from the Highland's mountains and moors. Charles thought himself safe. He was not.

There is no sacred ground for a suicide, but Fenella had no need of the church. She ordered a funeral pyre to be built for her daughter along the green banks of Loch Awe, directly beneath a stony crag that looked down upon the shore.

On the day of Rose's funeral, Fenella stood upon that crag, waiting for the sun to set. She wore the Macnachtan tartan around her shoulders. The evening wind toyed with her gray hair that she wore loose under a circlet of gold, gray hair that had once been as fair as Rose's.

At Fenella's signal, her sons set ablaze the ring of bonfires she'd ordered constructed around Rose's pyre. The flames leaped to life, and so did her anger.

Did Chattan think he could hide in London? Did his father believe his son could betray Rose's loving heart without penalty? That her life had no meaning?

That Macnachtan honor was a small thing?

"I want him to feel my pain," Fenella whispered.

Her daughters Ilona and Aislin stood by her side. They nodded.

"He will not escape me," Fenella vowed.

"But he is gone," Ilona said. "He has become a fine lord while we are left to weep."

At last the moon was high in the sky and the bonfires' flames were hot and strong. They feasted on the wood, making it crackle and sending sparks and ash into the air.

The time was right. Nain had said a witch knows when the hour is nigh—and this would be a night no one would forget. Ever.

Especially the Chattans.

The fires had drawn the curious from all over the countryside. They stood on the shore watching. Fenella raised her hand. Her clansmen and her kin fell silent. Her son Michael, laird of the Macnachtans, picked up the torch and held it ready.

Fenella brought her hand down, and her oldest put fire to the tender of his sister's funeral pyre.

'Twas the ancient way. There was no priest here, no clergy to call her out—and even if there was, Fenella's power in this moment was too strong to be swayed. It coursed through her. It was the beating of her heart, the pulsing in the blood in her veins, the sinew of her being.

She stepped to the edge of the rock and stared down over the burning pyre. The flames licked the skirt of Rose's white funeral gown.

"My Rose died of love," she said. She whispered the words but then repeated them with a commanding strength. They carried on the wind and seemed to linger over Loch Awe's moonlit waters. "A woman's lot is hard," she said. " 'Tis love that gives us courage, gives us strength. My Rose gave the precious gift of her love to a man unworthy of it."

Heads nodded agreement. There was not a soul around who had not been touched by Rose. They all knew her gift of laughter, her kindness, her willingness to offer what help she could to others.

Fenella reached a hand back. Ilona placed the staff that Fenella had ordered hewn from a yew tree and banded with copper.

"I curse Charles Chattan."

Raising the staff, Fenella said, "I curse not just Chattan but his line. He betrayed her for a title. He tossed aside handfasted promises for greed. Now let him learn what his duplicity has wrought."

The moon seemed to brighten. The flames on the fires danced higher, and Fenella knew she was being summoned. *Danse macabre.* All were equal in death.

She spoke, her voice ringing in the night.

"Watchers of the threshold, Watchers of the gate, open hell and seal Chattan's fate.

"When a Chattan male falls in love, strike his heart with fire from Above.

"Crush his heart, destroy his line;

"Only then will justice be mine."

Fenella threw her staff down upon her daughter's funeral pyre. The flames now consumed Rose. Fenella could feel their heat, smell her daughter's scent—and she threw herself off the rock, following her staff to where it lay upon Rose's breast. She grabbed her daughter's burning body and clung fast.

Together they left this world.

*S*ix months to the date after his wedding, Charles Chattan died. His heart stopped. He was sitting at his table, accepting congratulations from his dinner guests over the news his wife was breeding, when he fell facedown onto his plate.

The news of his death shocked many. He was so young. A vital, handsome man with so much to live for. Had he not recently declared to many of his friends that he'd fallen in love with his new wife? How could God cut short his life, especially when he was so happy?

The only clue to his being unwell was that he had complained of a burning sensation in his left arm. It had been uncomfortable but his physician could find nothing wrong with him.

However, Chattan's marriage was not in vain. Seven months after his death, his wife bore a son to carry on the Chattan name . . . a son who also bore a curse.

And so it continued. They tried to stop the curse. Generation after generation attempted to break the witch's spell, and did not succeed.

Such was the power of Fenella.

Prologue

Camber Hall
Glenfinnan, Scotland
November 15, 1814

What had started as a gentle mist was turning into sheets of rain when they least needed it.

Portia Maclean charged up the attic stairs in a race against the leaks in the roof.

"Cold, drafty, leaky house," she muttered, stomping on each step in her frustration. There were two buckets up there that were probably full from the rain the day before. She had been hoping she could put off the chore of emptying them. Now she was on a race against Nature.

The attic was not her favorite place. It smelled of must and was full of wooden boxes, crates, trunks and old furniture from what seemed to be centuries of previous tenants.

Portia could not stand the smell of dirt and decay and she hated cobwebs. She always held her breath when she came up here and prayed she never saw any of the spiders she knew had to be lurking in the rafters. Spiders that watched her, waiting for an opportunity to *jump* down upon her.

A shiver went through her at the thought, or at imagining any of the other multiple-legged creatures that lurked with those spiders.

The first bucket was close to the staircase and was, as she had suspected, almost full. She pushed the bridge of her wire spectacles up her nose, waved away a wet cobweb dangling from the ceiling, and picked up the bucket handle with both hands. She lugged it to the small window overlooking the front drive. Humidity had swollen the wood—again—so she had to give the sash a few pounds of her fist for it to open.

She poured the water out, returned the bucket to its place and went in search of the other in the far corner where the attic was darkest, even in the afternoon.

Anxious to finish this unpleasant task so she could return to the fire in the kitchen, Portia wound her way around the accumulated boxes, trunks, tables and crates toward the steady drip of water dropping into the bucket. Here was where the roof leak was the worst.

Portia found the bucket and made quick work of emptying it, closing the window when she was done. She was hurrying to place the bucket back under the leak when a streak of white blazed across her path.

She stumbled backward in surprise, reaching out for the first available surface to catch her balance, and ended up tipping a precarious stack of junk down onto her. She fell to the floor in a crash of wood and billows of dust.

Coughing, Portia needed a moment to grasp what had happened to her and to be certain she was all right. The noise of her fall had been so loud, she was surprised her mother and her sister hadn't heard and come to check on her.

Instead, all was quiet save for the rain on the roof. Her younger sister, Minnie, was probably down in the kitchen, and their mother . . . well, Lady Maclean might be in the bedroom almost directly below where Portia was now, but rarely stirred herself for anyone.

Portia wiggled her toes and her fingers. Nothing was broken. She was all right . . . but what had that flash of white been? She was a practical woman and not given to flights of fancy, well, other than her very reasonable distaste of bugs. If she saw something, then there was something. But before she could investigate, she needed to dig herself out of this mess.

She shoved a wooden crate off her legs. It had been filled with old shoes, clothes and hats, none of it salvageable. She and Minnie had already investigated the attic last June when they'd first moved in. She lifted the box and set it on top of a trunk and was just turning to pick up the empty bucket off the floor, when a book fell onto the floor right in front of her.

A book. There were never enough books to read in the house. It was a heavy, leather-bound book and so aged, the binding was falling off its spine. Portia forgot about the bucket and the leaks. She took the book and hurried back to the window so she could inspect it better in the light.

The book was handwritten. The paper was yellow and brittle. She had to be careful with it. There were pages and pages of writing. Perhaps poetry? She adored poetry—

"It's recipes," she said, disappointed. She frowned again, attempting to decipher the faded handwriting. Yes, recipes, but not the sort she was familiar with. "How to remove warts," she read and then curled her lip in distaste at the instructions to make a mash of onions and potatoes and apply to the wart for no less than ten days. "The whole poultice will stink after that period of time," she mumbled to herself. She turned a few more pages, and her imagination was captured. There were recipes for strawberry wine and what to say when surrounded by a toadstool ring to protect one's self against evil. Who would have imagined toadstool rings were evil?

" 'Queen of the Meadow, take this evil from this house,' " Portia chanted and then hummed her disbelief. She wasn't superstitious. Toadstool rings were toadstool rings. They harbored no magic, or at least not the ones she tromped through.

She flipped more pages and found one that was wrinkled and the ink smeared as if someone had shed tears over the recipe titled, "To Reclaim True Love." The word "Charles" had been written in the margin. The name wasn't in the same handwriting as the recipe, so perhaps this spell had been used. Perhaps some woman, years earlier, had pined for Charles.

Portia wondered if, after the spell, he'd come back to her. And if he'd been worth it!

Love was a mystery to Portia. Her sister was in love with Mr. Oliver Tolliver, the valley's physician, but who knew what would become of it.

Right now, Minnie was pining because Mr. Tolliver had not called in three days. Portia thought the man was busy with his duties. A doctor was always at the beck and call of his patients, and she'd told Minnie as much. Minnie was not convinced. She feared he had lost interest.

Portia herself had never been in love, and after witnessing Minnie's miserableness waiting for Mr. Tolliver these past few days, was grateful to have been spared. Then again, her father had taught her well that men could be selfish creatures with no thought of using women and then discarding them. After all, wasn't that what he'd done with his own family?

Of course, since she was seven and twenty and lacked a dowry, the likelihood of Portia ever marrying was long past. She was a penniless spinster, an old maid. She'd made her peace with it.

That didn't mean that she didn't find this love spell fascinating—

Her thought broke off with insight. Love spell? Yes, this was a book of spells.

Fascinated, Portia flipped through more pages. The toadstool chant wasn't the only spell that made her chuckle. There were spells to rid a house of demons—she should share these with Reverend Ogilvy—and to keep people she didn't like from crossing her path. She wondered if she could use that on the daughter of her landlord the duke. The very pampered and petty Lady Emma, daughter of the Duke of Moncrieffe, had lorded over the valley as the reigning beauty until the Macleans had arrived. Minnie had usurped her place, and Lady Emma was not happy.

On the inside front cover page of the book was a list of women's names. Most were unreadable. However, the last one on the list caught Portia's eye. *Fenella*. If ever there was a witch's name, Fenella was one.

At that moment, Portia's musings were interrupted by the sound of a small meow.

Portia cocked her head, unsure if she had heard correctly. How could a cat find its way into the attic?

As if answering her question, a small white cat climbed onto the lid of a trunk close to Portia's right hand.

Or at least she thought it was a cat. The body, tail, and sweet face were all catlike. However, the ears were different. They folded over, giving her head a flat roundness, much like the shape of an owl's.

The ears weren't the animal's only different feature. She had the largest, most expressive eyes

Portia had ever seen on a kitty. They, too, were owlish in expression: all-knowing, all-wise . . . with a touch of almost human understanding.

Portia shook her head, thinking she was being far too fanciful now.

The cat jumped to the floor. She walked around Portia's skirts and rubbed her face in them, purring softly.

Portia was charmed. She set the book aside and picked the animal up. Kitty weighed next to nothing. "So you are the culprit for the knot on my head." Portia smiled and the cat seemed to smile in return. "What beautiful eyes you have, kitty."

The cat closed her eyes and rubbed her cheek against Portia's hand, begging for a pet.

"Would you like some milk?"

Those expressive eyes came open. The cat made a sound that could only be interpreted as agreement and leaped down from Portia's arms. She trotted to the stairs before turning as if to ask Portia if she was coming.

"I suppose you do," Portia said with a laugh. "But wait. I must put this bucket in place."

She carried the bucket to the corner of the attic. The cat waited for her to finish the chore, taking a moment to gracefully groom herself.

A pet was exactly what Portia needed. She and

Minnie had never had one. Her mother wasn't fond of animals.

But they were in Scotland now, her father's ancestral home. Their lives had changed in so many ways . . . so perhaps it was time they had a pet. Besides, Lady Maclean left her room only for church and visitors, so keeping the cat a secret would not be that difficult.

Portia walked to the stairs and sat on the floor, fears of spiders forgotten. The cat climbed into her lap. "Owl," she said. "I shall name you Owl."

The cat purred approval.

Portia would have gone down the stairs, but Owl jumped from her lap and ran back to the window as if to remind her that she had almost forgotten the book. Portia laughed at the cat's almost humanlike sensibilities and at herself for imagining them.

"Thank you, Owl, I don't want to forget it," she said. "How else shall we know what to chant when we see a bat?"

The cat purred her approval and followed Portia down the stairs.

Chapter One

"Portia, take your eye spectacles off your nose right this minute. You know I don't like you to wear them around me. Or around anyone," Lady Maclean complained as she fluffed her pillows so that she could sit up in bed before Portia set the breakfast tray on her lap. Her ladyship's blonde hair was tucked into a lace cap, and her lace Spanish vest—a short jacket that served no purpose that Portia could tell—covered her lace nightdress. She rarely rose before noon.

"I need to see them to see, Mother," Portia responded dutifully. They had this conversation practically every day.

With an impatient sound, Lady Maclean declared, "You see fine without them. They age you, my girl. Not that you aren't old enough, but a woman shouldn't want to call attention to the fact. I don't understand why we haven't received our invitation to the Christmas Assembly," she announced, her mind shifting into another sequence of thought without pause. "They couldn't *not* think of inviting us."

Oh yes, they could, Portia thought as she walked over to the window to open the draperies.

When the Macleans had first moved to Glenfinnan, her mother had made it clear she thought herself better than the Scots even though they undoubtedly knew all too well what a scoundrel her husband and Portia's father, Captain Sir Jack Maclean, truly was. After all, Black Jack Maclean had grown up in these parts, and one thing Portia was learning about country society was that there were no secrets.

Lady Maclean sighed wistfully, "I always adored Christmas. The parties, the dinners, the gaiety."

Portia didn't remember the parties, the dinners or the gaiety. As far back as her memory went, they usually spent the season being shuttled back and forth among relatives who didn't really want Black Jack's family. "I like not having all those relatives around. It is good to be under our own roof."

"Even in Scotland?" Her mother sniffed her opinion and sipped her tea.

The day outside was overcast with the threat of rain. Portia wondered what the weather would be like in mid-January, when, she'd been told, it finally, truly would go cold. Would the rain change to sleet? She could go out in the rain but sleet was not to her liking. She began straightening the room.

The family only had one servant, a local named Glennis who did the cooking and the wash. Portia and Minnie managed the rest of the house. Minnie saw to the garden and Portia took care of the chickens, cow and pony. It was a good life, far better, to Portia's thinking, than the one they'd left behind in England.

"Your eyes are weak because you read too much," Lady Maclean said, returning to her earlier complaint. "If you would stop reading, you wouldn't need them."

"Minnie reads as much as I do and she doesn't wear spectacles," Portia argued.

"Poor Minnie," her mother said in another lightning-quick change of thought, "how are we going to find her a suitable husband if we are not invited to the Assembly? We must go."

Portia smiled at that concern. "Minnie has *found* a suitable husband," she reminded her mother. She crossed to the bed. "Her affections are fixed on Mr. Tolliver. You may not think him suitable enough—"

"*He is not.* I will not let her throw herself away on a mere physician."

"He is well respected and comes from a good family."

"He is ugly," her mother pronounced, munching on her toasted bread.

This was dangerous ground.

Minnie was a true beauty, with the round, guileless blue eyes and the blonde hair that had once made their mother famous. Wherever Minnie went, heads turned. When they had first moved to Glenfinnan, the sitting room had been full of young bucks, until they'd realized Minnie had set her cap for Mr. Tolliver.

Oliver Tolliver was of middling height, had a pouch around his middle and had a hairline that was receding rapidly. He was also one of the kindest men Portia had ever met. She understood how he could capture Minnie's affections. Portia believed them made for each other.

It would also be hard to find a man as handsome as Minnie was beautiful. Portia thought this without jealousy.

Of course, life could be difficult being constantly compared to such a beauty—especially by one's mother. Portia's hair was brownish with untamable curls she could only manage by pulling them back to the nape of her neck. Not even braiding brought them under control. Her nose was straight, her eyes were blue—but there wasn't anything remarkable about her features. She was also far less buxom than her sister.

And she wore spectacles.

In spite of their contrasts, she was proud of her sister and loved her dearly. "Minnie sees the measure of the man beyond his looks," Portia said. "And I think better of her for it."

"And I think she has an obligation to her family to marry well," her mother muttered before taking another drink of tea. "She's our one chance, Portia. Without a good marriage from her, we are sunk. How thoughtless of your father to leave us without anything."

"We'll manage fine, Mother. Let Minnie marry the man she loves." And hopefully he would call again soon. It had been almost two weeks without a word from him. Portia continued to assure Minnie that her gentleman had not forgotten her.

Lady Maclean gave a snort. "That will not happen." She set her cup down on its saucer and smiled. "You see, I had a private conversation with Mr. Tolliver when last he called."

All of Portia's senses went on alert. Her mother could be very resourceful when she wished. "She loves him, Mother," Portia restated. "In fact, she is quite concerned that he has not called lately. I tell her that he has probably been very busy. His profession is not one with regular hours."

The self-satisfied smile spread across Lady Maclean's face, and Portia's suspicions grew. "You warned him off," she accused her mother.

"He's not worthy of her."

"How did you do it?" Portia demanded, spreading her arms wide. "You are either here in this room or in our company at all times."

"You girls are not as attentive to me as you wish to believe. I had a moment alone with him the last time he called. It did not take long for me to say what I wished to express to him."

Portia let her arms fall to her side in exasperation. "How could you do that to Minnie? She loves him."

"Love is not for those of our class, my daughter. We each have obligations. We marry for the benefit of *family*. God gave Minerva beauty for her *family's* benefit. She needs to marry rich. After all, I want my sugar."

The last statement startled Portia. "Your sugar?"

"I like sugar in my tea," Lady Maclean announced as if stating the obvious. "We have not been able to afford it since we moved to Scotland, and I find that unacceptable."

"So Minnie must be unhappily married so you can have sugar? This is beyond selfish, Mother."

"This is being practical."

"But she *loves* him," Portia all but shouted. "And he loves her."

"Obviously not as much as you assume. It only took a word from me to set him off her. Trust me, Portia, it pains me to cause any of my daughters the slightest bit of unhappiness, but we must be sensible."

Portia looked at her mother, who was dressed in lace and lounging on a bed that had seen finer days. They lived in a house that was cold and drafty, and so she dared to ask something they had never discussed before, "Didn't *you* marry for love, Mother?"

Lady Maclean's gaze shifted away from her. She reached down and picked at the shawl around her shoulders, rearranging it before raising guileless eyes and admitting in a quiet voice, "And so I know of which I speak."

Crossing her arms, Portia looked away. "When were you going to tell Minnie what you'd done?"

"I see no reason to do so. If he doesn't call, she

will forget him, especially when we go to the Christmas Assembly and all the men flock to her."

"But how will she dance with a broken heart, Mother? Minnie isn't shallow. She cared deeply for him."

"She will learn to care for another" was the tart reply.

There was no answer to that.

Suddenly, Portia couldn't stay in her mother's presence one more second. She picked up the overflowing laundry basket and left the room.

"Please shut the door," her mother called. "I hate the draft in the hall."

Portia was happy to comply, slamming the door behind her.

However, alone on the other side, she all but collapsed against it.

Her mother exhausted her.

"And poor Minnie," Portia whispered to herself. She must tell her what their mother had done.

At that moment, a door opened and Owl came down the hall, her tail high in the air as she trotted up to Portia. So far she had managed to keep the cat's presence from their mother. Of course, Owl was a very independent creature. She could disappear for days at a time and then present herself whenever and wherever she wished.

Portia knelt to gather her pet up in her arms, asking, "What am I to say, Owl? How will I tell Minnie that Mr. Tolliver has deserted her? And all because of what Mother said. She'll be heartbroken. Then again, what sort of true love is he to abruptly drop her just on Mother's say-so? He probably understood our circumstances and ran. After all, how can he support all of us?" She hugged the cat close, feeling her heart beat. "I don't know what we shall do, Owl. Things are not good—"

"Are you talking to your cat again?" Minnie asked, her voice light with teasing as she came up the stairs. At the top step, she paused and tilted her head, her smile turning to concern. "Portia, are you feeling all right? Your face is very pale."

Owl struggled for release and Portia set her down before turning to her sister. "Minnie," she started, ready to confess what their mother had said to Mr. Tolliver, when Owl gave a loud, forceful meow as if in warning and bumped into her leg.

Portia looked down at her pet in surprise. The cat's expressive eyes seemed to urge her to silence. It was the most unusual impression.

"What is the matter?" Minnie asked.

"Nothing," Portia answered. She pulled her gaze away from Owl.

"Dear, I worry about you," Minnie said with great concern.

"You needn't," Portia answered. "I'm fine, or I will be."

"Perhaps not. We have a visitor. Mr. Buchanan is here and he is being very formal." Minnie lowered her voice as if not wanting it to carry where their mother could hear. "Are we behind in the rent?"

Mr. Buchanan was the Duke of Moncrieffe's man and managed all of his properties, including Camber Hall. It was a bad sign when a man was formal around Minnie. Usually they doted on her. Portia handed the laundry basket to her sister and untied the apron at her waist. "This will not be pleasant," she muttered.

Minnie understood that the answer was yes. "How far behind are we?"

"A month, so far. Uncle Ned will send money soon. I know he will," Portia repeated, more to reassure herself than anyone else. Their mother's brother Edward was their sole source of income and he was more than a bit unreliable in keeping his promises. It was he who had suggested the move to Scotland. She thought he believed that her father's relatives would be willing to help. However, although many had known Black Jack, few admitted they were related to him.

Portia forced a smile on her face and went downstairs.

Mr. Buchanan waited in the sitting room. He stood by the cold hearth, his hat in his hand. He still wore his heavy coat, and his boots were caked with mud. She'd have to sweep the wood floors once he left.

He was a head shorter than Portia and had a balding pate. He tried to hide his baldness by combing his hair from one side of his head to another. Portia thought it silly but tried not to give away her thoughts in front of the man.

"Mr. Buchanan, what a pleasure that you have come to call," she said, entering the room. "Please, have a chair." She indicated the two chairs and settee that were the room's main pieces of furniture. There were also several side tables.

"This is not a pleasure call," Mr. Buchanan answered in his thick burr. He took a step toward Portia. "I am so sorry, Miss Maclean, but I must have the rent. Your family is in arrears."

"I am sorry, Mr. Buchanan, that we have fallen behind. Certainly you can understand how precarious a position we are in. You know my father was a war hero—"

"'Tis why the duke offered you this establishment, Miss Portia. He knows your difficulties, but he means to be paid his rent. I need something, coin, household goods, something. I don't want to throw you out."

"Perhaps I should speak to the duke himself," Portia suggested, putting the right note of hauteur in her voice. Her mother wasn't the only one who could put on airs. Granted, Portia's workday dress might be frayed at the hem and her hands rough from housework, but her pride was intact.

"I wish you would," Mr. Buchanan said. "Frankly, I don't believe he would receive you." He shifted a glance toward the hall where Minnie hovered anxiously. "If I may speak plainly?"

"I pray you do."

He sidled over to Portia, lowering his voice. "I don't believe Lady Emma is happy you are here. Your sister is too attractive."

Portia frowned. "Lady Emma has no grudge against us," she said, knowing that was not true. "And Lady Emma is attractive as well."

"But not as lovely as Miss Minerva. It is embarrassing how headstrong and jealous my employer's daughter is. She is also his one weakness. He cannot deny her anything. There has been talk since you all arrived in the kirk that Miss Minerva outshines Lady Emma."

Portia was aware of this. "But my sister is no

threat to her. Her affection is fixed on Mr. Tolliver."

"That's not the word being bandied about in the valley. They say your sister rejected Mr. Tolliver. There are many hard feelings toward your family. Mr. Tolliver is very well respected, and, pardon my saying this, Miss Portia, you are English. We expect the English to be fickle."

"Minnie is *not* fickle," Portia shot back at him in an angry whisper. This is what her mother's meddling had wrought. " 'They' are wrong in what they say. My sister is steadfast in her character and her affections and you can tell them that. As for your rent, tell the duke he shall be paid."

"When?"

Portia hated that word, especially from landlords.

"May I have two weeks? We are expecting funds from family members. I don't know what has delayed the mail," she lied, suspecting Uncle Ned had not sent a shilling. "It will arrive any day."

"Portia, is everything all right?" Minnie asked from the doorway.

Portia looked at her lovely sister, whose brow was furrowed in concern. "All is well, dear." She turned back to Mr. Buchanan and gave him a ferocious frown. "Two weeks?" she demanded.

"*One*," Mr. Buchanan answered. "I value my position and can't have too many questions asked. Contact your relatives. Sell something. Do what you must. The duke will hold off Lady Emma's demands if you are right with him."

"I shall be."

"I did not mean to be a burden to you, Miss Portia."

"I understand." She found it difficult to unbend toward him. He was speaking out of kindness and with the truth. It didn't make his message any more palatable.

"I shall say good day to you then." Mr. Buchanan left the room.

Minnie saw him out and then returned to the sitting room. "We need money, don't we?"

"Oh yes. It seems the duke's daughter is jealous of your beauty."

"My beauty?" Minnie scoffed. "What nonsense. I've seen Lady Emma. She's lovely."

"But you are lovelier, dear, because you are beautiful inside as well. Lady Emma would like you banished from anyplace near her."

"You are jesting."

"I'm not."

Minnie's face had gone pale. "I can't leave. I can't leave Ollie."

"I believe there is something else I must tell you," Portia said. Owl was wrong. Minnie needed to know. She drew her sister over to the settee. As gently as Portia could, she explained what their mother had done.

Predictably, Minnie did not take Mr. Tolliver's defection lightly. She burst into tears and then tore up the stairs to confront their mother. In the sitting room, Portia could hear the angry argument. Moments later, her sister still noisily crying, she slammed the door on the way out of their mother's room and then slammed her own bedroom door.

Lady Maclean came downstairs. She was still wearing her lace dressing gown. She stopped in the doorway when she saw Portia, and smiled, pleased with herself, before turning and climbing the stairs for the haven of her room.

Owl jumped up on the settee beside Portia.

Portia ran her hand over the animal's silky fur. "You warned me not to tell her," she confessed to the animal. "But she had a right to know. She was waiting for him, Owl. She loves him." She paused and asked, "Why isn't life easier, Owl? Why must Minnie and I always be the ones who wait. I just wish something would happen. I'm so weary with all this worry about money and Mother and Minnie's happiness. I can't continue like this. I don't want to."

The sting of tears in her eyes surprised her. She angrily brushed them away, frowned at her cat, and confessed, "I just wish life held something more. I can't believe this is all there is, one day just like another . . ."

Owl nudged her hand with her pink nose as if in commiseration.

"I know, I shouldn't wallow in pity. It's just sometimes, Owl, I wish my life wasn't the way it is. Maybe sometimes, I wish there was a man by my side who could deal with Mother and Mr. Buchanan and Uncle Ned. A man with heart and courage and kindness, but not too gentle. Not like Mr. Tolliver. He is sometimes fastidious. But I'd want a man of a more robust measure. Someone *exciting*." She shook her head at her silliness. "I'm being foolish, but yes, there are times I long for someone. Times I'm lonely." She pushed the bridge of her spectacles. "I'm old. I'm what I am. This is my life."

She looked around the bleak room with its worn furniture and bare floor. "It is not so bad." She stroked the cat's back. "It's good actually. All is good," she repeated to convince herself.

Owl arched her back, wanting to enjoy every inch of Portia's pat.

"I should be like you and savor each moment as it is, shouldn't I? The best thing to do right now is carry on . . . and write my *uncle*." Portia put all her frustration about the situation in that last word. He was far from a loving relative.

She rose and walked over to the writing table. She hated begging. *Hated* it. But what else could be done?

Her letter to her uncle was not a newsy, pleasant one. She'd written those before to no avail. This time, she was direct. She let him know the family was in desperate straits and reminded him of the sum of fifty pounds a year he'd promised them when last they had a serious discussion. It should be enough for them to live in Scotland. *Otherwise, we may need to return to London and become a burden to your household*, she penned thinking that might be threat enough for her bachelor uncle.

Portia took a coin to frank the letter, put on her cloak, and went out the door to walk to the Glenfinnan House to post the letter. The clouds in the sky had grown heavier. There would be rain, but after so many months in Scotland, Portia never let the weather stop her from doing anything. Owl followed her to the end of the drive before disappearing into the woods.

There wasn't much to Glenfinnan other than the Glenfinnan House, the home of Laird Macdonald. However, the Scots in the River Finnan

Valley around Loch Shiel considered it a village, and so Portia had come to think such as well. The community itself was spread over the country-side. The Christmas Assembly would be held in Borrodale's barn. Portia had never seen the build-ing but had been informed it was a fine structure and unlike any barn she could imagine.

Portia had also discovered, after so many years of living in town, that she liked country life. Yes, Scotland was damp and cold, but the air was clean and there was freedom here as well. She'd not be able to walk the road unescorted in London, even considering her age. She also liked that the Scots didn't stand on ceremony. Clan alliances were more important than titles, and so the children of Jack Maclean had been, albeit somewhat tepidly, welcomed even though they spoke with English voices.

Exercise and fresh air heartened her spirits.

A plan of action began to form in her mind. She would find a way to contact Mr. Tolliver and con-vince him of Minnie's love. And Uncle Ned would honor his pledge and send money. She just had to think positively—

The sound of a galloping horse interrupted her thoughts mere seconds before the animal came charging around the bend. A huge, dark beast with hooves the size of mallets, and it was right upon her.

Portia barely had time to blink, let alone move. Indeed, her feet had suddenly grown roots to the ground.

The rider was a man in a greatcoat, the brim of his hat pulled low over his face as protection against the wind. He rode as if driven by some unseen power. Both he and the horse noticed her at the last possible moment, and there didn't seem time to save her from being run over.

Chapter Two

 $\mathcal{P}$ ortia threw her hands up in the air to protect herself . . . but the accident did not happen. Hard hooves did not strike her.

The rider pulled back with all his might, heaving the giant horse away from her. The steed reared and twisted midair. The flailing of hooves was so close to Portia's head she could feel their movement in the air and smell the sweat of the beast.

Then, out of sheer athleticism, the horse turned away. It started to slide, losing its balance on the muddy road, but regained his footing.

The man never lost his seat. Indeed, he barely moved. He rode as if he and the horse were one.

She lowered her arms, amazed she was safe.

The horse pranced in place, the white of its eyes rolling. The rider's scowl was so deep and angry it was more frightening than the near accident.

"Don't you have sense to stay out of the road?" he demanded in a harsh voice that could have belonged to the devil himself.

He didn't wait for her defense but put heels to flank and went riding away in a flurry of hooves and dirt, the hem of his greatcoat flying behind him like a cape.

Portia watched him go . . . and then came as close as she ever had in her life to fainting.

"Miss Maclean," she heard a man shout. "Are you all right?"

Dazed, Portia turned toward the sound to see Laird Macdonald's gardener Robbie running toward her.

"I saw what happened," Robbie said in his brogue. "I was thinking for certain you were going to be trampled."

"I was as well," Portia said. Her legs had begun to shake.

"Here, miss, take me arm."

Gratefully, Portia did as suggested. He led her toward the stone manse that served as Laird Alexander Macdonald's seat as well as an inn since the laird proudly honored the Highland custom of an open house.

Laird Macdonald was a young man and had great plans for Glenfinnan. These included the building of a proper inn and a monument to his ancestors who had served the Jacobite call. It appeared almost complete. The tower and building overlooked the loch and could be seen from the house.

Portia thought it rather silly of the laird to build such a tower. Yes, she had Scottish roots but held English loyalties—and the '45 uprising was not something she thought a prudent man should commemorate. Of course, her opinion was not shared by most of the valley and she kept it to herself.

Then again, no one had ever accused Laird Alexander Macdonald of Glenalladale of being prudent. He was a rake through and through, a man who owed everyone money, including the Bishop of Lismore. Fortunately for Portia's peace of mind, the laird had been spending the majority of his time in Edinburgh, or else, such was his reputation, they would have had to lock up Minnie.

Mrs. Margaret Macdonald, the laird's housekeeper, held the door open for them. She was a robust woman with a frizz of strawberry curls beneath her mob cap. "I saw what happened. I was looking out the window and I saw that bounder almost bowl you over. Here, come in, Miss Maclean. A bit of whiskey will make you feel right," she promised in her lilting accent.

Before Portia could blink, she'd been gently set

in a chair before the fire in the sitting room, and a dram of amber whiskey had been pushed into her hand. "Drink," Mrs. Macdonald ordered. She and Robbie had poured a dram for themselves as well.

Portia took a tentative sip. Whiskey drinking was not a habit she'd cultivated yet. It seemed to her that everyone, man, woman and child across the countryside, indulged in whiskey a wee bit too much. However, this time the whiskey was appreciated. The smoky flavor of it did not put her off, and the warmth that spread to her limbs helped restore her frayed nerves. Her legs stopped shaking and she found breathing easier.

"Who was that man?" she asked the servants.

"A *Chattan*," Robbie answered, spitting the word out.

"A Chattan?" Portia repeated.

"Yes, he's Colonel Harry Chattan. And they are not all bad, Robbie," Mrs. Macdonald said. "There is a good line of them."

"Aye, the Scottish ones. Fought alongside us in '45. But he's of English line. Traitors all," Robbie said, spitting in actuality this time, aiming for the hearth. Portia was surprised Mrs. Macdonald didn't want his hide for spitting in her clean house.

The rain threatening all morning finally came.

The sound of it made this meeting in the sitting room more intimate, and slightly more sinister.

"What would an English Chattan be doing in Glenfinnan?" Portia asked.

"He's *witch* hunting," Mrs. Macdonald said.

For a second, Portia wasn't certain she'd heard her correctly. She almost laughed until she realized the Scots were serious.

Robbie had taken a seat on a footstool close to Portia's chair. He placed a knowing finger against the side of his nose. "And well he should."

"Has he found any?" Portia had to ask, expecting the answer to be no. There was no such thing as a witch.

"We steered him to Crazy Lizzy, but he wasn't satisfied," Mrs. Macdonald answered.

"Lizzy is not a witch," Portia said. "Granted she's not all there, either." Crazy Lizzy was an old woman who lived in a hut in the woods. She spent the day talking to herself but she was harmless. Portia tried to take a food basket to her at least once a week, and she wasn't the only one. Mrs. Macdonald was known to send loaves of bread to the poor soul.

"I know that," Mrs. Macdonald said, "but the man was offering three hundred pounds sterling. I thought it worth the effort."

Portia almost fell from the chair. "*Three hundred pounds.*" With three hundred pounds, the rent would be paid and they wouldn't have to worry about money for years. No more worries, no more debtors, no more struggle.

"Why is he looking for a witch?" Portia asked.

"Because he is cursed," Robbie answered, sitting back on the stool and crossing both arms and legs.

"Cursed?" This time Portia did laugh. Neither Robbie nor Mrs. Macdonald joined her.

"You can make light of it, Miss Maclean, but be certain the English Chattans don't. 'Tis all Charles Chattan's fault. He handfasted himself to a Scottish lass but betrayed her love when he and his kin went running to England to marry him to an English heiress."

"When did this happen?" Portia asked.

"Hundreds of years ago," Robbie answered.

"Then why does it matter?"

Robbie stared at her as if she was a fool. "It has never stopped mattering," he said. "The Scottish lass took her own life. Everyone knows the story."

Mrs. Macdonald nodded agreement.

"I don't know it," Portia said.

A gleam came to Robbie's eyes. He had the Highlanders' love of a good tale. He uncrossed his legs and leaned toward her. "The Scottish lass's love was true and when Chattan betrayed her, she threw herself from a tower."

"Aye, sad thing it was, the poor little dear," Mrs. Macdonald said.

"Did this happen here?" Portia asked.

"No one is certain," Robbie answered. "The lass was known as Rose of the Macnachtan, and a bonny lass she was. They say she was the most lovely flower in Scotland and had a gift."

Portia frowned. "A gift?"

"For the sight," Robbie answered. "For things that we mere mortals cannot imagine. Her mother was a witch and a powerful one, they say. She had her daughter's beautiful body burned on a shore of a loch and she stood on a rock overlooking the funeral pyre. On that rock, she cursed the English Chattans before she leaped from that rock onto her daughter's own burning body."

No image could be more horrifying to Portia's always active imagination. The room had seemed to darken. The flames in the hearth leaped and danced as if saying, *Yes, it is so.*

"How are they cursed?" Portia asked Robbie.

"When a Chattan falls in love, he is struck dead. The witch wanted to curse them good. She wanted them to suffer for *all* time in the way she suffered."

Logic scoffed at the story. This could not be true.

And yet, here, in this room, with Mrs. Macdonald's head nodding to the particulars of Robbie's story, Portia would not be human if she didn't feel a shiver of foreboding.

"Did the faithless lover, this Charles, die?" Portia wanted to know.

"He did," Robbie assured her.

"And are the Chattans still dying?" Portia wondered.

Robbie smiled with ghoulish delight. "Chattan is here looking for a witch, isn't he?" He sat back, reaching for his whiskey. "We used to have many Chattans in these parts. We lost a good number of them in '15 and in '45. Almost wiped out the clan. They were puny fighters. A good number left with John Macdonald when he went to the colonies. Of course, the English Chattans don't care. They've been living the good life in London and beyond, counting their money and the *days* they have left." He cackled his pleasure.

But Portia's mind was no longer focused on the curse. Perhaps it was the whiskey, or maybe the rain and the telling of the story, or perhaps it was her own desperate circumstances . . . but an idea began to form, an idea so daring, it shocked her.

"And this Chattan almost ran me over because he couldn't find a witch?" Portia heard herself asking.

"I don't know, Miss Maclean," Mrs. Macdonald said. "The post left a letter for him here. He read it, crumpled it in his hand, stormed out of the house, and went tearing away as if no one else in the world mattered. Oh, foul of mood he was, and that's why he almost ran you down."

"He must have received bad news," Portia said.

Robbie dismissed the idea with a sharp wave of his hand. "Who cares what news Chattan has received? I say good riddance to him. He had clansmen die fighting in '45, and not a member of his family lifted a finger to help them."

Portia smiled agreement but she didn't have a care about Chattan loyalties. He was a wealthy man looking for a witch—and she was a woman with a book of spells.

She really hadn't had a chance to read the book all the way through. She and Minnie had studied it one night and had a grand time. There were all sorts of recipes in it. The most amusing were the potions and poultices that promised to heal everything from a wart on the sole of one's foot to a broken heart, each using the same three ingredients—moss, something called "dittany of crete," and sage. The sisters had surmised it was the words one chanted that mattered, and the feelings when they were said.

Then, there were the more "witchy" recipes that were for those who dabbled in spells a good Christian would not touch, unless she was desperate for money.

It had been those spells that had made both her and Minnie uncomfortable. The book had been tucked away beneath Portia's bed and had not been pulled out since.

Portia thought of the letter to her uncle and knew it would not be answered, just as her previous pleas to him had been ignored. If her family was to survive, she needed to be bold.

"Is the Englishman staying here?" she asked Mrs. Macdonald.

"No, he's with that English general that moved to the valley, say what? The early part of the summer?"

Portia's heart sank. General Montheath.

The general had been a childhood acquaintance of her mother's and had nursed an unrequited love for her all these decades and had sought her out on the flimsiest of excuses. When they moved to Scotland, he had not been far behind. However, he never called upon her. Instead, he hovered around her every chance he could, such as at church, moving with a stealth that made Portia and Minnie believe he feared pressing his attentions in any manner lest their mother banish him completely.

In truth, their mother was oblivious to such slavish devotion. She ignored him. Portia and Minnie felt a bit sorry for him—Minnie more so than Portia. If the man would call or take some sort of action, Portia could have been more sympathetic to his suit. As it was, she thought him a touch pathetic.

Of course, that didn't mean she couldn't act on the plan hatching in her mind.

It was so clear to her. So simple.

She could become the witch.

And the results might save them all.

Portia rose from the chair. "I must be going. Thank you for your assistance," she said to Robbie and Mrs. Macdonald. "I'm feeling much better now." She started for the door, pulling her cloak hood up over her head.

"But it is still raining," Mrs. Macdonald protested.

"Merely a mist," Portia answered, and then she remembered the letter to Uncle Ned. She pulled it from her pocket along with the coin. It wouldn't hurt to send it. "I brought this for the post."

Mrs. Macdonald, who had risen along with

Robbie to see her to the door, took the letter from her. "I'll see to it."

"Thank you," Portia said, and practically dashed out of the house.

The rain had let up, but even if it hadn't, Portia would have left. Her mind buzzed with details, fears, hopes. She'd not felt so alive before in her life.

Her step was hurried in her anxiousness to return home and grab the book of spells from its hiding place. However, as she topped a knoll in the road, she felt compelled to stand there a moment.

From this point, she could see the length of Loch Shiel hemmed in by the dramatic peaks of the mountains Moidart, Ardgour and Sunart. Not far off the shore, St. Finan's island was an oasis of firs and pines.

The rain-laden wind whipped across the waters before carrying itself up and around Portia.

She'd liked Scotland from the moment they'd arrived. She felt as if she belonged here. Of course, there was nowhere else to go. If she did not find a way to stay at Camber Hall, then she, her mother, and her sister would be forced to be a burden upon relatives. Such a fate was unthinkable.

At that moment, an eagle took flight over the

loch. It spread its wings and glided through the air above and around St. Finan's, and she experienced the thrill of destiny.

It was a sign. A blessing . . . or so Portia wished it to be. Had it been mere happenstance that the book of spells had fallen into her hands? She did not know, but she knew what she was going to do with it.

She would become the English Chattan's witch. She would become *Fenella*, the name of the last woman to sign the inside page of that book. Fenella. It sounded witchy.

And she would claim—no, earn—the Englishman's three hundred pounds.

Did her conscience bother her at pretending to be what she was not? She thought of the man who had almost run her over, the angry scowl, the rough voice.

She'd find a way to be at peace with herself. Having enough fuel to keep the fires in Camber Hall burning and plenty of food in the larder would be a good start.

His brother was dying and there was nothing Harry could do about it—not until he found someone or something that could break the curse.

For the first time in his life, Harry knew fear, a fear he attempted to escape by giving his horse Ajax, a mighty bay that had carried him into many a battle, his lead. It felt good to gallop, to release his frustration to the wind. Harry had never failed at an assignment before, he'd promised himself he wouldn't fail, and yet time was passing far too quickly.

The letter from his sister, Margaret, had not been hopeful. She'd urged him to act with all haste. His brother, Neal, was growing weaker, even as his wife grew larger with child. Margaret wrote her greatest frustration was how happy his brother, Neal, and Neal's wife, Thea, were: *They accept the inevitability of the curse and Neal behaves as if he does not even want to fight it.*

Well, Harry did. Neal was the finest man he knew. There had to be a way to break the curse. There *must* be.

He and Ajax raced over the moors, Harry's mind working furiously on all he had done, all he had learned. He'd come to Glenfinnan because it had been the home of Charles, the first Chattan cursed. There must be a clue here, something that would give him a direction. He sensed it was true, and Harry always trusted his gut.

But in a week's time, he'd not learned anything

except that Highlanders have long memories—when they wish to do so.

He'd met many who knew something of the curse and many more who still thought of his family line as traitors since they'd turned their backs on Scotland to marry into the English.

At first, Harry had tried reasoning. After all, over the past two hundred years and more, many a Scotsman had married an Englishwoman. But local lore was such that he discovered his ancestors unforgiven.

"They talk as if they could have won the rebellion in '45 with my family's help," he muttered at Ajax after they had run their fill.

Ajax was tired. He wanted his oats and his hay and didn't care much what the Highlanders thought of him.

Surprisingly, Harry did. He felt comfortable here, and if his brother's life wasn't at stake, he would have enjoyed himself.

As it was, he needed to move on, to continue his search. He just didn't know which way he should go.

It was dark by the time he returned to Montheath's house. A groom offered to help Harry with his horse but he saw to his own mount.

Monty had held dinner.

"You shouldn't have waited," Harry said, sinking down into a chair at the overladen table and finding himself quite hungry. He'd taken a moment to wash, while informing his man Rowan that they would leave at first light; however, he still wore his riding clothes and boots. Monty was equally casually dressed. This was a simple supper between two bachelors. A good fire burned in the hearth, the bread was fresh, and the leg of venison was still sizzling from the spit.

"You are my guest," Monty said. "Of course I would wait." He and Harry had fought in many campaigns together, although Monty was an artilleryman through and though. He liked the powers of guns.

Now, Monty was retired. He was some twenty years older than Harry and had seen far more fighting on numerous continents. He had a whippet-lean body and a full head of white hair. He was also a bit cross-eyed and he had a very strong nose, making him rather unhandsome. Harry didn't care about looks. Monty was both fearless and cool-headed under fire.

Monty also had an abnormal fondness for dogs. He must own at least ten of them of various and sundry lineages. Outside, inside, everywhere, the house was surrounded by dogs. One or two were at his heels wherever he went.

Monty could have chosen anywhere to live, but he'd chosen this quiet spot of Scotland where he didn't have family or close friends. Indeed, Harry and Monty had come upon each other by chance. Harry had just arrived in Glenfinnan and been riding down the road, and there had been Monty, riding in the opposite direction. He hadn't hesitated in inviting Harry to stay with him. Harry had asked him why he was in Glenfinnan but Monty had been unusually closed-lipped.

In truth, Harry's problems were so large, he did not have the luxury of worrying over his friend's concerns. So he'd let the subject drop.

"I shall be leaving on the morrow," he said to Monty as he speared a healthy-sized piece of venison for his plate. He shook his head at the servant offering peas. Harry was fond of any food as long as it wasn't green. "I have appreciated your hospitality."

"You *can't* go," Monty said.

Harry looked up in surprise. "I must. You know I am here on a mission."

"Are you certain you have met all the witches in the area? There are quite a few."

"There aren't any," Harry said flatly. He chewed

his food a moment without tasting it. He had no appetite. Food was something he needed for the strength to continue his search. "Well, save for that lonely old woman who lives in a hovel and chatters to herself all day. Crazy Lizzy is her name." Harry had given her ten pounds. He'd felt sorry for her. "They may look, and smell, like witches, but they are not. The woman I'm looking for is the one who placed the curse on my family. I'm searching for Fenella, or someone connected to her."

"You carry on about this Fenella as if you believe her still alive, even after hundreds of years."

"I know she is," Harry answered. "Some part of her must be alive or the curse would not be as strong as it is."

"Then you must stay right here in Glenfinnan. This is a very mystical part of Scotland. I think you should stay." A servant poured ale in Monty's tankard, and the general reached for it immediately.

Picking up his own glass of sweet cider, Harry shook his head. "I can't, Monty. My brother is growing weaker. I had a letter from my sister today. We don't know how much time he has. I must find a way to save him or he will die."

"Your brother. Yes," Monty said, his expression

stricken. "I forgot him. Sorry, sorry." He reached for a piece of venison off his plate and absently began feeding his dogs from the table.

A cold dog nose nudged Harry's arm. He gave the dog a pet and shooed it away, a bit concerned by Monty's behavior. His old friend would not forget such a detail as Harry's purpose for being in Glenfinnan. "Monty, is there something the matter?"

The general drained his tankard, held it for a servant to be refilled, and then motioned him away, saying, "Leave us." He waited until the door had closed behind the servant before leaning across the table. "I need your help, Chattan. I've put off asking since you have concerns of your own, but I'm desperate. I thought when I met you that here was exactly what I needed—a man who can claim any woman he wishes."

Harry didn't challenge the description. It was true. Women flocked to him. They always had.

It wasn't vanity for him to admit that he had looks they liked. It was a statement of fact. God had blessed him with a face and form that was pleasing to the ladies. And he had used them to his own advantage—until he'd set out upon this quest.

Now, he was beginning to wonder how he

could have been so shallow. Of course, he was free of the chains of opium and he couldn't remember the last time he'd taken a drink. No, that was a lie. He remembered all too well and he hated himself for it.

But he was curious why Monty thought this an asset. Monty was an avowed bachelor, or that was the impression Harry had gained.

"What's amiss, Monty?"

His friend sat back in his chair. A terrier jumped into his lap. Monty absently petted its head as he said, "I need you to help me attend the Christmas Assembly."

"A dance?"

Monty nodded vigorously.

Harry shook his head slowly. "I can't wait around for the dance, Monty. My brother's life is at stake."

"The dance is in four days, Chattan. You can wait four days."

"I don't remember you eager to attend any dances back when I served under your command," Harry said. "You usually avoided them."

"I did," Monty said. He pushed the dog off his lap and threw the animals another piece of meat. They yapped and snarled over it. "Not my thing."

"Then why must you attend this dance?" Harry

asked, leaning forward and resting his arms on the table.

"Because *she* will be there."

"Who is she?" Harry had to ask, intrigued.

"Lady Ariana Maclean."

"Maclean?" The name sounded familiar.

"Do you not remember Black Jack Maclean?" Monty said to prod Harry's memory.

Harry pushed away from the table. "That sorry rascal! He was married? I pity the woman he took for a wife."

"I do as well," Monty said. "Her life has not been easy."

"Does she know he had at least two families on the Peninsula?" Harry asked. "The man was a scoundrel. He wasn't even a good officer. He spent most of his time as far behind the lines as possible."

"He was a coward," Monty agreed. "But he was an even worse husband."

"To *all* his wives," Harry had to quip. Everyone in the regiment knew Maclean lived with different women as man and wife. He wasn't the only one to do so. Many soldiers did—but the practice had never set well with Harry.

"Aye, he was bad . . . and I hate what he did to Ariana." Now it was Monty leaning across the table. "Harry, you should meet her. She's the loveliest female that has ever graced this earth. Since first we met, there hasn't been a day of my life when I haven't thought of her. Not a day that has passed when I haven't wanted her."

"Why, Monty, you are in love."

"*Yes*. Yes, yes, a hundred times yes. I love Ariana Williams."

"That was her maiden name?"

"Her family lived not far from mine. I was first introduced to her when I was fourteen and she twelve."

"And you have loved her all this time?"

Monty sadly nodded yes.

Harry studied his friend in a new light. He was no fan of love. One couldn't be given his family history. His parents had both been cold people, until his mother died and his father had gone mad over an opera dancer whom he had made his second countess. And then the curse had claimed him. His father had died soon after the marriage.

Now Love was claiming the life of his brother.

But Monty's declaration was a complete puzzlement. "If you were so enamored, why didn't you speak up before she married Black Jack?" Harry asked.

"I tried, or I wished to do so. I'm not good with words."

"You are speaking clearly right now."

"But I can't speak to *her*. And then she chose Maclean over me. I tried to warn her but ended discussing the weather instead, and I had a hard time doing that."

"She made a poor choice. Being shot in a duel by an angry husband is not an honorable death."

"Yes, the Portuguese are not as reserved about adultery as we British are," Monty agreed. "The worst is that he had resigned his commission." One of the dogs put his paws on the table to catch his master's attention. "Down, Jasper," Monty said, pushing him away and then offering a crust of bread.

"So the family has nothing?" Harry shifted in his chair. "Well, it is the rare man who can afford three families."

"I don't know if Ariana is aware of what a scoundrel her husband was. They say the reason Ariana moved her family to Scotland was because it is less expensive to live here. I love her, Chattan. I love her completely and honestly and secretively. I want to change that. I want her to know. I could do so much to help her family, if she would let me."

"Then speak to her," Harry advised.

Monty raised tortured eyes to Harry's and said, "No. I'm afraid to even call on her."

"Why? What are you waiting for?" Harry demanded. "She needs a man to support her and you are one of the best. You have position, you have fortune, and she has your heart. What woman could resist such a man? None that I know. Call on her tomorrow. Make a declaration. Neither of you is growing any younger."

Monty gripped the edge of the table. "I can't face her alone. When I think about it, I'm petrified. I can't talk, I can't think, I can't move." He raised a pleading gaze to Harry. "But I *could* face her at the dance if you would speak for me."

"Oh no," Harry said. He held up a hand warding the suggestion away.

"You *must.*"

"I must *not,*" Harry replied. "I have done this before, Monty. I've had friends ask me to speak to their ladyloves for them and it has never ended well."

"But I'm not just *any* friend."

"That you aren't," Harry agreed, "which is all the more reason I should decline. I like you, Monty. Maclean's widow will like you as well, in fact more so. Be yourself, be kind, be attentive, and she will be yours."

"I'm tongue-tied around her," Monty lamented.

"You don't have to do much. Just go to the dance with me. Be there for support."

"Monty, I can't stay here that long—"

"It's in *four* days—"

"My brother is *dying*. I can't stay. My quest is for an end to this curse. Once I've found what I'm looking for, I'll return to Glenfinnan and go to however many dances you wish and talk to any number of women. But right now, I can't, sir, and I beg of you to understand."

The general's back stiffened. He would not meet Harry's eye as he said, "Have it your way then. I shall wait. I've waited decades already."

The pronouncement ended dinner. Harry's appetite had left him. He did not like disappointing an old friend. Then again, he didn't understand all this nonsense over a woman. He rose from the table. "I value our friendship," he said. "I have always respected you when under your command. I apologize, Monty, but my brother's life is a higher priority." '

"Of course it is," Monty said. "I understand. I'm just—" He broke off as if words failed him. He attempted to smile. It was a pathetic thing.

"Do you know your Shakespeare, Monty? 'Love is merely a madness, and I tell you, deserves as well a dark house and a whip as madmen do,'" Harry quoted.

"Yes, she makes me mad. But it is my own fear that disturbs me. I would rather face French cannon than make a fool of myself in front of her."

"You can't make a fool of yourself in front of a good woman," Harry said. "They are the kindest of creatures and amazingly forgiving."

"She's all I've ever wanted, Chattan. I fear the risk of losing any contact with her."

Harry studied his friend. The man appeared done up, and yet Harry could have sympathy only to a point. He rose from the table. "I shall return and help you, but I must go."

However, before Harry could leave, a servant entered the room carrying a silver salver bearing a letter. "Colonel Chattan, we found this on the front step. It is addressed to you."

"Left on the front step?" Monty said. "Did they knock on the door? The dogs didn't make a sound."

"They were all in here, sir," the servant said. "You know how they are during the dinner hour. And we didn't hear a sound from outside. It was by chance we looked outside and found the letter."

Harry took the letter. It was addressed to "Chattan." The stationery was thin and cheaply made.

He broke the wax seal, unfolded the letter, and what he read changed everything:

Meet me at the Great Oak, tomorrow, midnight.

Fenella

Chapter Three

Becoming a witch was no easy trick.

Portia obviously couldn't dress as herself. She would not want that scowling Englishman to know who she was. She also needed to convince him she was a witch—but how did a witch look?

She could wear rags like Crazy Lizzy did, but she decided she didn't want to be that sort of witch. And she knew she would have to do something to hide her face.

After finishing her tasks around the house, she disappeared to her room to give proper consideration to her costume. She had excuses ready in case her mother or Minnie asked questions, but they weren't necessary. Her mother had deemed today would be one of "those" days, which meant she would not come downstairs at all.

And Minnie was still mourning the loss of Mr.

Tolliver. She had cared deeply for the man. Portia had tried to buoy her spirits the night before but her sister was disconsolate.

"You will see him at the Christmas Assembly," Portia had said. The desired invitation had finally arrived the evening before and their mother had been very pleased after remarking on the poor form in delivering invitations at such a late date. Apparently, the kirk committee had a bit of a spat, so all the invitations had been late. Most in the valley assumed they would be invited, so for most the lateness didn't matter.

Not so Lady Maclean.

However, now she was happy and insisting that Minnie would be the belle of the ball.

Portia hadn't involved herself in their discussion. She was too busy plotting how to be a witch. But she had taken advantage of the messenger and had asked him to deliver "Fenella's" letter to General Montheath's residence. The lad had been happy to comply for a small coin and even pleased to be sworn to secrecy.

Over supper, Portia smiled at Minnie. "With this invitation, you now have the opportunity to talk to Mr. Tolliver and explain that Mother does not speak for you."

"Shouldn't he know for himself?" Minnie

asked. "Shouldn't he have cared enough for *my* opinion to speak to *me* himself and express his concerns?"

Portia didn't know what to say to those charges, and her silence was damning.

"I don't want a man in my life who is like Papa," Minnie said. "He treated Mother as if she was just a chair in the dining room. I expect far more respect." With that very sage declaration, Minnie left their table. When Portia went up to her room, she heard crying as she passed her sister's door.

Was it any wonder then that Portia threw herself into becoming a witch?

With the money she received from the English Chattan, they could even return to London, although Portia would resist the idea, or they could provide a handsome dowry for Minnie that would make Mr. Tolliver wish that he had been more steadfast. So becoming a convincing witch, or at least one worth three hundred pounds, was very important.

Owl helped. The cat lay on her bed and served as an audience as Portia tried on one outfit after another.

Since she didn't want to be an ugly witch, she decided to consider the classics she loved so much.

There was Medusa with a head full of snakes. No thank you.

Cicero, the beautiful temptress who turned Ulysses' men into swine. As appealing as it would be to turn this Englishman into a stout pig, Portia didn't see herself as a temptress.

Finally, she decided to design a wood sprite theme. She took an old work dress in brown sacking and stitched holly branches to the skirt. The sharp points of the leaves made the dress prickly and the material heavy, but Portia was willing to sacrifice her comfort.

A visit up to the attic yielded a swath of old, musty plaid that Portia threw around her shoulders. No one would expect to see her in plaid. She was too English.

However, her true find in the attic was a monstrous, wide-brimmed hat woven of straw. Portia adored it. She bent the brim so that it would hide her face and decorated the crown with some of the plaid and more holly.

Gazing at her image in the mirror, she thought the effect quite stunning.

"What do you think, Owl?" she asked as she twirled herself around.

Owl's response was to jump down from the bed and rub herself against Portia's leg, purring.

Changing out of the prickly dress, Portia sat down on the floor, pulling the cat in her lap. "All right. Now for a spell." She reached under the bed and brought out Fenella's book. "The man is looking for a spell to break a curse, Owl. There must be something in here that I can say and earn the money with some honesty."

The cat didn't respond but curled up in her lap and went to sleep, one eye opening from time to time to check on Portia.

For the next hour, she studied the book—and found nothing. There weren't even curses in the book.

But there was one strange little recitation for removing all obstacles. The instructions said it had to be recited five times. *"Power of All Beings abound,"* Portia read aloud. *"Clear my path that I may walk, Clear my eye that I may see, Depart all that would stop me from being free."*

She frowned, scratching a place on her neck where the holly leaf had pricked her. "That doesn't sound witchy." She set Owl aside and came to her feet. She crossed to the mirror above her chest of drawers and said the curse again, holding the heavy book with one hand.

No, this wasn't working.

Portia set the book on the wardrobe and practiced being a witch. She tried different voices and postures. She worked at keeping her hat low over her face while raising her arms and calling out, *"Power* of *All* Beings," to dramatize the spell.

Eventually, she reached the point where she could repeat the poem and not feel silly. In fact, she was rather proud of her witch.

Darkness fell early this time of year. Portia carefully tucked the hat inside a black cloth bag she'd used whenever her family moved. Her plan was to steal out of the house as Portia but change in the woods once she'd reached the Great Oak, a landmark many knew located deep in the forest.

Satisfied she had done all she could, she went downstairs for dinner, only to learn from Glennis that her mother had already received her supper tray and that Minnie had said she was too indisposed to eat.

"Poor thing, she truly cared for Mr. Tolliver. She isn't taking the new information we heard very well," Glennis said in her soft brogue. She was of Portia's age with a head of red, curly hair and sky blue eyes. They were in the kitchen with only their candles and the hearth for light. It was a cozy atmosphere and one for confidences.

"What new information?" Portia asked, wanting to know what Glennis knew.

"About Mr. Tolliver," Glennis said. "He's been keeping company with a lass in Fort William." She set a plate of stew on the table for Portia.

"*What?*" Portia was shocked. How do you know this?"

"My aunt is his housekeeper. She said he's been traveling to Fort William several times a week since last he called on Miss Minnie. He always bathes and dresses well before he goes."

Portia had to close her mouth that had dropped open. "Why, that ugly toad," she said, the words spilling out of her. "How dare he treat my sister that way."

"We'd all thought she'd sent him away," Glennis said. "But when I saw her this afternoon, I realized it couldn't be true."

"Her affections were firm," Portia said, stoutly defending her sister. She took her seat in front of her dish of stew. "Mother interfered and I believe she said some things to Mr. Tolliver that were not true—however, I am shocked that he has changed his heart so quickly." *Were all men the same? Were they all like her father?* "When I hear of how shallow men are, I am *thankful* I am on the shelf."

"They are not all that way," Glennis said, drying her hands on the apron over her skirt. "My Jamie is a good man and a fine husband."

"Well, you must have the only one," Portia said, picking up her fork. She needed to eat so that she had her strength for traipsing around the woods. "This is not the first gentleman Minnie has placed her trust in and been disappointed. There was a young man in London who disappeared after Father died and he discovered the severity of our circumstances." She didn't shy from speaking this way in front of Glennis. She owed the maid back wages, which she was determined to pay, and so they had already shared a blunt, difficult conversation.

"The heart doesn't know defeat," Glennis said. "Hers will love again. And you may fall in love yourself, miss."

Portia shook her head. "I've yet to meet a man who made me feel 'love.' Then again, I am not a giddy creature. I've met handsome men, but never one who has touched my heart. And I'm of an independent spirit," she announced. "I don't think I was meant to marry."

"But aren't you ever lonely?" Glennis asked.

"No," Portia answered, a touch too quickly. Loneliness was not something she could let herself dwell upon. "I have responsibilities and a busy life. I haven't time to be lonely."

"But don't you yearn for a man you can lean on?"

Portia thought of her father. "A man is the last person I would lean on."

"What of children, Miss Portia? Don't you want them?"

That question was too personal. Too frank. Portia rose from the stool. "I don't know," she admitted. "I don't think on it often."

"I think about it every day," Glennis said, picking up Portia's dish and tossing the contents into a bin. She scooped sand from another bin and scrubbed the dish with it. "Jamie and I want wee ones, but we haven't been blessed yet."

"Well, I've not felt that yearning," Portia said.

"Sure you have," Glennis answered. "Every woman has it."

Portia shook her head, but didn't speak. How could one explain to a person as blissfully happy as Glennis that not all lives were uncomplicated? That Minnie might search for love, but Portia didn't believe in it. She couldn't after watching her parents' marriage. It had been a sham. Her father hadn't given a care for any of them. Minnie didn't truly remember a time when he'd been around, but Portia did. He'd been more of a visitor than a family member.

And Portia had spent too many years scrambling to make ends meet when he'd not send money to support them to have any respect for his memory. She was better off alone, although there were times she wished she wasn't *so* alone.

Then again, one couldn't be hurt when one was alone.

This was not something spoken of to the cook.

"Good night, Glennis," Portia said instead, and picked up her candle.

"Sleep well, Miss Portia. I shall see you in the morning."

"Yes, thank you," Portia said, and escaped to her room.

The house was dark and quiet, and Portia was too nervous to sit and wait passively for the clock to move forward.

Reasoning she wanted to arrive at the oak early to don her costume and see that all was as she wished it, she put on her dress of holly leaves, covering it from prying eyes with her heavy wool cloak. She drew on her gloves and raised the cloak's ample hood over her head to hide her face. Picking up her bag stuffed with her hat and plaid, she left the house.

She worked in the barn every night after dark but she'd never left the property. It was a brave thing she was doing, going out on her own into the night, and an exciting one. She still wore her spectacles although she fully intended to remove them once she reached the Great Oak. If she kept them on, the Chattan might discover her identity if he asked questions. Not that many women wore spectacles in the valley.

The ground was wet and spongy beneath her feet as she left the path and walked into the woods. Clouds covered the sky, but the full moon peeped out every once in a while to guide her way. All was eerily quiet. A fog drifted across the ground and the trees took on sinister shapes.

Portia refused to let herself think nonsense about ghosts and spirits and dangers, although her pulse was racing madly. What she was doing was a gamble, but didn't they say fortune favored the bold? And she truly had no other choice. She needed money.

She was almost to the end of Camber Hall's property when she noticed a white object hovering on a tree stump. The object moved, jumping into the brush.

Portia gave a start, her hand going to her throat, but a small meow told her how silly she was being.

"Owl, you gave me a terrible fright."

The wee cat answered with another of her light, complacent meows.

Portia forged on. Owl followed at a distance,

disappearing into the brush from time to time. In truth, she welcomed the cat's comforting presence.

After a half hour of hard walking, Portia reached the Great Oak, which was a landmark in this section of the woods. Since the oak was on the way to Crazy Lizzy's house, Portia knew it well. The tree was set off the path and stood by itself, tall and majestic.

However, tonight, as she entered the clearing surrounding it, she received a surprise. The clouds had opened around the moon, painting the area a silvery light and highlighting the toadstool ring around the tree.

"Toadstool rings are not evil," Portia whispered to herself. Still, its presence brought out a superstitious uneasiness Portia did not know she had.

A toadstool ring *was* witchy.

Yes, they could be found all over, but not this time of year.

The chant in Fenella's book came to Portia's mind and she found herself repeatedly murmuring, "Queen of the Meadow, take this evil from this house," as she approached the Great Oak.

The tree was barren of leaves and its trunk was so wide around that it would take the arms of two men to encircle it. Therefore the toadstool ring was enormous.

Portia stepped inside the ring and put her bag on the ground. She raised a hand to lower the hood of her cloak so she could put on her hat, when a deep male English voice behind her said, "Hello, Fenella."

Portia froze. She dared not breathe, let alone move. She was not prepared. She still wore her spectacles, but at least her cloak covered her head. And there was no time to make presentation of the dress she'd labored over all day.

"*It's not midnight*," she said, blurting the first words that came to her mind, and then chastised herself because she hadn't used any of the special voices she'd practiced.

"I wouldn't be a good soldier if I did what was expected, would I?"

She pulled the hood of her cloak lower over her face to hide her spectacles and slowly turned.

He was a dark shadow against the forest. The shadow moved and changed into a tall, broad-shouldered man in greatcoat and boots.

The time had come. She could not show fear or allow herself to feel it. She had come this far to play a part, and so she would.

Portia raised a gloved hand and, using the witch's voice she had practiced that day, said, "And I wouldn't be a good witch if I let you have your way. *Begone* with you. We have no more business between each other."

*H*arry had not anticipated being dismissed.

None of the women presented to him as witches before had dismissed him. They all wanted the money or they had been sad and lonely.

Another difference—this witch was young. Very young. All the others had been crones. In spite of the long cloak, he could tell she had a slender figure, and her arm moved with natural grace.

A small white cat who appeared not to have ears had come to sit on its haunches beside her as if offering protection. A most unusual cat. Then Harry realized it did have ears that had dropped forward, and almond eyes that watched him as if daring him to take one more step.

The wind rose, rushing through the clearing and up and around them, and Harry knew in that moment, in a way that defied logic and common sense, that he was supposed to be here. That he was meant to meet *this* woman.

Harry wasn't given to flights of fancy. He was not even particularly superstitious—and yet there was a connection between him and this woman so strong that it *could* have survived two hundred years.

She was the one. She was Fenella.

This was the woman he'd been searching for. He recognized her deep in his bones.

He'd even overheard her chanting as she approached the tree.

"Wait," he said. "I . . ." He paused, and then removed his hat and fell to his knees in front of her. She held his brother's life in her hands. "I beg a moment of your time."

Her head turned slightly as if she didn't quite believe him.

"Please," he said, softening his voice. "Please" was a new word to Harry. He commanded and others obeyed. But then, since he'd started this quest, he'd had to make many changes.

"I have come so far and searched so hard for you," he said. "Please, hear my plea."

Her arm came down. She drew herself back toward the haven of the tree, as if uncertain, her face hidden in the shadow of her hood.

Accepting her actions as a sign that she would listen, he launched into his petition. "My brother's life depends upon your goodwill," Harry said, throwing all pride away. "He's a remarkable man. A better man than myself. He has fallen in love, Fenella. You know what that means."

She did not reply, but kept her head down. He wished he could see her face. The cat at her feet didn't blink but stared all the harder.

"Lyon and his wife are going to have a child. He has everything to live for, Fenella. Everything. He does so much good for the world. You have extracted your price for your daughter's death. It has been almost two centuries. Let it be, Fenella. Let it be. Let your clan and mine be at peace. Neither you nor I can bring Rose back."

The witch stood silent as if she was part of the tree and nature around her. She'd lifted her head ever so slightly as he spoke and he was shocked because she appeared to not have eyes. Instead, moonlight glinted from where her eyes should be. Again she lowered her head. Harry didn't know if she was agreeing to his request or merely considering it.

Harry swallowed and pushed forward, putting all his conviction, all his love for his brother in his words. "If you must claim one last life, let it be mine. I'm a worthless soul. I am burdened by my own senseless, selfish actions. I've cost many good men their lives through my rashness and vanity. I deserve to die. In fact, death would be a blessing. But my brother, Fenella, my brother merits happiness. I admire him before all other men. Lift the curse. You have had your revenge. And if it is more blood you wish," he whispered, spreading open his arms, "let it be mine."

*P*ortia did not know what to make of this startling declaration.

Did he truly believe that one person could claim the life of another with something as simple and silly as a curse?

Or that there were such creatures as witches?

Paganism was long dead in Scotland . . . or was it? He spoke with conviction, with belief.

And there was something unworldly about this moment. There was the moon, the drift of fog, the wind in the trees, and this warrior of a man on his knees in front of her.

Now that he was no longer scowling as he had been the day before, she could see he was a handsome man, big-boned and with strong features that spoke of a deep character. His hair was overlong, as if he had not had time to seek his barber. It curled around his ears.

Even in the moonlight, his eyes burned with his sincerity.

And she was afraid.

He reached into his greatcoat and pulled out

a small leather drawstring bag that he tossed toward the toadstool ring. It landed heavily at her feet. Owl pounced on it immediately, believing it a toy. The cat batted at the purse strings, and then, placing a paw upon it, lay down upon it, claiming it for her feline self.

"There are fifty silver pieces in that purse. I offer two hundred and fifty more if you will remove the curse," he said. "If that price is not enough, name what you want and I will pay it. I am a wealthy man but my money means nothing to me if I must watch my brother die."

Portia had meant to take advantage of an arrogant man. Instead, she found herself facing a contrite one. A wounded one. This man suffered. He was in pain.

The spell she had been practicing that afternoon rose to her lips, unbidden by conscious thought. *"Power of All Beings Abound, Clear my path that I may walk, Clear my eye that I may see, Depart all that would stop me from being free."* Her voice didn't even sound like her own.

"You will lift the curse?" he asked. Straight, masculine brows had come together. This man was nobody's fool, and here she was playing him for one.

"I will think on it," she whispered.

His jaw tightened. "I cannot accept that answer. I demand certainty. I'm paying for it."

Here was the man who had almost run her over.

Portia shook her head. "I shall *think* upon it," she repeated, matching the challenge in his voice with steel in her own.

He studied her a moment as if weighing his advantage, and then bowed his head. "As you wish. We shall meet tomorrow night?"

The Chattan was taking charge again, but Portia discovered her knees were shaking. Holding her own against him in this encounter was taking its toll.

"Tomorrow, midnight, *and not before*," she answered. "Now go." As if to second her command, Owl hissed at him.

He nodded, placed his hat on his head, and rose to his feet. Portia dared not to take a breath until he had walked away.

Owl did not move. The cat was listening, and Portia trusted her. She did not move as well.

A few minutes later, she heard a horse moving through the forest. The Chattan must have tethered it a good distance away so she would not be alerted to his presence. The horse's movements faded into the distance, and Portia could release the breath she had been holding.

She knelt to the ground, her legs almost unable to support her.

Owl rubbed her back against Portia and purred her pleasure.

Portia reached for the purse. It was heavy in her hand. She untied the drawstrings and poured the gleaming silver into her hand. This was a small fortune. It was one year of support from her Uncle Ned. They would be able to pay rent and back wages and hold on for another year of their tenuous existence. It would be a good Christmas.

Portia didn't linger but picked up her black bag and hurried home. She was very lucky that he had not seen her face, or at least she prayed he hadn't.

She took off the dress, stuffed it, holly leaves and all, in the bag with the hat, and hid the lot under her bed.

After a restless night when she had dreams of knights in armor kneeling before her and wild horses running her over, Portia cooled her impatient heels until late morning to announce to her mother and Minnie that she had heard from Uncle Ned. Her letter and his money to them must have crossed paths in the post, she said, because here was what he had promised.

Minnie was still very quiet and sad and behaved as if money didn't matter—but her mother was thrilled. "We need a new frock for Minnie if she is to attract notice at the Christmas Assembly."

"I'm not going to the Assembly," Minnie said.

"Oh yes, you are," Lady Maclean announced. "No daughter of mine will go into hiding for a mere country physician. You were destined for better things, my girl."

"We have plenty of dresses," Portia argued. "We don't need new."

"It's not you I'm buying for," her mother said. "It's for your sister. We need her to marry well, or do you want to spend a lifetime of begging Ned for money?"

"I'm not going to marry," Minnie announced. "I'm going to be just like Portia. Alone and content."

Portia had opened her mouth to speak, but found words deserted her. *Was she content?* Certainly she was alone.

And why did Minnie's assertion make her feel hollow inside?

"Minnie," their mother said, "you mustn't waste time licking your wounds. Mr. Tolliver ran too easily. It was a test, you see. Any man worth his salt would have fought for you. You want a man who is more stalwart. And you want to look your very finest when Mr. Oliver Tolliver sees you again, which will probably be at the Christmas Assembly."

The last argument won Minnie over.

Pride was a funny thing, and Portia could see that their mother had struck just the right chord to raise Minnie's.

Minnie's chin lifted. "You are right. If I don't go, then he will know how much he has hurt me."

"That's my girl. Portia, hitch the pony cart. Minnie and I are going to Fort William."

"Mother, please," Portia said. "We don't have money for this."

"Nonsense," Lady Maclean said, plucking the coin purse right out of Portia's hand. "We don't have money to *not* do this. Consider it a sensible investment in our futures."

"I won't let her spend it all," Minnie promised Portia. Now that she had a purpose in mind, that of showing Mr. Tolliver how foolish he was to let her go, color had returned to Minnie's cheeks. "We just need lace and ribbon. It won't cost much. I assure you it won't."

"At least let me keep twenty pounds for the back rent and the next quarter," Portia said. She'd also be able to see to Glennis's back wages.

"If you insist," Lady Maclean answered, and counted out the coins, but she kept the rest. She and Minnie put their heads together and started sharing ideas for updating dresses they already had.

Portia stood there, listening to them carry on . . . and realized they would soon spend what she had. And then she would need to find more. Always searching for more.

And she felt very guilty that she had deceived the Chattan only to have her family spend, spend, spend.

She was not surprised when they returned from Fort William with the information that buying lace and ribbon for old dresses had not been enough. A new dress had to be made for Minnie, and of course it had cost extra since the seamstress had such a short amount of time to create it.

And her sister had wanted it. In the space of hours Minnie had changed. She'd gone from the heartbroken sister to a woman who felt scorned. Certainly their mother had worked her magic.

Oh yes, and Lady Maclean had purchased a few "necessities" for herself.

That night, Portia didn't go to the Great Oak.

She'd never intended to. After all, she was not a witch. She could not give the Chattan the spell he wished. And she could not return his money. It was almost gone.

And so she lay awake, Owl curled into a contented ball at the foot of the bed, while she stared at her ceiling, praying fervently that the Englishman would forgive her for playing him false.

The problem was, with the image of the man on his knees in front of her burned into her memory, she doubted if she would ever be able to forgive herself.

Chapter Four

The "witch" had deceived him.

Harry had been cheated. The realization had come to him slowly. He'd rejected the idea at first. He'd wanted her to be a witch. He'd wanted her to have the power to save his brother.

He stood there in the middle of the night staring at the Great Oak, willing it to conjure Fenella. He'd waited for *three* hours before he realized she would not come. Three hours spent cramped and hidden, three hours when he'd dared to let himself *hope*.

And now? He realized the woman might have been some charlatan who had heard of the money he'd been offering. He was humiliated. Cheated. He'd even posted a letter to his sister, Margaret, to take heart, that he believed he had found Fenella. He hated thinking of the false hope he'd passed on to his brother.

Harry was not a man one crossed. He hated double dealing. Even in the military he was known for wanting the truth, no matter how ugly. Only then could he make a reasonable decision.

Damn, he needed a drink or the blessed relief of opium. His game leg had started aching and he was angry enough to tear the head off of someone.

He had to have a release, and for a wild moment, he vented his anger by kicking the tree and stomping on the toadstools, silly, childish gestures, and yet he was in such a rage he needed a release of some sort. *He had believed.* What a fool he'd been!

Harry had even fallen to his knees in front of her. He'd *humbled* himself.

He marched off, collected Ajax, and tore off across the moonlit countryside as if the devil was at his heels.

No, he *was* the devil! When he found "Fenella," she would rue the day she had thought to cheat him—and he *would* find her.

And he tried.

For the next twenty-four hours, he wore himself and Ajax to the bone, searching for the woman who had deceived him. She was here somewhere. He knocked on doors, paid bribes, followed every path through forests, over moors, along the shoreline.

Did he know the Scots didn't trust him? Oh yes, he did, but Harry was beyond caring what they thought. Every fiber of his being was intent on finding this woman.

Of course, his decision to stay had pleased Monty.

"So you *will* be able to attend the Christmas Assembly. That's good. That's good," Monty said, rubbing his hands. "Do you have something suitable to wear?"

Harry frowned at him, thinking his friend insane. "I am not going to any dance. That is not my purpose here."

"But you *are* here. It's tomorrow evening. You should go." He paused to add, "You know I need you. And it is the Christmas season, a time when we should gather for good company."

"*No.*" Harry ran a frustrated hand through his hair and attempted to soften his tone. "I'm sorry, Monty, but I'm not feeling in a festive spirit. I don't care if Christ himself was present at that dance. I'm failing my brother. I've never failed before. I've cost lives, but I have *never* failed."

"I only thought since you were here . . ." Monty's voice drifted off and Harry couldn't help but pity him, standing there alone, surrounded by his dogs who wagged their tails, eager for his attention.

Harry raised his hands to protest and then let them drop to his side. "I must leave on the morrow. I travel to Edinburgh."

"To what purpose?" Monty asked.

"There is a man, William Donan at the university in Edinburgh, who specializes in folk stories about kelpies and witches. Perhaps he can give me information."

"You don't know *where* you are going," Monty answered, his doubt about the idea clear.

That was true. But he had exhausted every avenue in Glenfinnan.

"I'm trying my best," Harry said, speaking more to himself than the general. He looked to his mentor. "I'm sorry, sir, that I can't help you. Once I've found a way to break the curse, I shall return and we'll sweep every woman in Glenfinnan off her feet."

"I don't want every woman," Monty responded. "I want just one, and I don't know if I'll ever have her." He turned away from Harry. "Go on. You've been wanting to leave. You need to carry on. Don't worry about me. We are both good soldiers and understand that there is always a calling higher than our own personal desires."

"I wish it was different, sir," Harry said.

Monty's response was a wave of his hand. "Just don't fall in love, Chattan. It's worse than hell."

Harry could answer that he had already lived his own personal hell, one made up of a love of a different kind, but there was nothing more that could be said that would make the situation better. He turned and left the room. As he passed the dining room, the cut glass of Montheath's wine and whiskey decanters gleamed in the room's lamplight. Harry gripped the stair railing. His leg was tight with pain and tension from too many hours in the saddle. A dram would make life easier.

Or make it tortured.

He'd fought hard to overcome his vices. He would return to them someday, but not until he had saved his brother. With that promise, he forced himself to climb the stairs.

His valet, Rowan, was waiting with hot compresses for his leg. The servant had been with Harry since his service in India. One day in Calcutta, he'd begun following Harry and had soon made himself indispensable. Over the years, the small man with the dusky skin, unflinching amber brown eyes and impeccable, accented English had proved himself trustworthy, and was greatly valued.

"How did you know?" Harry murmured, so grateful for his valet's foresight he could have wept. The moist heat immediately eased the cramping in his leg.

"The cold damp is not good for your muscles, Colonel," Rowan answered, sitting Harry on the edge of the bed and helping him remove his coat and boots. The manservant had also kept a steaming pot of water on the hearth and in short order had a cup of special "tea" made of dried lemon rinds, basil and honey.

Harry took a good sip, feeling the lemon's oil settle in his chest before saying, "I can't find her, Rowan. I've searched every inch of this damned place. Fenella was probably a fraud. I can't believe I was hoaxed."

"She is one of many who were not true, Colonel."

"Yes, but the first one who made me believe she was real."

Harry stared at the fire. Montheath liked a wood fire. Harry appreciated this choice.

"What do you do now, Colonel?"

What did *he do now?* "It's not the money. I don't care about throwing my money on the woman," Harry answered. "But I can't believe I was so wrong. I could feel her power, Rowan. She wasn't like any of the others I've met. And her eyes, Rowan, they were like small moons. I know that sounds odd but it was the image I gathered."

Harry shook his head. He was starting to sound foolish. "We go to Edinburgh," he informed Rowan. "There is a gentleman scholar there who is said to know a great deal about witches and the like. We'll leave at first light."

"Are you certain, sir?"

Harry gave a sharp glance to Rowan. The manservant had never questioned him. "Do you believe we should stay?"

Rowan didn't answer immediately, taking his time hanging Harry's jacket in the wardrobe. Harry waited. He expected a response.

The manservant turned and then said quietly, "There is something here."

"Something or someone?" Harry demanded. He had met mystics in the East. He'd often wondered if Rowan was one, if that was the reason the man had taken up with him, because Rowan had certainly chosen him, not the other way around. But he'd never asked. He did so now. "Rowan, why did you follow me that market day in Calcutta? Why did you choose me?"

"You are a good man, Colonel."

"There are many good men. I'm also a man who is fatally flawed. I've proved it many a time since you've known me."

"You are a *good* man."

"But why, Rowan? Why did you choose me?"

Rowan came over to Harry. He squatted in the native way. His somber gaze met Harry's troubled one. "I killed a man." He didn't wait for Harry to comment but said, "The man deserved to die. He was evil. But I had to atone for my action. I asked goddess Maya for guidance."

"Maya?" Harry repeated. There were thousands of Hindu gods. He'd not heard of this one.

"The Spider, the spinner of magic. She weaves the web of our lives. I asked her what I should do now because no one saw me kill this man. No one questioned me."

"Do you regret killing him?" Harry asked.

Rowan shook his head. "He killed my father for our family's land. He deserved his fate. His karma. He knew I would come, but he was a powerful man. I gave an offering to Maya and she told me to go with the next man I met. It was you, Colonel."

"*She* told you?"

A knowing look came to Rowan's brown eyes. "If you listen, the gods will speak to you."

"I doubt that, Rowan. I've been beyond God's hand for too long."

"Listen. Ask Maya."

The soft command hovered between them.

"I'm not a praying man," Harry said carefully, "to my God let alone any others."

Rowan shifted his weight. "Perhaps, sir, it is

something you should do. Every man must have a belief. How else does he understand his karma?" He bowed, rose, and withdrew from the room, shutting the door behind him.

The silence in his wake was unsettling. The servant had been with Harry through two continents. He'd been quiet and unassuming, never asking anything, never challenging—until now.

Harry looked around the room, at the draperies and bed curtains, at the bare floor and the wardrobe. He was alone, and yet perhaps Rowan was right. Perhaps there was something more here. Something he didn't understand.

But he did believe man controlled his own fate. His karma sprang from the decisions he made, the actions he took.

And Harry didn't look to a Hindu deity for assistance.

No, he was a lone wolf. It was how he'd survived. How he wanted to be.

As for God? Harry and God had not been on good terms for a long time. The last time Harry put trust in the Unknown was on a battlefield at Vitoria when he'd charged French cannons. He'd gone alone, leaving orders that his men were not to follow him . . . but they did.

One man could have made it across the field. A

troop of them were easy targets. Harry had survived. He and the mighty Ajax took the cannon—at a tremendous cost. His men had followed him. He'd prayed that day when he'd turned to see his men being mowed down by French guns, but there had been no God to answer his prayer. They had all died.

And strong spirits and laudanum had helped him face the disaster. He blamed himself. He'd been their commander. If he could have done it again, he would have been wiser. He would have understood the depth of their loyalty. Indeed, he was the one who had set the example of disobeying orders that they had used to follow him.

Harry rubbed his thigh where he had been wounded. He would have gladly given his leg if it would have saved the lives of those valiant men.

And Rowan spoke to him of karma . . .

Harry blew out the candle, slid beneath the sheets, and laid his head on the pillow.

Rowan had not come to him by chance. That was one thing Harry did believe.

Of course he dreamed of the battlefield. He couldn't stop the dreams. They haunted him, except this time was different.

She *was there.*

Although he could not see her face, he knew it was she. She was a glorious creature, hovering above the field as he watched his men being slaughtered.

And Harry wanted her. He was hard and ready for her. He reached up, the French artillerymen he'd slain watching him with curious expressions, their faces white in death.

Just when Harry thought he could touch her she moved—no, floated—away from him, drifting to the plains beyond the battle.

She was swathed from head to toe in a great cloak that moved around her slender frame, the moon in her eyes. She had no hands, no feet, no face, and yet he knew *her.*

And there was fire now, all around them. The flames leaped to the heavens but he felt no heat or fear.

He heard her laugh, the sound seductive, inviting. This was not the sound of a witch. It was the song of an angel. Again he reached for her. His hands went right through her.

And then Harry wasn't in the dream. He was in his bed and he sat up, puzzled. She pushed him back down upon the mattress. He could feel her, but could not see her.

She leaned forward. He sensed the movement as if his eyes were closed.

He knew he was still dreaming. This was not real.

Her head dipped toward his. He wanted to open his eyes, and yet he feared what he would see. She would have no face, only shadows—

And then her lips touched his. He felt the roughness of her tongue against his lower lip. The touch was real, wet, strange, abrasive—

Harry came awake with a start, realizing he *was* being kissed—but not by a woman.

A cold nose brushed his skin. Again the rough tongue stroked his lip. He reached up what was on top of him and flung it away from him.

A small body landed on the floor.

His senses on alert, Harry reached under his pillow for his knife as he rolled out of bed and held it out, ready for the intruder.

No one attacked.

He knew he'd been dreaming. Damn, his body was still hard and the blood flowing through his veins hot. The embers in the fire in the hearth sent a warm glow through the room. He held his breath, listening. He was not alone.

And then he heard the small meow.

A cat?

"Oh God," Harry said, raising the back of his free hand to his lips and wiping them clean.

What would a cat be doing here in this house that was a haven for every dog that came its way?

Harry put down the knife, pulled on his breeches, and reached for the candle. He walked over to the dying fire to stir the embers, lit the candle off of them, and turned toward the bed.

The cat jumped up onto the bed, a cat with an unusual round head and ears folded over. Fenella's cat.

Or was it Fenella? The cat's eyes seemed to view him with a wisdom as old as the soul.

Cautious now, Harry took a step forward. "Here, kitty. How did you come in here?" His door was shut. The window was closed as well.

The cat came to its feet, arching its back and hissing at him. Harry stopped. "How did you make it in here, kitty, past all Monty's dogs?"

The cat's lips curved into what Harry would swear was a smile, and then it jumped down from the bed and ran under the wardrobe in the corner of the room.

Harry followed, falling to his knees and reaching under the furniture to drag the cat out, heedless of claws. And yet, as he stretched his arm in every direction, he felt nothing.

Harry brought the candle down as far as he could so that he could peer beneath the wardrobe. The cat was not there.

He came to his knees and searched the room.

There was no sign of the cat. The window was still locked. Harry looked behind the drapes and under the bed.

No cat.

It had disappeared.

He even went so far as to open the door. The hall was empty and all was dark and quiet. Not one dog in the house stirred.

Just to be certain, he went to Monty's door and pounded on it. It took several knocks and shaking of the knob to wake his friend.

Monty in his nightcap cracked open his door, squinting against the light. A few of the dogs came out to check Harry. They didn't give him more sniffs than usual and didn't seem to catch a whiff of something different in the hall.

"What is it?" Monty asked, his voice sleep hoarse.

"Do you have a cat?"

"A what?"

"A *cat*," Harry repeated.

"Don't like the damn things," Monty said. "The dogs would tear it to shreds."

"Your pups don't seem on guard now," Harry murmured.

"On guard for what?"

"A cat."

Monty shook his head. "You've been dreaming. I have no cat here. May we discuss this in the morning?"

"Yes, of course."

His friend shut the door.

Harry returned to his room and sank down on the bed. There was no cat here and yet he had touched it. The animal had been living and breathing and not a dream.

He crossed over to the bedroom's desk, set down his candle, and pulled out pen and paper. Dipping the quill into the well, he began to write furiously everything he remembered from the dream.

His brother and his wife had dreams as well. They kept a record of them in a journal because they believed Fenella threatened them in their dreams. Harry had read what they'd written. There had been images of fire. He'd had fire.

However, his had been a dream of seduction.

And that strange little cat with its folded-over ears had not been a figment of his imagination. He wasn't a fanciful man. He believed what he saw, and he'd seen that cat, had felt the roughness of its tongue and the weight of its body.

He was close to Fenella.

Suddenly, the overwhelming emotions he'd experienced with the witch the night at the Great Oak were no longer a trick of his mind. They had been real.

And then he had a flash of insight. *He hadn't been able to see her face, but there had been the moon in her eyes. It had been a reflection—in person and in the dream.*

"She wore spectacles," Harry whispered, not believing he could have missed something so obvious. A witch with the need for eyeglasses.

A witch who wanted to seduce him.

Harry set aside the pen, knowing now that he didn't need to search for Fenella. She was coming for him.

He jumped up from the chair at the writing table. He charged into the hall and began banging on Monty's door with his fist.

"What is it now?" Monty demanded throwing open the door. "Are you being attacked by more cats?"

"The devil take the cat," Harry answered. "I'm going with you to the dance tomorrow night."

Chapter Five

"Whatever you do, Portia, do *not* wear your spectacles," Lady Maclean ordered in a furious whisper as they came into sight of Borrodale's barn. She, Portia and Minnie rode in the pony cart all bundled up in their sensible woolen cloaks over their finery. Portia was driving.

The barn was a huge stone building and the site of numerous dances through the year, although this was the first the Macleans would attend. Tonight the building was lit with what seemed to be a hundred torches. A crowd was already gathered, and the sound of music and laughter could be heard all around.

"Yes, Mother," Portia murmured with a hint of annoyance.

"Then take them off now," her mother said.

"Wouldn't you rather I see where I'm going this

last bit of the way?" Portia demanded. "Or shall we just trot over people?"

"Oh, what nonsense," Lady Maclean said, plucking the lenses right off Portia's nose. "You see perfectly well without them." She tucked Portia's precious glasses into her reticule.

Portia didn't see "perfectly well" . . . but she did see well enough. Unfortunately, she found she could develop a headache if she went without them for too long.

Minnie didn't say one word and hadn't most of the day. She seemed caught up in her own sad world. As Portia drove the cart to where the other vehicles were lined up, Minnie stirred and looked to the barn.

Their mother smiled. "He will be sorry," she promised Minnie in a soft voice.

Minnie nodded, her expression grim.

Portia assumed they were speaking of Mr. Tolliver and found herself sympathizing with him. It wasn't as if he'd abandoned Minnie. Their mother had warned him away, it wasn't as if he'd run. He was not the sort of man who had time to fight over a woman. He was a *doctor*. But she knew better than to express her opinion at this point—and if Minnie didn't care so much, then she wouldn't be believing the worst in the man. Women always fretted over whether a man liked them when they cared. Of course, Portia had never fallen in love, and wasn't likely to at this late date, so she couldn't speak from experience.

Local boys came running to help them with their pony, Honey, and watch the cart for them. Portia gave them a coin and then followed her mother and sister inside. She was several steps behind them, so she had a good vantage point to see everyone's reactions to Minnie's arrival.

The spirit was merry in the barn, which was like no barn Portia had ever seen before. The interior was enormous, with patterned stone floors and high ceiling beams. There was room for vehicles and equipment. Of course, everything, including the animals, had been moved out.

The rafters rang with music, laughter and greetings, and the place, especially by the door, was an absolute crush. Everyone of importance in the valley seemed to be there.

The guests were all in their finest. There was a kilt here and there, and most of the men and women proudly sported a bit of plaid in this once hotbed of Jacobite sympathies.

Lighting was provided by oil lamps hanging from the barn's beams. The musicians were two gentlemen with pianoforte and violin. One wouldn't think that such a small group could create enough sound to be heard above the conversations, but they did. The dancing was already going strong. Long tables decorated with evergreens and holly leaves, and holding punch bowls and platters of food, lined the wall farthest from the entrance. Portia feared what the dancing would be like after all the punch in those bowls had been consumed, although it appeared a good number of the guests had been tippling before they'd arrived.

Expectation and excitement were in the air. There was no class structure here. Everyone in the countryside was all decked out in their finest and had gathered in this barn to celebrate the season.

Lady Maclean led their way into the barn. Such was her presence, people created a path for her. Or perhaps they were taken aback by the three large, green ostrich plumes she wore in her hair. The hair decoration was common in London, but not so much here in the Highlands, and the Scots acted as if her mother was some grand peacock who had arrived to strut in their midst.

However, what started people whispering, what made them step back and really take notice, was not their mother. It was Minnie.

It started with the younger men—clearly still

in their teens—who stood at the door to assist guests with their cloaks. Portia watched in fascination as a red-faced lad offered to help Minnie with her cloak, his voice cracking with nervousness as he spoke to her. Minnie, oblivious to the trueness of her beauty, smiled, and the poor lad almost swooned from being the focus of her attention. His hands shook as he helped remove the garment from her shoulders.

And then a hush seemed to fall over all the males within a ten-foot radius around Minnie as they took in how incredibly beautiful she was.

The dress was perfect for Minnie's figure and probably worth the goodly amount of money paid for it. It was a snowy white muslin decorated with layers of lace and trimmed with white ribbon. The cut emphasized the fullness of Minnie's breasts and the gentle curve of her hip. She wore a white ribbon at her neck and had styled her blonde hair in loose curls high upon her head.

The crowd, which at first had reminded Portia of nothing more than a group of happy puppies climbing all over one another, took on form as men caught sight of her sister and stepped forward.

They were blocked in their pursuit by Lady Maclean, who, with a rap of her fan upon her gloved hand and a shake of her ostrich feathers, let it be known that this beauty was chaperoned. So of course the men queued up to make their introductions and pay their respects to Her Ladyship before receiving a nod to speak to her daughter.

At first, Minnie appeared startled by the fuss she'd created. Her nature was such that she didn't see herself as others did. She didn't realize how truly stunning her looks were.

Minnie started to turn to Portia as if searching for support, but then her gaze riveted on a sight beyond Portia's shoulder.

Portia turned to look directly where her sister stared. Mr. Tolliver stood off by a punch table, speaking to two not-uncomely women. He acted very interested in what they were saying and seemed not to have noticed Minnie's arrival.

So then Minnie did what every woman in the room would have done, she began flirting with a vengeance and in short order was being led toward the dance floor where the dancers were taking positions for the next set.

"May I help you with your cloak, Miss MacLean?" Portia heard a man ask. "Seems a pity you haven't joined us yet." She turned to see it was a smiling Mr. Buchanan.

"Thank you, sir," she said. She'd been so concerned for her sister, she'd not seen to her own needs. As for her mother, Lady Maclean was holding court with the young men left behind. She was obviously keeping a tally. There would be much reliving of this evening for months to come.

The duke's man removed her cloak, saying, "We don't stand on much ceremony here, not for the Christmas Assembly. As you can see, it is open to one and all. What's important is that we enjoy a bit of merriment."

"I'm looking forward to the evening," Portia answered.

"Even introductions are easy," he advised her. "As the punch bowls empty, we become very friendly. Beware. The lads will dance your feet off."

"I thank you for the warning, sir." Of course, Portia rarely danced. Not any longer. She was too old.

Certainly, she didn't expect to cause a stir in any form close to her sister. Her dress was a creamy muslin she'd worn to a family gathering years ago during better times. It was trimmed in green ribbon so she thought it festive . . . although she did feel a bit too aged for the gown. The dress had been fashioned for her younger self. Her hopeful self.

And because she hadn't any expectations for the evening, she hadn't done anything with her hair other than what she normally did. She'd just pulled it back with a matching ribbon from her dress. She wished she had her glasses. She could see, but they had also come to offer protection over the years. They made it easier for her to be the plainer sister.

"I have the money we owe for rent. We don't want to upset the duke's daughter any more than we already have, but I warn you, sir, Minnie is going to be an uncommon success tonight."

"You are right, however, I'm not certain Lady Emma cares about the competition your sister may give her for being the belle of the countryside. As you can see, her attentions are firmly fixed, which is one of the reasons so many of our bucks came running to claim your sister's attention." He nodded toward the other side of the barn as he spoke.

Portia had been introduced to Lady Emma at church. The girl was all of eighteen with creamy skin, black-as-a-raven's-wing hair and blue eyes— just the sort of Scottish lass troubadours would have lauded in songs.

She was also willful and condescending. Portia usually steered clear of her, as did Minnie.

But right now, all of Lady Emma's attention was claimed by a man, a tall man, one who was familiar to Portia—the English Chattan.

For a second, all Portia could do was stare. Mr. Buchanan was introducing his wife to her, a pretty woman with merry eyes, but Portia listened with only half an ear.

The Chattan was more handsome in the lamplight than he had been in the moonlight. He was dressed as all the other men were here. Some wore evening dress but a good number more wore breeches and tall boots. Of course, the boots were shined and their best clothes pressed, however, the Chattan wore his with the unmistakable air of a Corinthian through and through.

Many of the young men this evening were already aping his manner. They lacked the money to purchase buff-colored breeches of material woven so tightly they hugged his form perfectly or leather boots that fit so well they seemed a part of his legs.

His jacket was a deep, dark blue so that the neck cloth at his neck, tied in the most current fashion, appeared an even more brilliant white. His waistcoat was red, as if to bring a cheery note to the festivities.

Of course the one thing the Scottish lads could

not copy no matter how hard they tried was the Chattan's military bearing, developed, no doubt, over years of discipline. There was a touch of gray at his temples, something she could not have seen during their meeting beneath the Great Oak.

But it was his eyes that claimed all her attention. He was a keen-eyed man—and he was looking right at her.

Portia's breath caught in her throat. Her first instinct was panic. He must not recognize her. He couldn't.

And yet, what if he did?

She murmured some words to excuse herself to Mr. and Mrs. Buchanan. She feared she cut Mrs. Buchanan off in mid-sentence but what else could she do?

She had to gather Minnie and her mother and tell them they must leave immediately.

It would be a challenge, but their very lives— no, *Portia's* very life—might depend upon it.

Blending in the best she could with the crowd and keeping her head down, Portia worked toward where her mother was gaily chatting away. She dared to glance over her shoulder, hoping that she had been mistaken and the Chattan had not been staring at her.

Oh. No. He was *still* watching her.

Lady Emma had noticed he was not completely attentive to her and turned to see why.

Portia ducked her head lower. She had reached the dance floor. Her purpose was to catch Minnie's notice. However, as Minnie's young man preened at having such a lovely partner, she was looking over at the punch table where Mr. Tolliver stood alone studying the contents of his drink glass. He appeared as heart bereft as Minnie.

If he would look up, he would see Minnie's longing . . . and Portia decided what he needed was a good talking to, something to counter her mother's insensitivity, but it wasn't going to happen tonight. They needed to go home with all possible haste—

Portia almost walked into him before she saw him.

The Chattan stood right in front of her.

She looked up, frightened. He bowed, a short, courteous movement. "Miss Maclean, I beg the opportunity to introduce myself to you. I'm Colonel Harry Chattan. I knew your father."

Portia didn't dare speak. She didn't know if she trusted her voice. In any second, she expected him to denounce her, to accuse her of stealing, of lying, of pretending to be *a witch*.

He was going to expose her, right there in front of everyone—

Another man's voice interrupted them. "Miss Maclean, would you dance with me?"

Portia whirled around to face the speaker. Mr. Longacre was the caretaker at church. He was some thirty years her senior with an earnest expression on his face. She flashed him a brilliant smile. "Of course I would," she said, delighted to be whisked away from the Englishman, but then Colonel Chattan proved he had other plans.

I'm sorry, I've spoken for this dance," the colonel said—and then *he* took her arm.

Portia's temper flared. "I did not hear you ask to dance," she said.

Colonel Chattan directed her to their place on the dance floor. "That was my intent," he said. "And you should be honored. I don't dance."

She latched onto his statement as her escape. "Oh, well, then we don't need to," she said, and would have turned and walked away but he captured her hand.

"I need to talk to you," he said, his voice low as if he didn't want anyone else to hear.

Her blood rang in her ears in fear. "About what?" She'd squeaked the words out, actually squeaked.

Before he could answer, the music started, and the caller of the dance announced, "A kiss to the ladies." Portia barely registered this unusual command when Colonel Chattan leaned forward and kissed her cheek.

Startled, Portia drew back. The touch of his lips had been like a small jolt of electricity.

If he felt the same, he didn't show it. Instead, he said almost apologetically, "It's the rule of the Christmas Assembly. To start the dance, the lads must give the lasses a peck. I believe it is a capital idea."

And she realized she hadn't been the only one kissed. All the dancers, even the married couples, had kissed. Most were demure kisses and some not so. Minnie's partner had been overenthusiastic, and those close to them were laughing at her skillful handling at cutting short his efforts.

Heat rushed to Portia's cheeks. She'd been kissed before. Twice, when she was much younger and she'd had suitors. That was before her father's death. They'd been kind, considerate men who hadn't aroused much passion in her.

But Colonel Chattan was different.

He was the sort of man who could make *any* woman's blood race, and Portia was no exception, except she should be. She must be on guard and not let his lips close to her again.

And then Colonel Chattan took her hand and the dance began.

It had been a long time since Portia had danced. The set's figures were simple and the caller good so that everyone knew what to do without the music being overshadowed. Portia was out of practice and felt very self-conscious, but she would have been that way with any partner, albeit more so with him. He had a presence about him that threatened her in a way she wasn't certain she understood.

He knew how to hold a woman's hand. He didn't grip too hard or too lightly. He wasn't a skipper or hopper as some of the gentlemen dancers were. In fact, he moved with an athletic grace, despite favoring his right leg.

Nor did he count the steps to himself under his breath as the gentleman to his left did. Or step on her toes the way the gentleman to the right did to his partner.

And Portia found herself relaxing. She actually smiled. Minnie caught her eye and gave her a sisterly grin in encouragement. The music was merry and fun, the dancers were lighthearted, and Portia couldn't help but enjoy herself even when Lady Emma managed to move herself and her partner over to where Colonel Chattan was.

And then the dance was over.

He bowed.

She curtseyed.

He reached for her arm—

"Was that not the best fun?" Lady Emma asked, stepping between Portia and Colonel Chattan. "But I do enjoy a quadrille."

"Yes, it was good," he answered, again reaching for Portia.

"The next dance will be a reel. You know you owe me a dance, Colonel," Lady Emma said, her voice dropping, becoming coy.

Portia didn't wait to hear what else was said. She took the young woman's distraction as an opportunity to escape among the other dancers leaving the dance floor and those moving toward it.

Colonel Chattan had not denounced her. That was a blessing and she would be wise to not give him another opportunity. She was still intent on gathering her family and leaving, until she noticed Mr. Tolliver slip outside. He went alone, his head down, his shoulders slumped.

Had he seen Minnie's partner kissing her so enthusiastically? Certainly he could not escape noticing that Minnie was being courted by what seemed to be the entire male population of Glenfinnan.

Across the crowd, Portia located her mother's

bobbling ostrich plumes. Minnie was there. The brief smile the sisters had exchanged was gone from her face. Another eager lad was offering his arm, and there was a line waiting. A line of men who would not make her happy.

Minnie's feet would be danced off her legs before this night was out. However, instead of the dance being a moment of social triumph, Minnie's sadness was hard to witness.

The only one pleased with the turn of events was Lady Maclean.

There were many reasons God created big sisters, and the most important, in Portia's mind, was for them to speak for their younger siblings.

It didn't seem right that two people who had so enjoyed each other's company were now apart, and all because neither spoke up.

Portia understood Minnie couldn't run after Mr. Tolliver. It would not be seemly.

But Portia could.

She dismissed her concerns about Colonel Chattan. They were unimportant in the face of True Love.

Without a word to her mother or anyone else, Portia walked out the door in search of Mr. Tolliver.

There were quite a few gentlemen gathered

outside around the door. They stood in the torch-light, sharing a bottle that they passed between them. Mr. Tolliver was not among their number.

"Here, lass," one of them said. He was Augie Macdonald, the farrier. "Take my plaid and keep your shoulders warm."

Portia gratefully accepted the offering and continued on her way.

Horses nickered at her as she moved past them. The ground was soft but not wet, and even if it had been, she would not have thought of her dancing slippers. She was on a mission.

And then she caught sight of Mr. Tolliver. He had on his hat and was standing by his horse. He was giving a coin to one of the lads who watched the horses, and Portia had to hurry or he would leave. She hastened her step.

"Mr. Tolliver, please, I beg of you to wait."

He turned to her. His shoulders stiffened, but he was a polite man.

"How may I be of service, Miss Maclean?" he asked.

Portia glanced at the boy and his friends who were listening with big ears. "Please, sir, walk with me a moment?"

"Of course." Mr. Tolliver nodded to the boy to continue watching his horse and offered his arm.

Portia directed him toward the trees to the side of the barn. There was a pond here and tables had been set out. Other couples lingered around them so Portia didn't think their presence would be too remarkable. However, to ensure they were not overheard, she moved as far from other people as she could. She didn't need to worry. Those others were too caught up in their conversations to eavesdrop on Portia's.

She faced Mr. Tolliver. "Why are you leaving the dance so early?"

He didn't pretend to misunderstand her meaning. "You know why I'm not."

"No, I don't." She drew a breath and plunged in with the question uppermost in her mind. "Do you not admire my sister?"

"Of course I do."

"Above all others?" she demanded.

There was a beat of silence. Portia could feel the man struggle with himself. "You know I have deep affection for her."

Portia wanted to groan her frustration. She hated when men and women kept their distance with words. She herself liked to cut to the heart of a matter. That was how one managed to see things done.

"She has been waiting for you to call."

"I mustn't. She will be wiser to find a better man."

"Oh, so you can't abide her."

He appeared startled at her suggestion. "Who could not like your sister?" he said. "She is one of the stars in the heavens. She is gracious and kind and lovely. The most perfect woman God ever fashioned."

"Is that why you *ignore* her?" Portia surmised, her tone making it clear he didn't make sense.

Mr. Tolliver lifted his chin and straightened his shoulders. "I'm not ignoring her. I am setting her free."

"Free of what?"

"Me."

There, he'd finally admitted it, and now Portia was determined to set him straight. "I know what my mother said to you. I am deeply embarrassed—"

"She was right—"

"She was *wrong*." Portia placed her hand on his arm. "Mother is, well, *funny* in her conclusions. I don't agree with her emphasis on the superficial. Nor does Minnie. My sister admires you greatly. She may appear to many to be happily dancing, but I know her best of all, and her heart is breaking. She holds you in the deepest affection, sir. She doesn't love lightly and she loves you."

He released his breath with the same fervor of a man who had just witnessed a miracle. "I love her."

"Then I would not be standing out here in the dark, Mr. Tolliver. Or planning to return home early. I believe you should return to the barn and ask Minnie to dance."

The kindly doctor took a step away. "If only I could. There is another matter that your mother took me into confidence to speak, and I must hold my tongue, but I understand her concerns. Minnie could do much better."

"Are you talking about the fact we have no money and she expects Minnie to marry well to provide for us?"

He blinked at her bald speaking.

"Mr. Tolliver, are you afraid that my mother and I will be a charge to you? That very well could be true. We are done up. However, my mother and I will manage. We understand that you and Minnie will need to set up your household."

"I would gladly take you all on," Mr. Tolliver said, surprising Portia. "I would be honored to do so. Although finances would be tight."

"It is not anything we are not accustomed to."

"I know," he agreed sadly. "And you all deserve better. That is what your mother forcefully impressed upon me."

"To Minnie, sir, *you* are the best," Portia said softly.

"Because she is so kindhearted. But look at me. I'm half a head shorter than she is. I have a big nose and if I'm not careful, I'll have a big gut as well. My idea of an entertaining evening is a good book and my bed. I own one horse, a small library, and will never be more than a country doctor. I like it here. These mountains, this valley is my home. Minnie is a woman who could outshine the best of them in London."

"I don't know why I'm arguing with you," Portia said, deciding to put a touch of big-sister bullishness in her voice. "And you are right. My sister is very lovely in person and in her nature. She could crook her finger and a half dozen of the most handsome men in the valley would be on their knees in front of her. She's demonstrating that this evening. However, she fell in love with a country doctor who believes her nature so shallow she doesn't know her own mind. Yes, yes, yes, you are right. Well, begone with you, Mr. Tolliver. I tried to serve as a friend and sister to both of you, but I see it is hopeless. You do not care for her—"

"I do. I do, I do, *I do.*"

"Then prove it by going in there and asking

her to dance. In fact, dance with her twice. She will say yes and everyone will know she's chosen you."

"Your mother does not approve of my suit."

Her mother. Disgust rose like bile in Portia's throat.

"My mother . . ." Portia had to pause, fearing what would spill from her lips. "She is not a happy person," she said, amazed at her considerable restraint. "She was not happy in her marriage and swears she married for love. This is a terrible thing to say of one's dam, but I don't believe the woman knows how to love. And since we are talking about the family, you should know my father was a feckless wastrel who I can barely remember because he had very little to do with his family for almost fifteen years. One shouldn't criticize one's parents, but I believe in the truth. Now, decide, sir, do you love my sister enough for her to defy her parent? Because if you don't, say so and I shall walk away." Portia turned as if to make good on her promise.

Mr. Tolliver caught her arm. "I love your sister with all my heart."

"Then go into that dance, sir, and *stake your claim*. Make her a *happy* woman."

She didn't have to repeat herself. He went hurrying off, tearing off his hat as he did so, and Portia was very proud of her handiwork.

What she didn't realize was that she had an audience until he started clapping.

The sound caught her off guard. She'd been so involved in her argument with Mr. Tolliver, she had ignored her surroundings. Now she realized everyone else had gone inside, save for a lone man sitting at a table close at hand.

Colonel Chattan.

He had her isolated. She could shout for help if she needed it, but would she be heard over the music?

Portia feared the time for a reckoning over her pretending to be a witch was at hand.

But when he rose from the chair, it was not to hurl an accusation. Instead, he said, "Well spoken, Miss Maclean. And now, I shall ask you, what else will you do for love?"

Chapter Six

 $\mathcal{M}$iss Maclean's eyes widened at his question and Harry smiled, pleased with himself. He liked the banter of innuendo, and he liked Miss Maclean.

Loyalty, especially to one's sibling, was a quality he admired.

He'd noticed her when she had first arrived, without realizing that here was the daughter of Monty's infatuation. She wasn't Harry's usual style. She was of medium height and pleasant enough looking, but not as buxom and not as knowledgeable as he usually preferred. She could have easily been dismissed as a woman on her way to spinsterhood, if she hadn't relegated herself to that role already. She was not comfortable in the dress she wore. She'd pulled on the neckline and had stood alone for a touch too long to show ease in large gatherings.

But what had first caught his attention had been the graceful movement of her cloaked figure. It had reminded him of Fenella, the witch. For a second, he'd thought he'd found his quarry.

And then she'd removed her hood, and he had been disappointed that she didn't wear spectacles.

When Monty had noticed Harry eyeing her, he had beamed with pleasure.

"See? Isn't she a paragon?" Monty had whispered.

Well, Harry wouldn't have gone that far. Any man with a red-blooded nature would have noticed Miss Maclean's sister first. She was truly a rare pearl. Blonde hair, huge doe-shaped eyes, full, full lips . . .

And then Harry had realized Monty wasn't speaking about either sister, but *their mother*, the woman sporting the impossibly tall ostrich feathers. He'd thought the fashion silly in London and ridiculous here in the country.

For her part, Lady Maclean had noticed Monty. She had looked right at him and then she had done the cruelest thing she could, she had turned her back to his friend. It was a nasty cut direct, and Monty had not taken it well. He'd walked away to drown his sorrows in a very potent punch. Such rudeness had not been necessary, especially from a woman as old as Lady Maclean.

And then she had compounded the insult by sending word through different friends that she was most anxious to meet Harry since she was certain he would like an introduction to her younger daughter.

Harry was determined to speak for his friend this night. He'd promised Monty he would, and he would deliver. But he would not speak to Lady Maclean. Grasping, manipulating stiff-rumped people always made him lose his temper. And he knew better than to approach the younger daughter. That would free wild speculation, fueled, no doubt, by Lady Maclean herself.

Instead, he'd decided to speak to the older daughter, the woman who had piqued his interest.

The woman who had practically run from him on the dance floor.

She was no happier to see him here, but this moment of privacy gave him the opportunity he needed to speak for Monty.

Miss Maclean glanced toward the barn as if ready to bolt, and Harry was puzzled. Her reaction was more than that of a woman with a dislike of him, although he'd never known a woman who disliked him. She was almost frightened. He could sense it.

"I've startled you," he said. " 'Twas not my intention. Please, may I have a moment of your time?"

"I don't see what I can do for you," she replied, and would have left, except she paused to add crossly, "It was rude for you to eavesdrop."

"Perhaps it was a lapse of good manners, but it was not rudeness."

"Says a man who was eavesdropping," she replied, taking a step away from him.

Annoyance froze his smile on his face. "Actually, I was awaiting my turn in line. Please, Miss Maclean, a moment of your time. That's all I ask."

She looked again to the barn and then turned to him with the same grim resignation on her face as he'd seen on men facing court-martial. "What do you wish to say?"

She was as direct as his sister, Margaret, who was also too shrewd to be teased or charmed. So he launched into the speech he'd been mentally rehearsing in his mind all evening.

"It is my great honor to count amongst my friends General Alastair Montheath. Do you know him?"

Her brows had come together in puzzlement. "You wish to speak of Montheath?"

"I wish to speak *for* him. I value his friendship and admire him as an officer and a gentleman."

Miss Maclean's whole stance changed. Her shoulders softened and she released her breath as if in relief.

Harry thought it a very odd reaction. *What had she thought he was going to say?*

"I know General Montheath," Miss Maclean said. "Or at least, I know of him. We have not been introduced but I am aware he has strong feelings for my mother. He follows her."

"Yes, I know," Harry said. "His is odd behavior."

"Decidedly," she agreed with a lift of her brow. "And you are going to tell me that he would like to call on my mother?"

"Yes, I was, or I am."

"He is wasting his time, sir. My mother is set against him and has been since they were children. She married another man. What more proof does the general need?"

"I can only say in his defense that the heart is a persevering organ. Not that I know. I'm as fickle as they come, so perhaps that is why I'm touched by his steadfastness. I knew your father."

That statement brought out a reaction in her. She crossed her arms, sidled a step away.

Harry hurried to continue, "I say this because I want you to know that Monty does not share the same character as your sire. He truly loves your mother."

"How can he?" Miss Maclean answered. "She is not very lovable."

Harry felt his jaw drop at such a bald statement and caught it in time before he appeared a yokel. "I beg your pardon?"

"I'm being honest, Colonel. If you do value your friendship with the general, persuade him to avoid my mother at all costs." She held up a gloved hand to stave off comments. "She can be very difficult. And although she is my parent, I rarely admire her. My conversation with Mr. Tolliver is because of my mother. She is attempting to make my sister's life as miserable as her own has been. I know I sound like the most perverse of children, and perhaps I am."

"I find you refreshingly candid," Harry admitted and had to laugh. "I, too, had a mother that was not pleasant."

"There is a wealth of meaning in that word 'not pleasant,' isn't there?" she guessed.

"A wealth of misery. She was not a happy person."

"Are any of us?" Miss Maclean asked, and then

sighed. "I should guard my tongue. However, be a good friend to the general, Colonel. Warn him off Mother. She's too selfish to consider anyone besides herself."

She started to walk away, but Harry found he didn't want her to leave just yet. He stopped her by being provocative, curious as to how her mind worked. There was a great deal of pride in this woman. "And what of you, Miss Maclean? What advice do you have for yourself?"

His words brought her to a halt. She turned. "What do you mean, sir?"

Harry closed the distance between them. "I mean no insult, but I can't help but wonder if you should take your own advice. You obviously care for your mother because you've set aside your life for hers."

Miss Maclean lifted her chin. "You are right. You *are* being presumptuous."

"It's a fault of mine."

A hard glint appeared in her eyes. "I wouldn't brag on it, sir. "

Miss Maclean wasn't one to back down. He liked that.

At that moment, a great roar of approval sounded from inside the barn, carrying with it the name "Tolliver."

Her manner changed. She went on alert and he was not important. "Excuse me," she said, already moving toward the building, her hips swinging with feminine determination.

Harry followed her at a slower pace. He sensed a mystery about Miss Maclean. Prickly people usually were hiding something. But what would *she* have to hide?

He found himself intrigued.

*A*s Portia headed for the barn doors, she overheard the Maclean name being shouted. Tolliver and Maclean. *What was going on?*

She also had needed to escape Colonel Chattan. She preferred the man as the scowling horseman who had almost run her over. She hated the image of him as the kneeling supplicant before her, begging for a solution for his brother, or this other man, the one who was as direct as she was and who valued his friends enough to speak for them.

He was also uncommonly handsome. She found it hard to concentrate when he placed all his attention on her.

One of the reasons she'd been able to accept being a spinster was that she stayed away from men like him. Men who made her pulse race a touch faster and who challenged her and who aroused her curiosity about them.

But she had yet to meet a man who actually seemed to understand her sacrifice for her family and that made him all the more threatening.

Mr. Longacre came out of the barn's door. "You aren't inside, Miss Maclean?" he said with his broad brogue. "Your sister has just accepted Mr. Tolliver's request for marriage. Hurry up or you'll miss it all." He lowered his voice to add, "Lady Maclean has swooned. Some of the lads caught her but she isn't right happy."

Portia flew into the barn, where Minnie and Mr. Tolliver were standing in front of the assembly, beaming at each other with undisguised joy. Her sister had never radiated more beauty than she did in this moment beside her beloved.

Everyone was offering congratulations. Of course, almost everyone had drunk a wee bit too much, so the very popular physician received many hearty slaps on the back as he helped his future bride down from the stage. Even the young men who had only moments ago vied for Minnie's attention seemed pleased for the couple.

The one person who was unhappy staggered toward Portia. "Are you ready to leave?" her mother said, her proud ostrich feathers now flopping forward. She pushed them to one side. "*I am.*"

"He's a good man, Mother."

Her mother snorted her opinion. "I must leave. General Montheath has been a nuisance all night."

"I think it is dear that he has carried strong feelings for you all these years," Portia said, thinking of Colonel Chattan's request.

"If I'd wanted him years ago, I would have encouraged him. He was nothing like your father. Not half as handsome."

"But, perhaps, the much better man?" Portia could not resist saying. "After all, he has position and fortune. Two things Father lacked at the end of his life."

"Your father was a gentleman."

"So is General Montheath," Portia answered. "Of course, Father was more handsome, but handsome can't take care of a woman."

Those ostrich feathers quivered as her mother's head snapped around to her. "And what would you know of it? What man do you have following you around? I will wait for you and Minerva outside."

Several people around them heard Lady Maclean's charge and now couldn't help but look at Portia with sympathy.

Feeling humiliated, Portia wished she had bitten her tongue. No good came of ever talking sense to her mother. Lady Maclean refused to see Black Jack Maclean realistically. Not that Portia doubted that her father had been dashing at one time, probably much like Colonel Chattan whom, she noticed, had rejoined the company.

Dear God, she hoped he didn't hear of this small scene with her mother.

At that moment, thankfully, Mr. Tolliver led a beaming Minnie over to her. Portia gave her sister a huge hug. "I'm so happy for you." She then turned to Mr. Tolliver. "Sir, you do not waste time."

"I took your words to heart," he confessed, his cheeks turning bright with color. "I walked right up to Minnie, apologized, and declared myself. I said I wanted to marry her, just bold as you please. There was a line of men waiting to dance with her. They all heard me."

"And they heard me shout yes." Minnie had hold of Mr. Tolliver's arm in a display of unbridled affection. "I am so fortunate. Thank you, Portia. *Thank you.*"

"I dislike spoiling the moment," Portia said, lowering her voice, conscious that many ears were listening, especially after the dust-up with her mother, "but Mother is waiting for us. She wishes to leave. I imagine neither of you said anything to her in private before agreeing to marry?"

Mr. Tolliver started to color, but Minnie quickly declared, "No, we didn't and I wouldn't have. She would never have given her approval, Portia. You know that." She moved closer to Mr. Tolliver. "Understand, I will not let her insult this man. I love him. She should never have interfered in the first place."

"Agreed," Portia said. "However, she is waiting outside for us to take her home."

"Of course I'll come," Minnie said. She turned to Mr. Tolliver and gave him one more happy smile. He squeezed her hand.

"I shall call on the morrow," he promised.

"I shall be waiting," she answered.

"I am so happy."

"I am happy as well—"

Portia stepped between them, or else they would be there all night. "Come, dear. We must face Mother."

"Yes, we'll be listening to an earful on the ride home."

Mr. Tolliver made a commiserating sound but let them go.

As she was leaving, Portia had to steal one last look at Colonel Chattan. He stood by the punch table. He didn't hold a glass in his hand, which was unusual for any of the males in this group. He was temperate and was still sober. The majority of the other men were not. After having a father such as hers, Portia admired that quality.

And then Lady Emma walked up to him.

Portia looked away.

*T*hey were barely out of sight of the barn when Lady Maclean launched into her recriminations. "How can you throw yourself away on a *doctor*? A mere doctor."

"No, he's not a 'mere' doctor," Minnie said. Portia had to admire the patience in her sister's voice. "He's a very special doctor. He has a heart as large as the valley and I am lucky to say that it is mine."

"But Colonel Chattan was at that dance," their mother said. "His brother is Neal Chattan, the Earl of Lyon, one of the wealthiest men in England. You were presented with a remarkable opportunity to make a brilliant match with Colonel Chattan if you had impressed him in the way I know you could. Instead, you are settling for a physician, and a country one at that. What sort of opportunities will your children have with a *doctor* for a father?" she demanded, a plaintive note in her voice.

"Happy ones," Minnie said. "Well-loved ones. I can't wait to hold them in my arms."

Lady Maclean shouted her frustration, a sound that echoed in the woods around them.

"Oh, Mother," Minnie said, using a coaxing tone. "Think about how nice it will be to have me close at hand to you and not running around London. Oliver will always live in this valley."

"I *wanted* you to run around London." Lady Maclean pulled her cloak closer around her. "And you needn't worry about caring for me. That is Portia's responsibility. That is her purpose in life."

Both Minnie and Portia looked to her in surprise. "Yes, it is," their mother insisted in her defense. "Every family needs one child who dedicates herself to her parents. After all, now that I'm a widow—"

"You have been alone for a long time, Mother," Portia interjected, indignation coloring her tone. Her mother's statement echoed Colonel Chattan's assessment, and Portia discovered, in this moment, she didn't like being so predictable.

And suddenly, she discovered she didn't want to be bundled off to spinsterhood. Yesterday, yes, maybe she had thought of herself ready to be set aside. Even before the dance she had thought of herself as on the shelf.

But at this moment, she was feeling, well, rebellious—and she didn't understand why.

What had changed?

"Yes, it is true I was alone," their mother said, "when your father was away in the service of his country."

"He was away spending his money on his own happiness without a thought or care for us," Portia said. "You may pretend it was something else, but I won't. We struggled to put food on our table even when he was alive. He's only been dead three years but I've barely noticed a change in our lives."

"Except I'm a widow," their mother declared.

"If I'd been his wife, I would have been a widow much sooner, such as the first time he stepped out of line," Portia announced, a declaration that earned a scream of horror from her parent, but Portia was in the mood to be ruthless. "In fact, you should encourage General Montheath, Mother. Then you will have a man who would truly take care of you."

For a second, Lady Maclean appeared ready for an attack of apoplexy.

"Mother, Mother, please, you are upsetting

yourself," Minnie said, but the words were directed at Portia as a command for her to ease off their parent.

Lady Maclean punctuated Minnie's chastisement by breaking into tears. "I don't understand what has happened to my girls. Minerva has contracted a marriage, announcing it in front of everyone without so much as a by-your-leave from me—"

"I'm sorry, Mother," Minnie said, sounding as if she meant the words. Such was the power of their mother's tears on her youngest.

"And Portia is trying to push me in a direction I do not wish to go. Why, you may ask? Because, apparently, she's tired of comforting me in my dotage. She wants to rid herself of me."

"You are far from your dotage," Minnie hastened to say. "And you will always have a place at Oliver's and my table."

But those promises didn't offer solace. Directing her comments to Portia, Lady Maclean said, "I know your father wasn't a good husband, but what could be done? I'd married him. I tried to make the best of things but I'm not like you, Portia. You don't need a man. You will survive one way or the other."

"Yes, I will," Portia agreed, her jaw tightening

with determination, even as she wondered—*She didn't need a man?* Where had that idea come from?

"And that is the worst," their mother said, "because it is not natural. A woman should be submissive and *you* are not in the least bit docile."

Portia pulled back on the reins so hard, Honey's front feet left the ground. She turned to her mother, stunned by the accusation. "I am perfectly *fine.*"

"Oh please," Lady Maclean said. "If you were fine, you would want a husband and a family—"

"I'm trying to keep *this* family together," Portia answered.

"Which is my original point. You are the child who will stay and take care of me in my declining years." And then she had the audacity to smile, because she'd neatly maneuvered Portia to where she wanted her.

And Portia realized the whole purpose of the argument had been lost. She really had only herself to blame. Why hadn't she tossed aside all worries for family years ago and encouraged one of those young men who had courted her?

Because she hadn't wanted either of them. Her gentleman callers had not pleased her. She'd thought them boring and had preferred being alone than with one of them. Perhaps she *was* unnatural.

The idea was unsettling. Almost as unsettling as her realization that Minnie didn't speak up to counter their mother's accusation. Did she believe Portia was unnatural as well?

Portia snapped the reins and trotted Honey home.

When they reached their front door, Portia broke her silence with a terse, "We're home."

"Yes, please don't be too long seeing to the animals," Lady Maclean said, rising and opening the door of the pony cart.

"Do you need some help?" Minnie asked.

Portia swiveled in her seat to glare as hard as she could at her sister who had not stepped up to defend her. It felt good to have a focus for her own discontent.

"Do you?" Minnie repeated, apparently unmoved by the glare.

"It won't take but a moment," Portia replied through clenched teeth.

Minnie ignored her ill temper. "Then I shall help Mother. I'll see you inside." Minnie hopped out of the cart.

"Yes, go help Mother," Portia echoed. Minnie waved off her mockery.

Portia steamed with anger as she drove Honey around to the stables. The pony, a milk cow, and two goats were stabled here. On the side of the barn was a coop for Minnie's chickens and geese.

Portia wasted no time putting Honey up for the night. In fact, she threw the hay into the stall.

But as she worked, her temper cooled, to be replaced by hurt.

Hadn't her mother seen her dancing with Colonel Chattan? Of course, he had a motive for asking her to dance, but her mother didn't know that. Mr. Longacre had asked her as well. There, that was two men who hadn't seen her as too old for interest . . . although Mr. Longacre was very elderly himself.

Yes, she was over five and twenty. Yes, she had a sharp tongue. But, no, she wasn't ready to be tucked away and ignored.

And she'd just realized that tonight.

Owl came into the barn with a meow of greeting. She jumped up on a keg barrel turned upside down.

"Is it wrong to want something more?" Portia asked the cat as she gave her a pet.

Purring, Owl arched her back and seemed to shake her head no.

Portia had to laugh. She gave the cat human qualities far too often.

But on this point, Owl might be wrong. Colonel Chattan's face rose in Portia's mind. He'd even smelled good. His shaving soap had some sandalwood in it but there was a masculine air about him as well. Handsome, intense, intelligent . . . and a man on a quest. Could there be a combination of qualities in a man more devastating to the female heart?

Or should she say *hearts*? He had created quite a stir with the women at the Assembly and she'd be wise to remember that some things were beyond her reach.

Portia left the barn and walked to the house, Owl trailing behind her.

It was a long time before she fell asleep, and when she did, she dreamed of dancing . . . in Colonel Chattan's arms. It was a silly dream. An impossible one.

*P*ortia overslept the next morning. She wasn't the only one. Her mother and Minnie were still abed. She made quick work of her toilette, weaving her unruly curls into one long braid and scrubbing her face. She reached for her glasses and then remembered her mother had not returned them the night before. She would ask for them back once her mother woke, and then wear them every day just to spite her.

Downstairs, Glennis was busy cooking and cleaning. "The day is half over, miss. I've not known you to hug your pillow."

"It was a late night," Portia murmured.

"And an eventful one. I hear you have news."

Portia smiled. "Yes, my sister has accepted Mr. Tolliver's proposal for her hand."

"He's a good man."

"Yes, he is," Portia said, buttering a slice of Glennis's fresh bread for her breakfast.

"Now we need to find a husband for you who is just as good."

Portia almost laughed. At least there was one person who didn't see her as completely on the shelf. "You'd best start on that task, Glennis," she teased. "It might take you most of your life."

"*Och*, it won't be that hard."

"We shall see," Portia said, and slipped out of the kitchen. She threw on her cloak and went to the stable. There was a chill in the air but the sky was blue with only a few clouds, and Portia felt her spirits lift.

Honey was ready to be turned out into her pasture, the goats trotting right alongside her. Glennis always milked the cow when she first arrived and before she left.

Portia took down the pitchfork to muck out the stalls. It wasn't unpleasant work. She enjoyed the fresh air and even the smell of hay and the animals.

Because the day was so fair, she started doing a bit of cleaning and tidying up, and it was at this task Lady Emma discovered her.

Portia heard the hoofbeats coming up the drive. They rarely had visitors. She was surprised to see their visitor was none other than Lady Emma, accompanied by a groom. The girl was dressed in a silver gray riding outfit with a sophisticated, brimmed hat, decorated with a white ostrich plume that would have made her mother proud.

Now if Portia envied anything, it would be Lady Emma's horse. The mare was a dainty dappled gray that made Honey appear a lumbering ox. She had a kind eye, big ears, and a smooth gait.

Instead of going to Camber Hall's front door, Lady Emma had spied Portia and came trotting up to the paddock. "Good morning, Miss Maclean."

"Good morning, Lady Emma," Portia said, feeling at a disadvantage with her hair curling wildly around her head in spite of the braid and her person covered in dust and straw.

She and Lady Emma rarely spoke other than a passing nod of acquaintance. Then again, Portia was nine years older than the girl and as far from society as one could be—especially wearing her work shoes and mucking out the paddock.

"I was out for my morning ride and thought it would be nice to call," Lady Emma said.

Camber Hall wasn't anywhere close to the duke's sprawling estate. Lady Emma had ridden out of her way to visit, and Portia's suspicions were confirmed by how lathered Her Ladyship's horse was.

Noting the direction of Portia's gaze, Lady Emma said, "Yes, he does need to be walked out. Marvin," she called to the groom, "help me down and then walk my horse."

The groom, a dark, brooding sort who wasn't much older than Portia, jumped to do Her Lady-ship's bidding. Having helped Lady Emma dismount, he took the horses off to walk up and down the drive.

Alone, Lady Emma glanced over to Honey with a critical eye. "What is it?"

"*She's* a pony."

"What sort?"

Portia's earlier good mood started to vanish. There was only one reason she could think of why Lady Emma would be here—the back rent. But why would the girl bypass Mr. Buchanan, who knew the rent was coming?

"She's of undetermined lineage," Portia said, resting the pitchfork she'd been holding on the ground, hoping that Lady Emma's appearance didn't portend bad news. "May I offer you refreshment?"

"I don't have time to linger." She faced Portia, her smile hardening on her face. No, this *wasn't* a social call. She still carried her crop, a feminine thing with a beribboned handle.

"Is there something the matter, Lady Emma?" Portia dared to ask.

"Yes, there is. I don't want you to have anything to do with Colonel Chattan."

Portia almost laughed. A duke's daughter believed *Portia* was competition?

"You need not worry, my lady," Portia said.

"But I do," Lady Emma said. She had the softest voice and liked to smile as she spoke as if she was being pleasant, but Portia sensed behind that smile were sharp, tiny teeth. "We all noticed his marked attention to you last night."

"Marked attention?"

"He searched you out. You were seen talking to him . . . outside."

"It is not what it appeared," Portia said.

"The colonel took his leave from the Assembly right after you left," Lady Emma said, an accusatory note in her voice.

Portia shrugged. "I have no idea why he chose to depart when he did, but it certainly wasn't because of me."

Lady Emma studied her a moment. She hit the palm of her leather-gloved hand softly with her crop. "You may be right." She smiled. She *did* have small, sharp teeth. "I, um, well, we are fortunate to finally have a man who has everything I've been searching for in a husband pay his respects to us in the valley."

"And what is everything?" Portia asked, curious, especially in light of her own wonderings.

"Handsome, well connected, wealthy, handsome—"

"You said handsome once," Portia pointed out.

"It is worth repeating," Lady Emma answered, and this time her smile was genuine.

Portia felt herself relax. "Well, he is all those things," she agreed.

"Yes, and perhaps I shouldn't jump to conclusions," Lady Emma said. "I mean, you are almost as old as he is. Why would he be flirting with you?"

Portia tried to smile, but was thinking perhaps she preferred the suspicious Lady Emma over the friendly one. "He was being polite," she said.

"Of course." There was an awkward silence. "Well, I'd best be going. Father will worry if I am gone too long."

"I can understand that," Portia murmured.

Lady Emma turned to signal her groom to bring over her horse—but two riders coming up Camber Hall's winding drive caught her eye.

Portia stepped forward, once more surprised by visitors. Then again, hadn't Mr. Tolliver promised to call?

But it wasn't Oliver Tolliver.

It was General Montheath . . . and Colonel Chattan.

Lady Emma slapped her crop against her palm, this time with more force. "It appears you have a caller, Miss Maclean," Lady Emma said. Her eyes had grown as sharp and pointed as her teeth. "I believe I will accept your invitation for refreshment."

Chapter Seven

Harry was not impressed with Miss Maclean's home.

The stone house was a bit shabby. Someone had attempted to bring order to the front shrubberies, but the rest of the grounds were overgrown. The drive itself had more than a few holes that Ajax disdainfully stepped over. There had been some painting done to the house's sashes but slates were missing on the roof. Harry wasn't a very skilled workman but even he could tell the roof had to leak, and it made him angry. The landlord should take better care of an abode housing three women alone.

He had convinced Monty that if he truly wanted to woo his ladylove, he must call on her. No more waiting for the fair damsel to come to him. Monty must go to the damsel.

Of course, Monty was scared witless at the prospect, so Harry had thought it wise to accompany him. Harry also found himself eager to spend some time with Miss Portia Maclean again. Their moment of verbal sparring and plain speaking had been the last thing he'd thought about before he'd drifted off to sleep. She was quite possibly the most contrary female of his acquaintance. There was something about her that he could not define, something that drew him to her.

Besides, he told himself, it was a good day for a ride.

And so, here he was, dressed for a casual call and an easy ride, while Monty wore a full dress uniform with his gold braid gleaming in the winter sun. Harry had suggested his friend was a tad overdressed. Monty had shaken his head.

"If I'm going to do this," he informed Harry, "it's going to be a full-on attack. I've always rigged myself out before going into battle. I am laying siege to Ariana's heart. I am going to give her my best until she sees we were meant for each other."

His best had included the intention of bringing *all* his dogs with him. The whole pack of them, large and small.

Harry understood that, in Monty's mind, the dogs were his clan, his trusted troops, but he had strongly suggested the general leave them behind. Monty had argued and they had compromised and brought one, Jasper, leaving the others penned in horse stalls lest they follow. They had howled their disappointment.

Jasper was not Harry's favorite dog. He was a long-legged hound with an overeager, rambunctious personality. Harry couldn't understand why Monty always wanted the dog close at hand. He owned better-behaved dogs—all right, they were just barely better-behaved—but he always made allowances for Jasper.

Of course, the dog had run ahead of them, as wild and bounding as an antelope, his ears flapping and his tongue hanging. Jasper noticed the activity by the barn before Harry and went racing over there first. He gleefully circled the groom holding the horses, ignoring the servant's air of bored insolence.

One of Jasper's favorite tricks to earn attention was to nip at a horse's heels. Ajax had put him in his place with a well-aimed kick.

Now, the dog attempted to nip at the gray the groom held. The mare snorted a protest and shifted away, revealing that her body had been blocking the view of the person of Lady Emma.

Harry cursed under his breath. The duke's

daughter had wanted him to call on her today, something he was determined not to do. He knew better than to play with innocents, especially those related to dukes. They were marriage bait.

And then he saw that Lady Emma was talking to Miss Portia Maclean, who appeared to be masquerading as barn help, although she did make a charming sight. She wore heavy boots and had flipped her cloak over her shoulders to reveal a sensible dress of forest green. Her curly hair created a halo around her head and her cheeks were rosy from fresh air and good work.

Harry just naturally directed Ajax toward her.

"I say, Chattan. Let's go to the door," Monty said.

"One moment," Harry murmured, and trotted over to the barn.

Both women watched him approach.

But before he could reach them, the front door to the house opened. The other Miss Maclean, Miss Portia's sister, came out on the step. He nodded to her.

"General Montheath and Colonel Chattan," she said in greeting. "Have you come to call?"

"We have indeed, Miss Maclean," Harry responded, and jumped from his horse. He tied Ajax at the post. Lady Emma had started walking toward him from the barn, a smile on her lips, and her fist tight on her crop. She was not pleased.

Miss Portia followed like a child who hated anything unpleasant.

Harry had to smile. "Good day, Lady Emma. Miss Maclean."

"How nice to see you here," Lady Emma said in a voice overladen with honey. "I was paying a visit to my friends Miss Portia and Miss Minerva, and had no expectation of meeting you here. How did you know what I was about?"

Harry had to marvel at the woman's ability to make it sound as if he pursued. "Lucky happenstance?" he suggested.

"Very lucky," Lady Emma echoed, sliding a triumphant glance toward Miss Portia, and as far as Harry was concerned, the game was on now.

There was no easier way to discourage a woman, even an aggressive puss like Lady Emma, than to pay court to another.

So he made much of shifting his gaze to Miss Portia, of smiling warmly, of moving into step beside her.

Miss Minerva had noticed the exchange, and a secret smile came to her lips. She was no one's fool. "Let me tell Mother you are here. Please, come inside."

"I must beg off," Miss Portia said. "I am involved in something else right now. Please forgive me."

"*Of course* we do," Lady Emma hurried to say.

"*I* cannot," Harry interjected. "I came specifically for a moment with you."

Miss Portia's eyes narrowed with suspicion. She recognized nonsense when she heard it. "I am sorry I may not accommodate your wishes."

"But you can," Harry insisted pleasantly. "Come inside, just for a bit. The general and I will not stay long." He took her arm so that she could not run off, and was also gallant enough to offer Lady Emma his other arm. "My lady?" He thought it a peaceful offering.

Lady Emma did not. She sniffed, her smile tight. "General, will you escort me?"

Monty was still on his horse. His glassy-eyed expression was one Harry often saw on the faces of green recruits. Moments before he had been telling Harry of all the gallantries he would visit upon Lady Maclean. He now appeared ready to pass out.

"General? You are joining us?" Harry prompted.

His friend responded to his voice. "Yes, yes," Monty said, and dismounted.

Miss Minerva had already gone inside, presumably to announce they had company. Lady Emma placed her hand on Monty's arm and together they climbed the three stairs to the front door.

Harry started to follow them, but Miss Portia pulled back. "What game are you playing?" she demanded in a low voice.

"Game?" he asked innocently.

"You know Lady Emma has her interests set on you. Don't use me to hold her off. You shall make my life miserable."

"And how is that?"

"She's my landlord's daughter."

If Miss Portia thought that news would bring him in line, she was wrong. "The landlord who hasn't repaired the slates in the roof? Or applied a bit of paint to the wood of this house?" He demonstrated his meaning by placing a hand on the door frame. The wood was rotted. Harry frowned. "This place is about ready to fall down around your ears. I should talk to Montcrieffe. He should *pay* you to live here."

"Don't you say a word to him." *Now* she had a grip on his arm. "Don't you dare. I like this house, and I'm thankful we have it."

"That doesn't mean he shouldn't meet his obligations."

She shook her head. "The world must be a very easy place for you. You have rank, you have privilege, you have money to burn on ridiculous notions—"

"What notions?" Harry asked, confused.

Miss Portia dismissed his question with a wave of her hand. "Whatever notion you wish. You are handsome, bold, and people come to you."

"You think I'm handsome," he murmured. "Kind of you to notice."

"I *haven't* noticed," she lashed out. "And can you not be serious?" She drew a breath as if to steady herself before admitting, "Life is not easy for those of us who are of the genteel poor. My mother insists upon appearances while I'm struggling to see if we can keep a roof over our heads. I am *very* aware we can fall much further than our present circumstances. So will you kindly stop the pretense of being interested in *me* and place your randy intentions upon Lady Emma, who will appreciate them."

"Randy intentions?" Harry almost choked on his laughter, which earned him another glare from her. He held up his hands as if begging for quarter. "If you think my being pleasant is randy, let me assure you, Miss Maclean, I can be much randier."

For a second, he feared he was going to be slapped. Her cheeks turned a becoming shade of red, and he enjoyed the moment. "I'd wager few people make you blush, Miss Maclean."

"Few people *want* to." She spat the words out, and would have stormed into the house, but he caught her arm.

"The simple truth is," he said, "I like you. You are rather easy to tease, but only because you want to pretend no one notices you. Well, you are out of luck with me."

Her lips parted, her temper replaced by surprise.

He braced himself, curious as to how she would respond to his honest compliment.

She disappointed him. She ducked her head, pulled her arm from his hold, and dashed into the house.

Harry was puzzled. Women didn't run from him. They flocked to him. They searched him out.

This one didn't, and he didn't understand why. There was something more between them, something he wasn't understanding.

Did she not feel the pull between them? And if she did, why did she fight it? Why not be pleasant and encouraging to him? Every other woman was.

Removing his hat, Harry stepped into the house. Monty was standing at attention in the sitting room to the left. Lady Maclean was not present. Her daughter Miss Minerva was playing the hostess and arranging the chairs to Lady Emma's comfort.

Miss Portia had not joined the others in the sitting room but was climbing the staircase off the hall as if to escape.

She was stopped by her mother.

Lady Maclean came to the top of the stairs, her blonde curls tucked into a lace cap, a cape of the same lace around her shoulders and her hands in fussy lace, fingerless mittens. Her daughter froze like a deer caught in a hunter's sights. There were some whispers between them. Harry strained to hear what was being said, and then Lady Maclean saw him. A broad smile of pleasure crossed her face. "Why, Colonel Chattan, what a pleasure." She started down the stairs and was such a force of nature, Miss Portia had no choice but to turn and go ahead of her.

Lady Maclean reached the bottom step. "I'm so happy you have called. I know my daughter Minerva is as well—"

She broke off with a frown of disapproval.

Jasper, that woebegone hound, had returned

from his nosey investigation of the barn. He was now on the hunt for Monty and had tracked him here. Sniffing the doorstep, he walked into the house, so enthusiastic his body seemed to be wagging his tail.

"*Out.*" Lady Maclean punctuated the word with a finger pointed to the door.

Jasper gave her a big dog grin and did not obey. After all, Monty never made him obey.

"I want that dog *out of here,*" Lady Maclean ordered.

Monty still stood at attention. He'd not moved a muscle, not even for his cherished dog. It was Harry who shooed Jasper out and closed the door.

"I can't stand the beasts. So uncouth, so filthy and annoying," Lady Maclean said. "I didn't know you had a dog, Colonel Chattan. I hope I didn't offend you."

"You didn't, my lady. The dog is not mine," Harry answered.

"Not yours?" she repeated faintly, and then her face drained of color as she realized the implications. Slowly, she turned to the sitting room.

Monty put back his shoulders, trying to look his best. "Good day to you, my lady." His voice shook slightly. He'd known he would not be welcome.

"You haven't changed," Lady Maclean said with a sniff. "Always with the hounds."

For a second, Monty appeared flummoxed; his expression was that of an officer losing the battlefield—and it made Harry angry.

"He has a champion pack of dogs," Harry lied audaciously. "The envy of not only Scotland but England as well."

Lady Maclean smiled her disbelief. She entered the sitting room and took a seat on the room's settee. "Please, sit here, Colonel," she said, patting the seat next to hers. Minerva, take the chair next to the colonel—" she started, but stopped as Lady Emma plopped herself into the indicated chair without so much as a by-your-leave.

Monty still stood, anxious and ill at ease.

"Please, sit here, General," Miss Portia said, directing him to a chair across from her mother. Harry knew she had not intended to stay. She'd hovered by the door but had now apparently decided to champion Monty's cause and counter her mother's rudeness. Harry silently applauded her. She'd saved him from having to make a stand that would be doubly harsh.

A tray of tea and slices of bread and butter was carried in by a rosy-cheeked maid.

"Place the tray on this table, Glennis," Mrs.

Maclean said, indicating the table closest to her, and began pouring tea.

Outside, Jasper barked. He had discovered the sitting room window and leaped in the air to let Monty know he was outside. His ears flapped in the breeze from his effort. The poor dog couldn't understand he wasn't welcome, much like Monty.

Harry helped his hostess pass the cups and saucers brimming with hot, strong tea, using the opportunity to place himself in front of Miss Portia as often as possible. She was determined to ignore him. Her actions didn't make sense. She was kind to Monty. Why couldn't she be more open to him?

Not once did he consider the fault might lie with Miss Portia. He'd learn to read people quickly and she was not one for airs like her mother or—

"Bread and butter?" Lady Emma said, lifting her nose at the offered refreshments. "How quaint." She held her portion in one hand as if afraid to take a bite.

"How delicious," Harry countered, and it was. The butter was fresh and the bread still warm. Monty had shoved all of his in his mouth with one bite.

"So, are you enjoying your visit to our corner of the world, Colonel?" Miss Minerva asked.

"I am," Harry said. "I don't know why the Scots

are considered such dour people. You all have been welcoming."

"That's because none of us in this room are Scottish," Lady Maclean said with a twitter at what she perceived as her own cleverness. "Lady Emma's line is English, as is mine."

"I would rather be anything but Scottish," Lady Emma said.

"Then how did you arrive in Glenfinnan?" Harry had to ask.

"Father bought this estate. He loves the sport here. Fishing, hunting. I can't wait to return to London," Lady Emma said.

"And we were victims of circumstance," Lady Maclean said, heaving a long-suffering sigh. "My late husband, God rest his soul, was knighted for serving his country."

That had been luck, Harry thought. He looked over at Monty. They both knew the true story. Black Jack had been in India and rescued the daughter of an officer in the East India Company from being kidnapped. It was an adventurous tale, although most serving with Black Jack knew he was the reason the girl had almost been grabbed by slavers. They'd been in a lovers' tryst. He wondered if the daughters thought their father a hero.

Miss Portia answered his question by saying, "He was a rogue, Mother. A rogue." The words had just burst out of her as if any hint of untruth was unbearable to her.

"You are speaking of your father," Lady Maclean chastised.

"I'm speaking of my sire, Mother. But he was never a father."

"Oh dear," Lady Emma responded in an amused tone. "May I please have some more *bread and butter*?"

"She is jesting, Lady Emma," Lady Maclean said. *"Aren't* you, Portia?" This was an unspoken command for Portia to mind her manners, but Portia Maclean was a rebel. She wasn't afraid to call things as they really were. She ignored the command by suddenly becoming interested in what was in her teacup.

Her sister jumped into the sudden void of conversation by saying, "I understand it doesn't grow truly wintry in Glenfinnan until around mid-January. Is that true, Lady Emma?"

"Yes, the days are mostly rainy but the temperature is generally mild until then," Her Ladyship replied. "I don't mind a bit of nip in the air."

Lady Maclean started on about how perfect London weather was, but Harry was not interested in conversation or anyone else in the room. He couldn't take his eyes off Portia Maclean.

He knew she was aware of him.

When she thought the conversation had gone on, she slid a glance in his direction, noticed that his focus was completely on her. She started to turn away and then stopped herself. She met his gaze with a level one of her own. Her eyes were more blue than gray. Clear eyes that didn't flinch from what was honest.

And then she looked away.

But Harry found himself unable to do so.

Her profile intrigued him. He liked her straight nose and flawless skin. Hers was a classic beauty such as that which could be found in Greek sculpture, a beauty that was often overlooked because of its serenity.

His musing was interrupted by a knock on the door.

Miss Minerva was instantly on her feet. "I'll see who it is," she said breathlessly as she almost ran from the room. She opened the door and then her lovely face broke into a wide smile. "Hello, Mr. Tolliver. Please come in." Harry recognized the name as that of the man who was now her intended.

"I hope I'm not intruding," Mr. Tolliver said.

"You could never do that," she replied. "Here, let me take your hat."

He handed a hat to her, but neither of them moved beyond that exchange. They stood staring at each other. They both had the silliest grins of pleasure on their faces, a sign that the couple was in love.

It was Miss Portia who gently reminded her sister, "Bring the man into the sitting room, Minnie. Or are you going to keep him all to yourself?"

Miss Minerva's eyes brightened at her lapse of manners, and a dimple appeared in her cheek. "I might just do that." Harry and Monty had both stood to greet this new guest.

"This is Mr. Oliver Tolliver," Miss Minerva said, pride in her voice. "He is our local physician."

Oliver Tolliver? What had his parents been thinking? Harry lowered his head to hide a smile, and then his eye caught Miss Portia's, but instead of freezing up on him, an answering smile came to her lips. She thought the name silly as well.

"Yes, I know Mr. Tolliver," Lady Emma was saying, offering her hand. "He was very helpful when I had the croup. Congratulations on your happy news."

"Thank you," Mr. Tolliver said. "I am pleased

you are feeling quite the thing now." He looked to Lady Maclean, who leaned back against the settee as if not wanting to be any closer than she must to him. "It is good to see you are in fine spirits, my lady," he said, a hopeful note in his voice.

"Yes. I am," she replied coolly—and Harry decided he really did not like her. He hadn't thought much of her before, but to be so rude in the face of her daughter's happiness? There would be no pleasing a woman such as Lady Maclean. Miss Portia had spoken truly when she'd advised him to warn Monty away. He would give his friend a good talking-to, as well as advising Monty to fall on his knees and thank the Lord he'd never married her. She'd peck a man to death with her tongue, and he now had some sympathy for Black Jack.

Harry moved forward to shake the physician's hand. "My congratulations as well. We have not met. My name is Chattan, Harry Chattan, and this is General Montheath."

But before anything else could be said, the screech of a cat filled the air, followed by a woof.

A white blur ran through the still open front door and into the sitting room, followed by Jasper, fast on the chase with every hound instinct he had in him. He dashed right between Miss Minerva and Mr. Tolliver, almost knocking them over.

The cat raced for the safety of the settee and Lady Maclean. Jasper didn't have enough sense to stop. He sent the table with the tray of refreshments flying into the air. The teapot landed right in Lady Emma's lap. The girl's cry of outrage was louder than the cat's screeching.

But nothing was as loud as Lady Maclean's furious demand to *"Take that beast out of here."*

Monty jumped into the thick of things. He grabbed Jasper by the scruff of his neck and began dragging the dog out of the room, muttering, "I don't know what has got into this dog." Jasper clawed at the hard wood floor in an attempt to gain enough traction to pull Monty back toward the cat.

Harry was about to point out the presence of the cat. However, words died in his throat once he had a clear look at the animal's folded-over ears.

Here was the cat who had visited his bedroom. The cat who was the sign that he'd needed to stay in Glenfinnan. The cat who'd been with the witch that night.

And the cat sought refuge from Miss Portia Maclean. She had covertly shooed the cat under her chair as if not wanting her mother to catch sight of the kitty.

For a second, Harry was so shocked he couldn't think. All that searching, and the woman he wanted was standing right here in front of him.

Portia Maclean *had* been avoiding him, but not because of spinster shyness. She was afraid he'd recognize her.

And on some level, he had. Of course, he had thought it was physical attraction, but now he knew differently . . . or did he?

Harry paused, unwilling at this moment to confront her. One should always be certain of one's enemy before making an attack.

Meanwhile, Monty was mumbling excuses and trying to keep control over his dog, and Miss Minerva and Lady Maclean were occupied trying to soothe Lady Emma's offended pride.

Portia Maclean had turned her back to the room, protecting her cat from Jasper, who continued to howl and struggle against Monty's hold although he was now outside. She couldn't see Harry's expression so she didn't know that he was aware his quarry was in sight.

But the cat knew. Her curiously shaped head popped up over her shoulder. She didn't look in the direction of the dog. She couldn't give a care.

Instead, the cat looked right at Harry. Her huge amber eyes seemed to gleam with a fiendish delight, almost daring him to speak out.

Fenella. She was here.

She was Portia Maclean.

Harry turned and left the house, but he would be back.

Chapter Eight

After the disaster of the afternoon, it took hours for Portia to calm her mother, who had demanded smelling salts, her dinner on a tray and a soothing hot bath.

"We've been humiliated," Lady Maclean had declared. "That boor Montheath and his dog have destroyed our social standing."

"I doubt that, Mother," Portia had answered.

"Did you not see Lady Emma? She practically ran from the house."

Portia could have told her mother that Lady Emma had left because Colonel Chattan had taken his leave and she was not, and never would be, interested in befriending the Macleans. But then, that comment would have set her mother off into new hysterics about losing her chance to wed Minnie to Colonel Chattan.

For her part, Minnie confessed she was delighted that their mother had something to rail against other than her intentions to marry Mr. Tolliver.

"I'm more worried over what Lady Emma will do," Portia answered. She'd managed to free her spectacles from her mother's grasp and now pushed them up her nose. It felt good to be able to see clearly again. A headache had been forming, but Portia didn't know if it was from going so long without her spectacles or from the stress of the afternoon.

"She can't blame us for what happened today," Minnie said. "We don't own the dog."

"Yes, but we hurt her pride," Portia answered. "Mother is also upset that we laughed over all the damage. She feels we are not sensitive to our social position."

"Oh posh," Minnie said with good humor. "The furniture was rickety to begin with. That table would have broken sooner or later. Of course, having the dregs of the teapot dumped into Lady Emma's lap would have upset anyone. Her riding habit truly was an exquisite outfit. I don't know that the stain can be repaired."

They were in the kitchen, tidying up. The sisters had sent Glennis home, telling her they could take care of themselves for dinner.

Portia had to suppress her laughter at the

memory. "It truly was a good moment when she stood up and put her foot right into the bread and butter plate and almost fell on her face. I know I shouldn't make sport, but the girl is like a medieval princess in this valley. What she says goes, and if she doesn't like someone, well, then 'Off with her head.' I am very tired of her petty jealousies and threats."

"Threats? She doesn't like one of us?" Minnie asked, looking up from where she was taking a boiling pot of water from the fire. "She has nothing to fear from me now," she said, a smile coming to her lips. "She may claim all the men in the valley for herself. Oliver is the only man I want. Oh, Portia, I can't believe I'm going to marry him."

"Does it not bother you how upset Mother is?" Portia had to ask. Minnie seemed almost carefree, something that was a bit out of character.

"Of course it bothers me, but she'll have you here and, well . . ." Her voice drifted off. She looked up at Portia. "I must live my own life. I love him, Portia. I can't *not* be with him. I don't expect you to understand. You are far too rational. You can't imagine how I feel."

"I was the one arguing *for* you and Oliver," Portia pointed out.

"I know," her sister said. "And I appreciate everything you've done. Truly, I do."

Portia wasn't so certain Minnie did. She focused on wiping the table with a linen cloth.

But she'll have you here. Minnie's words echoed in Portia's head. Once again, she felt trapped. Forgotten. Set aside.

Portia took the conversation back to its original thoughts and away from her own disturbing feelings. "Well, now Lady Emma may see us evicted from Camber Hall because of the scene this afternoon," she murmured.

"Oh, Portia, is the duke truly that petty that he would listen to her?"

Portia rubbed the top of the table with her hand thoughtfully a moment before deciding to take her sister into her confidence. "Her jealousies extend beyond you," she said. "Lady Emma made the trip over here today to warn me to stay away from Colonel Chattan. She believes he is interested in me."

Minnie laughed. "She doesn't know you at all, does she?"

"What do you mean by that?"

Her sister shrugged as if realizing she might be treading on tender ground. She started ladling hot water into pitchers to be carried upstairs for the bedrooms as she said, "He's a rake. And a womanizer. He may be dashing but he's too much."

"Too much what?" Portia pressed.

"Well, too much for you. You are not his sort of woman."

Portia didn't know if she liked the description. "What sort of woman is his sort?"

Again, Minnie shrugged as if realizing she might be on tender ground. She picked up two pitchers, preparing to leave the room and avoid the question.

"Is Lady Emma his sort of woman?" Portia asked.

A cautious look came to Minnie's eye. "I don't know. She has a dowry." She'd tossed that last off as if to explain away her comment.

But Portia was in the mood to take offense.

This afternoon, for a moment, she'd thought there was a connection between her and Colonel Chattan. She'd let herself consider that he might be attracted to her. Certainly, she had found herself attracted to him. That spark had been lit when she'd made the statement about her father, a strong one, to be sure, and had noticed a bit of admiration in the colonel's eye when she'd not apologized for her opinion of Black Jack.

And although Minnie was speaking aloud thoughts Portia had had about herself, the verdict stung. Her sister was usually more loyal. Perhaps the prospect of becoming Mrs. Oliver Tolliver made her believe herself better than Portia?

The bitterness, the hurt behind this sort of thinking was dangerous. Now might be a good time to put distance between herself and her sister.

"I must see to Honey and bring in the goats," she said, crossing over to where her cloak hung on a peg. She reached for the oil lamp and went over to the fire to light it.

"Portia, I didn't mean all what I said quite the way it sounded. It's just that Colonel Chattan is known for the lovers he has taken. They are the cream of the cream. Lusty women. Women who aren't good enough to polish your shoes. I hope I haven't upset you."

"You haven't," Portia said, carrying her lamp and moving toward the door.

"I know that tone of voice. You've taken offense. Please, Portia, I'm just saying someone like Colonel Chattan is not the sort of man for you."

Portia paused by the door, one hand on the latch. "What sort of man would be for me, Minnie?"

Her sister raised her brows and seemed to mentally scramble for words.

"Never mind," Portia answered. "I know that I'm long of tooth. I'm done. I was done before I ever started. But there was a moment this afternoon when I thought—" She stopped. She'd not told Minnie of meeting Colonel Chattan alone at the dance. Her sister had been too busy accepting Mr. Tolliver's proposal of marriage to worry about Portia's whereabouts at the time.

"Thought what?" Minnie asked.

"Thought I didn't know why the ladies were all so giddy around him," Portia finished.

"I understand why," Minnie said with a laugh. "He is handsome. I might be giddy around himself, except now I have my Ollie."

Portia smiled, but didn't feel any mirth. In her happiness, her sister was throwing darts at every insecurity Portia had and hitting them.

"I need to see Honey." Portia turned the handle and slipped outside.

The moon was rising and the night air felt good on her skin. She did not like fighting with Minnie. But she also didn't like her life very much right now.

Minnie would leave the house and someday have children with Oliver Tolliver, and Portia would have nothing.

Of course, she would be the doting aunt, but that didn't mean she didn't want something *more* out of life. Something of her own.

And just because she was older didn't mean that she didn't yearn in the way other, younger women did. Her head could be turned by Colonel Chattan, and it was. She wasn't as sensible as everyone gave her credit for.

She stopped and looked up at the moon, remembering how the colonel had appeared that night by the Great Oak, remembering him on his knees in front of her, begging her to take his life for his brother's. She'd never thought that a man, especially one such as he, for whom everything came his way, could be so noble. He'd meant those words. He would sacrifice himself for another.

And if there was anyone who understood sacrifice for a family, it was Portia.

Tears burned her eyes, born out of a longing for what she could not have.

Portia lifted her spectacles and swiped at her tears. She was being a goose. She'd come to terms with her fate a long time ago. She lived for Minnie and for their mother. That was it. Her purpose . . . and there was no wishing it away.

Resolution, that was what she needed. She must not yearn for what she could not have.

Setting her glasses back on her nose, Portia marched into the barn, and almost said something ugly when she realized she had not finished with her chores that morning. Lady Emma had interrupted her and then the events of the day had taken over. Well, work healed the troubled soul.

She hung the lamp on a peg in a supporting beam and set to work.

Quickly, Portia brought in the pony and the goats. She picked up the pitchfork and, to the sound of the animals munching, she started jabbing at the straw with all her might. Work relieved frustration. Work put at bay desires a woman such as she should not have. Work was what life was about, wasn't it?

"So at last I see the spectacles," Colonel Chattan's deep voice said from behind her.

Portia whirled around.

As if she had conjured him, Colonel Chattan stood in the door leading to Honey's paddock. He wore his greatcoat. He was hatless and his face was devilishly pale in the shadows. His eyes were two hard shards of light. He was angry.

And for a second, her heart quit beating.

He walked toward her. "Hello, *Fenella.*"

Portia wanted to take a step back. To run.

She couldn't move.

He moved into the circle of lamplight surrounding her, stopping when they were almost toe to toe. He placed his hands on her upper arms, squeezing, lifting her up until she stood on the tips of her toes. He stared into her eyes as if he could read her very soul.

She started shaking. He was too close, too powerful, too strong, too driven.

"Why?" he asked.

One word for which there was no easy answer.

"I'm not Fenella," she whispered.

He shook his head in disbelief.

"I'm not her," she insisted. "I wish I could help you but I can't."

"The *cat*," he said. "The cat is *yours*."

Portia shook her head. She didn't understand his meaning. "The cat? Owl?"

As if summoned, Owl padded into the barn with a low sound of feline satisfaction in seeing them there.

Heedless of the tension between them, Owl purred and rubbed her back against his leg.

"Yes, the cat," Colonel Chattan ground out. "I was almost fooled. I was going to leave Glenfinnan until you sent your cat to me. You wanted me to stay and so I did. Well, here I am, Fenella. What do you want to lift the curse?"

"I'm not her," Portia said, her voice faint. "I have no powers."

Owl now wove herself around and through

their legs, brushing against Portia's skirts and his boots, purring as she did so, the sound growing louder.

The air about them seemed to change, to grow warmer.

He was so close to her she could see every line in his face and the color deep in his eyes. "I didn't send a cat," Portia whispered.

A rush of heat, of desire rose between her legs. If she leaned forward, her breasts would graze his chest and they wanted to do so. They tingled in a way she'd not experienced before.

His grip on her arms tightened. His eyes had darkened. The anger turned to something she could not name. It was he who moved closer until their bodies fit together. She could feel his heat, his hardness.

She had never been this close to a man before.

Still Owl purred, the sound growing until it drowned out everything save the racing beat of her pulse.

He was handsome. Noble. A man unlike any other.

A man every woman wished to kiss.

A man who had captured her imagination in a way she'd not believed possible.

A man who brought his lips down upon hers.

Chapter Nine

This was madness.

Harry hadn't come here to kiss Portia Maclean.

He'd come here to throttle the truth out of her. He wanted Fenella. If she was not the witch, then he knew there was a link between them.

The lust of battle sang in his blood. He was a warrior. Here was his enemy—and yet, he could not take himself away from her.

Dear God, her kiss was sweet. Intoxicating in a way that no spirit or drug had ever been.

The moment his lips met hers, reason flew from his mind.

She smelled of fresh air, moonlight and the earth. It was a scent more potent than any perfume.

He'd been holding her arms. Slowly, he let her down to the ground so he could gather her up and kiss her more completely.

Her response was everything a man could ask. She was eager for his embrace. Her arms slid up around his neck to pull him closer to her. Her breasts flattened against his chest, and Harry found himself impatient with the barrier of his heavy greatcoat between them. He slid it off, letting it fall to the ground at his feet.

Was the cat still there, winding around them, purring?

Harry didn't care. A force as old as man drove him now. The roof of the barn could cave in on them and he would not break this kiss. He could not.

He slid his hand inside her cloak, circling her waist and pulling her closer to him. He was hard and anxious. Harry couldn't remember the last time he'd felt this excited.

Her waist was trim. He soothed his hand over the gentle curve of her thigh. She was lean and strong, a different sort of woman from the overly pampered ones he'd grown bored with in London. Her legs were longer than he had first imagined. His mind focused on those legs and on wanting them wrapped around his waist.

The kiss broke. They had been inhaling each other. He now kissed her cheek, her eye, her ear. His hand found her breast. The weight of it felt good in his hands. He circled the tight, hard bud of her nipple pressed needily against her clothing. Her breath caught in her throat. He was surprised again with how good she felt, and suddenly, Harry was done with seduction. He wanted her. *Now*. He'd go to pieces if he didn't have her.

He unbuttoned his breeches while burying his face in her neck and her hair. His erection practically sprang free from the confines of his breeches like a spring that had been compressed too long. He was hard and ready. Desire gave him the strength of ten men, and he was done with waiting. He'd never wanted a woman the way he wanted this one. His blood sang with need.

She was pulling at his clothing now, wanting the restrictions between them gone as eagerly as he did.

But he could not wait for genteel seduction. With an almost animal savagery, Harry lifted her up so she fit against him, pushing aside her skirts as he did so. She still wore her cloak. They were both still fully dressed. But none of that mattered. The moist heat of her body put him over the edge of sanity, especially when he realized she wasn't wearing drawers, any silly bits of muslin that annoyed a man when he knew what he wanted.

Harry entered her with one long, smooth thrust and buried himself deep.

She startled, stiffened, then struggled as if to push him away.

He couldn't stop. Not now. He wanted her too much. He'd never felt this strong of a bond with any other woman. She held him with a force he could not understand, but that he intended to thoroughly enjoy.

He began moving, cradling her in his arms as he had his way with her.

Portia Maclean ceased her struggles. Her body adjusted to his. She was tight, perfect.

Harry had to have more leverage. He leaned her against the wall of the barn, bracing her with his arms and thrusting, each drive taking him beyond where he'd ever gone before. He was whispering her name and telling her she was beautiful.

She made soft gasps that excited him more than any other sound.

Dear God, he would never let her go.

Her legs were around his waist now. She wore woolen stockings. Someday, he'd see her legs covered in silk. He was not ever going to let such a woman go. She was a magic creature in his arms and he was bewitched—

She cried out. Deep muscles tightened around

him. The force of her release almost brought him to his knees.

It seemed as if it would never end.

Like rings of water after a stone is thrown, the power, the intensity of this moment radiated from her and through him, until he could hold back no more. He let himself go.

Harry prided himself on being careful. He wanted no bastards, especially ones that could carry on the curse.

However, this time he was powerless to withdraw, and no completion could have ever felt better.

Slowly, he brought them both to the ground, holding her as if she were made of gold.

Silence stretched between them, a silence filled with the pounding of their own hearts. Harry didn't know if he'd ever be able to move again. Their mating had been unexpected but physical, demanding.

The best he'd ever experienced.

And then she broke the magic of the moment with a horrified "What have I done?"

She started to untangle herself from him but Harry would not let her go.

"Stop," he ordered as she struggled against him. "Stop."

She struck out at him. *"Don't touch me."*

"Miss Maclean, *Portia*," he said, wanting to calm her, and yet he was confused himself, especially when he realized she'd been a virgin.

God help him.

Harry was not one to deflower innocents. The evidence was damning. There was the stain of blood upon his breeches.

She noticed it as well. "Oh no," she said, her voice wavering as if she were ready to fall to pieces.

"It's not that bad," Harry hurried to say.

She gave him a look that would have made a clergyman run.

Harry warded off her anger with a hand. "It's not. Trust me. I won't let any harm come to you."

Her answer was to slap his hand away.

And Harry knew she had a right to be angry. He'd taken what had been only hers to give and had done so with wild abandon. But he had not been alone. She had been a willing participant and far from virginal in her desire.

Just thinking about what had been between them caused his body to stir with interest—

"The cat," he said. "Where is the cat?" Harry rose to his feet.

"Owl? What does Owl have to do with this?"

"That is no cat," he informed her. "The cat is Fenella." He was certain of it. Harry buttoned his breeches as he began searching every corner and crevice of the barn. The cat had just been there. The cat was still there. He could sense it, but he could not find it.

Portia had managed to come to her feet. She leaned against the wall for support, her face still alarmingly pale. "There is *no* Fenella," she said. "Fenella is the name in a book."

"A book?" Harry crossed to her. No one had mentioned a book. "What book?"

She shook her head. "One I found. Please, leave me."

But he couldn't leave, not after she had shared that tidbit. He took her by the arms. "Please, you must help me. What book did you find?"

"A book," she lashed out. "It's nothing important." Tears had come to her eyes.

The sight of her crying went straight to his heart. She was not the sort who broke easily. He'd hurt her and she was the innocent in all of this.

"Please, tell me about the book," he pleaded.

Her response was to raise her knee and practically geld him.

His sex was still sensitive from their lovemaking. Her blow was doubly effective.

Harry let loose his hold, bowed over in pain. Freed, Portia tore off into the night, escaping into her house.

Meanwhile, Harry could barely breathe. He wheezed and gasped, waiting for the pain to subside, helpless to chase her.

And what if he did? She was too distraught to help him.

Slowly, Harry came to his feet. He would talk to her on the morrow. She needed to think. He needed time to think as well. He didn't understand what had happened any more than she did.

But he did know one thing—he was coming closer to Fenella.

*N*o one was waiting for her inside the house, and Portia didn't stop running until she reached her room. She slammed the door behind her, afraid *he* was following.

For one long moment, she leaned against the door, her heart pounding in her ears, a hundred separate thoughts all jumbled and confused in her brain.

She placed a hand over her eyes as if to erase the memory of what just happened from her mind. She sank to the floor.

Her body still pulsed with the memory of being joined with him, of having him deep inside her, and she feared she was wanton—because she'd *liked* it. There had been a moment when the pain had been unbearable, and yet, she would have not let him stop.

Portia hugged her arms around her. So that was "making love" and it had earned its reputation. She'd never felt so alive, so *uncontrolled* before in her life.

She'd also ruined herself.

Fear raised its ugly head. Now what would she do?

She had thrown herself into the arms of the most notorious rake in the— Her mind froze, unable to think of how far and wide Colonel Chattan's reputation spanned, and then decided, yes, he must be the worst in the world! How else could he have seduced her so easily?

And she had thought he'd been angry when he'd first entered the barn. There had not been anger in his kiss. No, there had been hunger, and desire, and passion, and—

Making love was the most remarkable experience in her life.

Portia felt as if she had just opened a Pandora's box.

She'd liked it. He'd felt good inside her.

Even now a curl of yearning unfurled in her womb. She had lost her virtue, and besides being shocked and alarmed at what would become of her, she had a very strong desire to kick up her heels in joy.

So *this* was what life was about.

This was what poets meant when they scribbled about love. They were not speaking of some sort of staid, soulless wanting but of a complete, boundless celebration of two bodies becoming *one*.

It was an incredible thought, until she remembered that Colonel Chattan had a reputation for becoming "one" with a goodly number of women.

Portia stood up. She still wore her cloak. In the darkness of her room, she walked over to the window. It overlooked the barn.

The lamp hanging from a post in the barn had been blown out. All was quiet.

She strained to see him in the shadows, but he was not there, and she began to cry.

Portia knew she was undone.

No one would marry her now. She'd been *used*.

And, perversely, she wished Colonel Chattan would "use" her again.

Oh no—another *wanton* thought. If her mother

knew, she would fly into a rage. If Minnie knew, she would be sorely disappointed in her older sister.

And then Portia realized if anyone in the valley knew what had happened, she would be ostracized. Their opinions of her would change. She was the spinster, the daughter who would take care of her mother, her family. The daughter who did everything right and who had a stellar reputation.

She also had to be realistic. Colonel Chattan had no passion for her, although he had shown quite a bit of energy!

No, he'd been punishing her . . . she thought. Portia wasn't certain. When he had first confronted her in the barn, he'd been very serious, and then everything had changed. *Everything.*

And she didn't completely understand herself or her reactions to him. Such unbridled passion frightened her. And he frightened her because he could inspire it.

He also attracted her.

Of course, who knew how he felt now? She had not been kind to him. In her panic, her horror at her behavior, she'd kicked him, but she'd needed to have a moment to herself to think. He'd sounded like a lunatic with his talk of witches and possessed cats. She'd needed distance from him. She had to regain her perspective.

Her kick had accomplished more than she could have imagined. They'd always told her that was the way to protect oneself, and they'd been right.

Owl jumped up on her bed, interrupting her fevered thoughts.

Portia hadn't realized the cat was in the room.

She glanced at the door. Owl *had* been outside. No one would have let her inside . . .

Portia made an annoyed sound. Now Colonel Chattan had her suspecting the cat, and the idea was ridiculous.

Cats weren't witches. Witches weren't even witches. Portia was a modern thinker. Believing in spells and curses was the purview of the superstitious. The women labeled witches were often like Crazy Lizzy, lonely old women with baffled minds.

Owl had curled up in a tidy ball at the foot of the bed. She looked peaceful in the moonlight. And an overwhelming tiredness stole into every fiber of Portia's being.

What had happened tonight had been traumatic. It was too much to take in.

Portia climbed into her bed, fully clothed. She took off her precious spectacles and placed them on the bedside table. Using her cloak as a blanket, she sank down into the mattress and closed her eyes.

Owl moved up the bed to her, moving with a cat's light grace. She snuggled in next to Portia, kneading the folds of the cloak with her paws as she made herself comfortable. Portia fell asleep to the cat's contented purring.

The next morning, Portia woke up exhausted. It took a moment for her to realize she was still fully dressed. Her room was cold and muscles she hadn't known she possessed, *secret* muscles, ached in a way she'd never felt before.

And then it all came back to her.

She sat up with a start and covered her mouth with her hand as if to stifle a scream.

A knock sounded on her door. "Portia, have you overslept?" Minnie said. "We leave for church in an hour. Are you all right?"

Portia never overslept. And usually she was the one who knocked on doors, not the other way around. "I'm fine," she mumbled to her sister, surprised her voice worked.

"I'll take breakfast to Mother," Minnie offered. "Mr. Tolliver is coming over to escort us to services." She left. Portia could hear her walking down the hall for the stairs.

Church. She must prepare for church.

Portia untied the strings of her cloak that was still around her. She felt like herself, and yet she felt different.

"Owl?" Portia remembered the cat sleeping beside her. She looked around the room, but there was no answering meow.

Sliding off the bed onto her knees, Portia searched under the bed. No cat. Fenella's book was there, but no Owl.

And she told herself she was being silly. Cats had a hundred ways of going in and out of places. She was allowing her imagination to grow foolish.

Rising from the floor, Portia walked over to the washbasin. Of course the water was cold. She should have washed last night when Minnie had brought up the pitchers. She poured the water into a bowl and began undressing—and that was when she saw the bloodstain on her petticoat.

For a second, the room seemed to spin around her. "No, no, no," she said softly, and then she met her face in the looking glass on the wall.

The woman who stared back at her looked as if her world was about to come to an end. How foolish she had been. The rampant desire, the lust of the night before evaporated in the light of this new day.

"It's over. It's done," she told that image. "Don't think on it."

All would be fine; all would be well. She needed to carry on as she normally did. That was what she would do. It was all she could do.

Portia began washing her face. She picked up a cloth and scrubbed all over her body as hard as she could. Within the hour, she felt a bit like her old self, although she had no appetite for breakfast.

She was absolutely certain that her sister and her mother and even Mr. Tolliver could see a change in her, because she could see the change in herself. She was certain of it. Her eyes were darker, her skin lighter, her features older.

But no one else in her family seemed to notice.

And the barn where the deed had been done seemed remarkably normal. No signs of struggle or savage passion. Even Honey, who had to be a witness to the goings-on, greeted Portia with her usual nicker.

None of that stopped Portia from feeling guilty. Her penance was to worry as Mr. Tolliver drove them to the church meeting.

There was no church in Glenfinnan, well, no proper church as they'd had in London, which was something else for Lady Maclean to complain over. However, the Duke of Montcrieffe had a chapel on his estate, and his chaplain, a very kind man by the name of Reverend Ogilvy, read services each Sunday.

Portia was not truly thinking about where they were going and its implications, until they arrived and she saw the crowd gathered there. She was not up to facing very many people. She ducked her head and hurried to the chapel, running right into Lady Emma.

Her Ladyship looked positively fetching with a berry red velvet jacket over a creamy muslin gown. A cap of the same velvet was tilted at a jaunty angle over her perfectly styled hair.

Beside her, Portia felt dowdy and haggard—in more ways than one! Her Sunday dress was a sprigged muslin that had been out of fashion when it had been handed down to her by a distant cousin and her hat was the one she wore every Sunday for church. Nor was there anything "jaunty" about her.

"Hello, my lady," Portia murmured.

Lady Emma replied with a lift of her brow and a look down her nose. She moved on.

"Are you all right?" Minnie asked, taking her arm.

"I'm fine," Portia answered a little too quickly. Then paused, turning suspicious. "Why do you think something is wrong?"

"Just a sense I have," Minnie answered. "You've been so quiet."

"I have many matters on my mind."

"Is it about Lady Emma and our paying the rent?" Minnie said, dropping her voice lest any of the others around them overhear what she was saying. "I talked to Oliver. He said perhaps he can help. I mean, he doesn't earn much. Usually his patients pay him in turnips and bread, but maybe we can work something out."

Portia put her hand on her sister's shoulder. "Oh, Minnie, it isn't the rent." For a moment, she debated confiding in this person who was closer to her than any other.

However, the opportunity was swept away by their mother's approach. "I don't understand why we can't have a proper horse and vehicle. I mean, even Mr. Tolliver has one. You hold too tight to a coin, Portia. Too tight." On that pronouncement she swept into the chapel, and her daughters had no choice but to follow.

The service was long. Mr. Ogilvy enjoyed hearing himself speak and had a good bit to say. To-day's sermon was on the story of the Prodigal Son. Always before, Portia had cast herself in the role of the oldest son. Not today. She saw herself as the youngest son, the one who was hedonistic and enjoyed sensual pleasures and paid a price—

It was then Portia realized *she could be with child.* Chattan's child. And then *everyone* would know what she'd done.

The thought was horrific, especially when she remembered how Laird Macdonald's gardener had kept spitting at the mention of the name "Chattan."

Dear God, please don't let me be carrying his baby, she prayed. In fact, she'd never prayed so fervently in her life—and that was when she felt *him.*

The hair at the nape of her neck tingled.

Portia knew before she turned around that Colonel Chattan sat behind her. He sat *directly* behind her, and he was staring at her with an intensity that left no doubt in her mind, or that of anyone who noticed, that he was there for *her.*

Chapter Ten

$\mathcal{P}$ortia snapped her head back around to focus on Mr. Ogilvy in the pulpit.

What did Colonel Chattan think he was doing? He hadn't been to services since he arrived, and he showed up *this* day? Portia felt her temper rise.

If he was following her around because he wanted to repeat what had happened last night, he was going to be disappointed. He'd caught her in a weak moment. That woman who had so eagerly leaped into his arms was not *she*. She'd had a moment of madness but she was sane, sober and *remorseful* today.

By the time the services had ended, Portia had worked herself into such a state, she almost couldn't wait for a confrontation with Colonel Chattan, and then she saw Lady Emma.

Her Ladyship had realized Colonel Chattan

was in the chapel, and she was not pleased that he sat close to Portia.

Minnie leaned toward Portia. "Now Lady Emma is looking daggers at you. This is very odd, Portia. She is overreacting to a bit of spilled tea."

"Yes, it is," Portia agreed. "Now, if you will excuse me?"

She didn't wait for her sister's answer but brushed by her to leave the pew before Colonel Chattan could say anything to her.

Fortunately for her, he'd brought General Montheath with him. The general used this opportunity in church to corner Lady Maclean in the aisle and was attempting to converse. In fact, he seemed insistent he converse, as if he'd been gathering his courage all night for just this moment.

Her mother blocked the aisle, making it impossible for Lady Emma to move past her, and General Montheath blocked the pew so that Colonel Chattan couldn't leave.

Portia was free to leave and she did not dally. She fled the chapel and kept walking. Of course, Minnie had been following her and now caught up with her. "Portia, what is it? You've been acting peculiar."

"Nothing is wrong. I don't wish to linger. I want to leave as quickly as possible. I have chores."

"It's Sunday."

"There is no day of rest for women."

"Granted, but we usually spend a few moments visiting with our neighbors," Minnie said. "Only last week you claimed this was your favorite part of the Sunday."

"It is. Sometimes. I'm ready to go." Portia would have plowed on, but Colonel Chattan had escaped the chapel and had come up behind her.

Her traitorous body wanted to jump into his arms.

"Good day, Miss Maclean *and* Miss Maclean," he said to Portia and Minnie, as pleasant as one could be. He was obviously not racked with guilt over what had happened last night.

"How are you, Colonel?" Minnie said with great warmth.

"Very well, thank you. I believe my friend the general might be making some progress in the pursuit of your mother. I suggested he might actually muster the wherewithal to speak to her."

Portia glanced back at the door and was surprised to see that her mother was walking out with General Montheath and seemed to be listening to what he was saying.

"I'm surprised," Minnie admitted.

"He's determined," the colonel answered. He turned to Portia. "May I have a moment?"

Portia shook her head. "I'm so sorry. We are leaving."

She would have walked off but Minnie stopped her. "Oliver is not here yet and he is the one who drove us. Don't be in such a rush, Portia. You can talk to the colonel while I go see what is keeping Mr. Tolliver." She didn't wait for Portia's protest but hurried off.

Nor did Colonel Chattan wait to tell her what he wanted. "I need to see you."

"I don't believe that is a good idea," Portia whispered furiously. "Not after last night."

"Are you all right?" He sounded anxious as if he truly cared.

Portia didn't know how to respond, so she didn't say anything, choosing instead to study a point beyond him.

He made an impatient sound. "We can't pretend nothing happened between us. We should discuss it."

No, Portia definitely didn't want to discuss it with him. She was also not comfortable talking to him in such a public place. Lady Emma came into her line of vision. The girl's jealous eyes narrowed as she saw the two of them together, and Portia knew she was assuming the worst.

In this case, she'd be right.

Portia could feel him frown at her continued silence. "There is nothing to discuss," she answered, and would have walked off but he stepped in her path.

"I want that book," he said.

The book again.

"You can't have it," she said, annoyed and not quite understanding why. Apparently, concern for her wasn't his primary purpose in speaking to her.

"Name your price."

Her price?

"What price can you place on what it has already cost me?" she answered.

His expression changed. The determination in the set of his jaw softened, and in his eyes was the bleakness of regret.

And Portia wished she'd never spoken. It pricked her pride that he was sorry, because, actually, she wasn't. She hadn't realized that until this moment.

She began backing away, afraid of what she might reveal if she stayed there any longer. She was afraid he'd offer excuses. She didn't know what she wanted but it wasn't apologies.

And so she said the one thing she knew would make him leave her alone. "You can have the book."

Colonel Chattan gave a start as if he hadn't expected her to make the offer. "I'll come to your house—"

"*No.*" She couldn't afford to let Lady Emma confirm her suspicions. She glanced over to where the duke's daughter stood with several of her friends. They had their heads together, and Portia knew that didn't bode well for her.

She also couldn't let herself fall apart and imagine things that were not true. Colonel Chattan was reputed to have made love to almost every woman who had crossed his path. To him, she was no different from the others, and she mustn't let herself think otherwise.

Without facing the colonel, Portia said, "There is a shepherd's bothy not far from the Great Oak. I'll meet you there in two hours." She walked off without waiting for his answer.

*H*arry watched Portia march away, her back poker straight, and didn't know what to think. She'd dismissed him. No woman had ever dismissed him before.

They had made love last night with a passion he'd never known, and she had barely looked him in the eyes today. He'd known governesses who were more yielding than she was.

And they did need to discuss what had happened last night between them. He *wanted* to. *He*, the man who rarely discussed anything with a woman or anyone else.

"Chattan," Monty said, rushing up to him, "I followed your suggestions and they worked!"

It took a moment for Harry to pull his thoughts away from Portia Maclean. "My suggestions?"

"I tried to be myself around Ariana," Monty announced proudly. "I asked her a direct question and she spoke to me. We had a conversation."

"Did she speak kindly?" Harry had to ask. Lady Maclean had spoken to Monty before but not with the sweetness of her sex.

"*Yes*," Monty said as if that was quite an accomplishment. Harry started walking to where they'd tethered their horses, and the general fell into step beside him. "I asked her opinion about a soiree I'm having. I told her that I desperately needed advice from an accomplished and well-respected hostess as herself. I asked if perhaps she could give me a moment of her time, and she did."

"You are having a *soiree*?" Harry asked with disbelief. He mounted his horse.

"It's one of those words the ladies like," Monty said, climbing into the saddle of his own horse. "She didn't question my use of it. Anyway, the conversation went better than I could imagine.

Who knew that all I had to do was ask Ariana questions and then she'd answer me and we would be talking?"

"Monty," Harry said, concerned for his friend, "are you certain this is the woman you want?"

"With all my heart," Monty replied.

"Poor bugger," Harry said under his breath. He set Ajax down the road.

"I don't expect you to understand, Chattan. You aren't the sort of man who knows *how* to love or even values it."

This comment caught Harry's attention. "I value love."

"I challenge that," Monty said with his new-found confidence. "Tell me, have you ever been constant to one woman for, let's say, more than three weeks or even three days in your life?"

"What do you mean by 'constant'?" Harry asked, suddenly not liking this conversation.

"I mean that you are true and faithful to her. That you would cherish her."

"I've cherished many women," Harry answered.

"One at a time, Chattan. *One* woman, for a long period of time, and because you valued her mind and her opinion as well as her body. I don't believe you've even had a mistress."

"I didn't see the purpose to it," Harry answered. "Why focus my energy on one bit of muslin when there are all these others begging for me to notice them?"

"And that is why I know you've never been in love," Monty announced with a crow of satisfaction, as if he'd proven his theory correct.

"Maybe I don't want to be in love," Harry returned. "What good is it anyway? You've been miserable being in love."

"But today, I am ecstatic," Monty declared. "I spoke to her and she was civil. I just need to come up with a method to keep her that way."

"Yes, you can't have a 'soiree' every day."

Monty's pride in his accomplishment was so great, he dismissed Harry's sarcasm with a wave.

But Harry couldn't dismiss his friend's criticism. In truth, Harry was reaching the age when bachelorhood was no longer attractive. He'd noticed that once a man closed in on five and thirty, he became overly self-indulgent, spending his time on petty things that didn't matter like the cut of a glove or ridiculous jealousies. Harry was only a few years away from that age.

He'd never thought that way before, but since in Glenfinnan and sober, he discovered some of his attitudes were changing.

His brother had leaped into love once he'd met his wife, Thea. He adored her with all his heart and soul, and Harry had never seen Neal happier. He'd told Harry that life now held meaning whereas before it had lacked any sense of purpose beyond duty.

"Do you feel life has meaning now?" Harry suddenly asked Monty, curious as to his response.

The general turned to him in surprise. "I was just thinking that. I was looking at the passing scenery that I have seen a dozen times before, and it all looks new to me. There is no reason other than the pleasure I have in Ariana's speaking to me."

Harry took in the stately firs lining the road through Moncrieffe's estate. It all looked the same to him now as it had when they arrived. They were trees, and he doubted any emotion, even love, could make them seem different to him.

"Do you still believe I'm a madman, Chattan?" the general asked.

"Sir?" Harry said.

"The Shakespeare you quoted, saying love is akin to madness. I don't feel like a lunatic right now, Chattan. I feel bloody damn brilliant."

Harry was stunned by this change in his friend wrought from nothing more than a simple, courteous conversation with a woman who should have been more courteous before.

"One woman, Harry," Monty said as if reading his mind. "Try to value *one* woman. Then maybe you'll see that everything, even trees, is more than what you thought them to be."

Harry didn't care about trees, but he *had* been thinking of only one woman.

And Portia Maclean had made it very clear she wanted nothing to do with him.

A bothy was a stone cottage left open to all. They were built for shepherds and travelers alike. Anyone was welcome to use them, and bothies of all sizes and shapes could be found around the Highlands.

Portia had chosen this particular bothy because it was located away from any road or path. Nestled between two rolling hills, it was not easily seen. In fact, someone would have to search to find it. The bothy was also not far from the Great Oak and Crazy Lizzy's cottage, giving Portia the excuse she needed to go for a walk on a Sunday afternoon.

Mr. Tolliver had stayed for the Sunday meal Glennis had waiting for them after church. Lady Maclean had been so petulant about his continued presence that she had gone to her room without joining them.

"She's pouting," Minnie had told Mr. Tolliver.

"She doesn't approve of us. I should have asked her permission for your hand first. I should have been more proper."

Minnie had leaned forward and placed her hand over his. "She would have said no. She has some ridiculous notion that I would have caught the eye of Colonel Chattan and we would have all returned to London."

That statement had set off new concerns for Mr. Tolliver. "Do you *wish* to return to London?" he'd asked, and Minnie had laughed before assuring him she wanted plump, happy Highland babies.

Portia hadn't stayed to hear more. Their obvious love for each other was more palatable when she wasn't facing social ruin. She now knew everything they said about Colonel Chattan was true. The man was an unrestrained libertine. She knew because she had "libertined" with him.

After retrieving the book from its hiding place under her bed and placing it in a covered basket, Portia knocked on her mother's door. "Mother, I need to deliver some bread to Lizzy. You must come downstairs and chaperone Minnie and Mr. Tolliver."

"I'm not feeling well," came the weak reply. "You must do it. Oh, and bring me another piece of that chicken we had for dinner and some more peas. I find myself famished." Her voice had grown stronger as she spoke, and something inside Portia snapped like a twig that was too brittle.

"Mother," she said, "I am going out. Go downstairs and sit with your daughter and her intended. The chicken is in the pantry."

With those words, Portia turned on her heel and left. Ran, actually, because she'd never told her mother no. She'd always done as bid. But she had more pressing business right now and a flurry of conflicting emotions that were making it hard for her to focus on her own needs, let alone the demands of others.

She put on her cloak and went outside. The bothy was about a mile walk from Camber Hall. The fresh air and exercise felt good. It cleared her mind and gave her a moment to prepare for her meeting with Colonel Chattan.

This would be their first and last meeting. She'd already decided that. She would hand him the book and march off as quickly as possible. There was no use in lingering, because he might have ideas that she would be as unrestrained as she had been the night before.

Consequently, Portia had taken great care in

her appearance. She'd put one of her mother's lace Spanish vests over her shoulders so that her chest was covered. She'd pulled her untamable hair back as tightly as she could and pinned it severely. Finally, she wore her spectacles. They hadn't deterred him last night but they were one more barrier.

She tried not to think of the night before. She wanted to erase it from her mind and thought she had succeeded until she arrived at the bothy and saw his horse tethered and grazing there.

He had to be inside.

Portia gripped the handle of her basket with both hands. Her mouth had gone dry and her blood started pounding in her veins. She walked toward the stone cottage.

There was movement in the open doorway. Colonel Chattan had seen her arrive. He came out, ducking so that he didn't hit his head on the top of the door.

He wore his greatcoat open. He looked dashing, a man at home in the world whether it was a battlefield or an isolated stone cottage.

Portia reached for the book. All she had to do was hand it to him and leave. She didn't even need to speak.

And then they would be done.

He'd have what he wanted and she could return to her safe, predictable life.

A soft meow caught her attention. Owl had followed her. The cat now leaped up onto a large rock in the hillside.

If Colonel Chattan saw Owl, he gave no indication. His eyes were on her. He reached into his pocket and pulled out a coin purse. He was going to pay what he'd promised.

Portia was both thankful and insulted. It was hard to look in his eyes as she approached. There was something about him that drew her to him, and it was best if she kept her attention on anything other than how handsome he was or how masculine.

She held out the book.

He held out the money.

Portia reached for it as he reached for the book—and then, she didn't know how it happened, but she found herself in his arms.

And he was kissing her.

And she was kissing him back for everything she was worth.

Chapter Eleven

*M*onty's challenge for Harry to focus on one woman had not set well with him. After all, he'd spent most of his life avoiding the dangers of "one woman," a danger his brother had happily embraced.

After strong reflection, Harry had decided his wisest course would be to keep a distance from Portia Maclean.

He told himself he wouldn't be so strongly attracted to her if he'd been following his old ways of strong spirits and dozens of women. Back then, he'd not been picky about what woman he'd been taking to his bed. They had all been the same to him, or so he wanted to believe . . . because the realization that this pull, this attraction he felt for Portia Maclean, was something more than what he'd ever experienced before left him humble, vulnerable—emotions Harry didn't like.

And yet, right now, with her in his arms, he could not stop kissing her.

Nor was he the only one who felt this way. Her kiss spoke louder than words that even though she could be prickly in public, she was a more than willing participant now.

He swept her up in his arms and carried her inside the bothy, their lips still locked together.

Inside, he began undressing her. Her hands were as eager as his. She pushed his coat down his arms so that it fell to the ground. She tugged at his shirt. Her fingers found the buttons to his breeches. She untwisted one, then another.

He untied the strings of her cloak and brought her into the circle of his arms. Their kiss deepened as his fingers searched, then found the laces of her dress.

Harry knew all the tricks and tucks to women's clothing. It was not a difficult feat for him to unlace her dress. His reward was access to two of the sweetest breasts he had ever held.

Her skin was creamier and smoother than he could have imagined. The nipples were hard and pink. Perfect, really . . . just as she was. Perfect for him.

Portia ran her hands up his rib cage, pulling his shirt up as she made her journey. His neck cloth was still tied around his neck and he wore his woolen jacket.

Laughing, he said, "One moment, love. Not so fast." He tried to untie the knot in his neck cloth.

She drummed her fingers on his chest and kissed the sensitive underside of his neck, and Harry could not take it much longer. His fingers became clumsy, and he didn't want to fool with the knot when he had her to touch.

Portia was a wicked delight. She didn't hold back, on both opinions and desires.

Putting his arms behind him, he yanked at the sleeves of his jacket. He was trapped that way as she lifted his shirt more fully, stepped closer and pressed those luscious breasts against his skin.

Harry groaned, reveling in the feel of her, delighted by her boldness and innocent sensuality.

Her hands smoothed down his sides, moving toward his waist. She was kissing him now, her hand against his erection. Her fingers stroked sensitive skin, discovering and measuring the length of him before she held him in her palm, and that was Harry's undoing.

Who needed to be naked? Clothes served a purpose, didn't they?

Harry shrugged the jacket he'd not yet been able

to remove back up his shoulder and used both arms to lift her up to him for a kiss that would devour her if he had his way. He would swallow her whole . . . and he could not wait one moment longer.

He spread her legs around his waist and entered her with one smooth, strong stroke.

She was tight, hot, ready, and Harry rogered her for all he was worth. She drove him to madness. She had only to touch him for him to feel an overwhelming need.

Even that morning in church, he'd wanted her. He'd stared at the back of her head, the feeling, the smell, the heat of her controlling his mind.

Now he had her and he wanted his fill.

*P*ortia didn't want reason, or rules, or strictures.

She wanted *him*.

Wrapping her arms around his neck, she reveled in the sensation of her bare chest against his as he thrust deeper and deeper into his body.

He made her feel alive. She was on fire. The heat of their coupling threatened to consume her.

She moved with him, and yet found she had her own wants, her own desires, and only he could satisfy them—

A pinnacle of sensation started building inside

her. She'd felt it the night before but this was more powerful, keener.

Portia held tight, almost afraid of what was happening to her. This was so good, *too* good—

And then she found what she had been searching for. She hit *it*.

One moment, her body was of this earth and in the next she was part of the heavens. She was a shooting star. She was the *sun*. She was all that was perfect and wonderful.

Had she thought last night was what the poets praised? She'd been wrong.

This was what they celebrated.

He flew with her as well. He rocked her in his arms as her body exploded into a hundred different shards of sensation. He was buried deep within her and she felt the power of life flow from him to her.

Life. *Yes,* that was what this was. Portia was finally a part of life. Sweet, valuable, always-to-be-cherished life.

Of course, reality, the part of life she truly belonged to, returned with the cooling of her body's sweat, and a realization that once again she'd compromised her virtue.

What virtue?

She'd tossed that aside last night.

What she needed to do now was arrange her clothing into some semblance of normal and run from this place and this man as fast as her legs could take her—

"You had better not be having recriminations," his deep voice said above her.

Portia closed her eyes. She wished she could blame him for her shameful behavior, but she couldn't. She'd wanted him, and she'd had him.

"I need to go," she whispered.

"No, you don't," he said, his arms hugging her closer. Her legs were still around his waist. "I'm not letting you go anywhere."

"Please," she said, her throat starting to close on tears.

He stopped any other pleas she could have made with a kiss.

This kiss was different from the devouring ones of only moments ago. This was gentle, caring, understanding.

Slowly, her resistance vanished. He let her down to the ground and she stood in front of him, almost afraid of what would happen next.

He cupped her face with his hands. His palm was rough. He was no dandy but a man who used his hands, who almost took pleasure in it. He traced her lips with the tip of his thumb.

"You must believe me," he said, his voice low. "What is between us is different. It's not how things normally are."

Was he saying she was different to him from all the women he was reputed to have bedded?

She wanted to believe him.

He picked up her cloak. With caring reverence he placed it around her. It was then she realized her dress hung down to her waist. Her breasts were completely exposed to him. She started to pull her bodice up. He caught her hands.

"No, not yet."

Portia looked askance. She didn't understand.

"You are so beautiful," he answered.

Beautiful. No one had ever called her beautiful before. Minnie was the beauty. Portia was the less-than-attractive older sister, the one who would never marry without a dowry . . . and yet, in this moment, she felt beautiful.

He smiled as he touched the bridge of her spectacles, pushing them up her nose. "I like your glasses. I like you."

A warmth filled her that was more potent than even his lovemaking.

"I like you as well," she said.

He smiled, the expression transforming his face. He looked relaxed, younger, carefree. But then he turned serious. "The book?"

Of course, the book.

She had been a momentary diversion. One he enjoyed before he focused on what he truly wanted.

He looked past her to where the book had dropped to the ground when they had embraced. The money bag was there as well, and Portia was stunned to realize that she'd been so embroiled with him she could have forgotten something as important as money.

The colonel left her, tucking in his shirt as he went outside, and picked up both the book and her money. He left the basket where it lay.

Portia began straightening her wardrobe. Her hair was a mess. Her curls sprang every which way. Her body was still full of him. She tried not to think on it as she started searching the ground for stray pins.

He leaned against the door and opened the book, blocking her way to escape.

Portia waited a few moments, watching him turning the pages, a frown marring his forehead.

All was silent save for the sounds of his horse grazing outside and the fragile brittleness of the pages as he flipped them.

"I should be leaving," she said.

He raised his gaze, his eyes saying he hadn't comprehended her words.

"I should leave," she repeated. She did need to go now, while she had the good common sense to do so—and she would never cross his path again. Never, never, *never.*

The colonel might act as if this sort of explosive mating was normal for him, but it wasn't for her. She was developing a habit around him that was quite disturbing.

He held the book out. "I don't understand this," he said as if she hadn't spoken. "What is it? And where did you see the name Fenella?"

"It's a book of recipes," she explained. Seeing he didn't understand, she said, "Women write down recipes for curing bacon and remedies for healing a fever or setting a bone. They pass these books down from one generation to the next. This one is a bit unusual because it has chants and spells. Magic, you could say, although I doubt if any of the spells work." She took the book from him and turned the pages to show him what she meant. "I found Fenella's name in the front. In this book, I'm assuming that when it was passed from one woman to the next, the woman wrote her name in it. That's a common practice for such books, much the same as what you see in family Bibles."

The colonel stared at the list of faded names

ending with Fenella's. "It's an unusual name. It must be her. Why else would the cat be here? Tell me how you found the book."

Again, with the cat.

He could make a woman question his sanity. "I need to be going," Portia said, and would have slipped past him out the door except he placed an arm up to block her way.

"Please," he said. "This is important."

"My family will wonder where I am." She shouldn't stay here. Not alone with him.

"Where did you tell them you were going?"

Portia made an impatient sound at his commonsense response.

"Well?" he prompted.

"I told them I was taking a basket to Lizzy."

"Crazy Lizzy?"

"You've met her?"

"I have met every woman people thought could be possessed in some way or the other," he answered, and then took her arm, leading her over to a three-legged stool by the bothy's cold hearth. "Sit here and trust me when I say I will see you home, and well before dark."

Portia tried to turn back to the door. "That will not work. If Lady Emma catches wind of this, there will be an uproar."

He held fast to her arm, not letting her escape. "No one will see me return you home. And as for the duke's spoiled daughter, I won't let her harm you. I won't let anyone hurt you. Please, just a moment more of your time."

"There is no such thing as a witch," she said, the words bursting out of her. "And Fenella, who created your curse, is dead. Gone. She isn't a cat and she doesn't exist now."

"I understand your doubt," he said. "I would be the same way if I was not involved in this. But if I don't find a way to break this curse, my brother will die and his son will bear the mark as well and it will continue on. Please, stay a moment and hear the story. I'll see you home without anyone being the wiser. I promise."

She should leave . . . but curiosity led her to sink down to the stool.

"Thank you," he said, and he sounded as if he truly meant the words. He sat on the ground in front of her, crossing his booted legs so he could cradle the book in his lap.

"Fenella had a daughter named Rose who loved Charles Chattan of Glenfinnan. She claimed they were handfasted, which at the time, to Rose, was the same as being married."

"I've heard the story. It's common knowledge

amongst the locals. They think Charles was a traitorous scoundrel."

"I believe he probably cared for Rose but he didn't consider them betrothed. Or perhaps he did. We Chattan men are capable of being scoundrels."

He gave a self-deprecating smile as he said this, but Portia wasn't so certain he wasn't giving her a warning as well.

The colonel continued. "Charles's parents managed to contract a marriage to an English heiress for him. He chose to do as his parents asked, which was reasonable, especially for the day and age—"

"Protesting too much?" she suggested.

"Perhaps. I wasn't there, and I was teasing about Chattan men being scoundrels."

"I'm not so certain," she murmured. He frowned. "I was told she jumped from a tower." He nodded. "She had to have been heartbroken . . ." She paused.

"What is it?"

"Let me see the book." He handed it to her and she turned to the page with the spell and the word "Charles" written in the tearstained margin. "Could this be from her?" She handed the book back.

His reaction would have been the same if she had given him the crown jewels. "Yes, Rose could have written this." He traced the writing as if he could divine something of that woman from centuries ago.

Portia felt her eyes fill with tears. "Hers is a terrible story."

"It happened a long time ago," the colonel said.

"I know, but I can imagine how she must have felt." And Portia could, especially with him sitting so close. She barely knew him, and yet all he had to do was touch her and she threw aside convention and priorities. Of course, she didn't love Colonel Chattan. She hadn't known him long enough to love him . . . and she would not be so foolish as to do so.

However, she did understand how powerful Charles Chattan's betrayal must have been, given Rose's love for him.

"Tell me about the curse," she said. She'd remembered the story from Mrs. Macdonald's telling but she wished to hear what he had to say.

"Fenella was angry," he said, "and she wanted revenge. She ordered a funeral pyre built for her daughter's body. As a suicide Rose couldn't be buried on church ground, so Fenella honored the old ways. They say she cursed Charles Chattan as her daughter's body burned and then she leaped onto the fire itself and died with her daughter."

"That's terrible."

"And it was very effective," he agreed somberly. "She said that when a Chattan falls in love, he will die . . . just as, I suppose, her Rose died." He looked down at the page of the book again.

"And the curse always comes true?"

"Yes. Charles Chattan of Glenfinnan fell in love with his English heiress and dropped dead within a year of his marriage. His wife was carrying his son, a son that fell in love, and he, too, died, and so on. The pattern has been the same. A Chattan marries, his wife is with child, and then he dies. The pattern has been almost the same for nearly two centuries. My forebears have done everything they could think possible to break it."

"You say almost two hundred years? When has it been different?"

"With my father. Before his time, the Chattans had sought the advice of priests, cardinals, bishops, the pope, self-proclaimed witches, Gypsies and fortune-tellers. They tried not to fall in love, and have always failed. Each time they have left behind a son who bears the weight of the curse. My grandfather and his father married women they could not abide. It was a hateful life and one that led to their early deaths. My father followed in their steps, but he had a better temperament for keeping his distance from his wife. He'd been bred for that. Perhaps all of us have. You see, if death is the penalty for love, one learns not to love. One learns to guard his heart."

"I can imagine," she agreed.

"My father was the first of his line to have more than one son. There are three of us. My brother, Neal, myself, and my sister, Margaret. She is the first daughter to be born of our line in two hundred years. Then, after my mother died several years ago, my father did a very foolish thing."

"He fell in love," she surmised.

"Head tumbling over heels," he confirmed, nodding. "With an opera dancer far younger than even myself."

"And then did he die?"

"Within six months." He closed the book, leaning toward her. "He wrote a letter to us to be opened upon his death. He said loving his wife, Cass, was worth death. He said life had been empty before her, that he'd done more living in the months he was with her than all the fifty-some years before his marriage."

Portia sat a moment, studying him as she digested all that he'd said. His story was contrary to reason and nature. She could have dismissed it for a grand tale save his sincerity.

"My brother is in love," he said. "He's a good man, a noble one. I'm a wastrel and certainly of loose morals. I've cost men lives, drunk too much, had a taste for opium; I'm a sinner through and through and have deserved to die many times over. But Neal is one of the finest men in England. He doesn't deserve this fate," he said, tapping the cover of the book. "Especially for loving his wife, Thea. He should have a chance to see his son grow to manhood. If I don't find a way to break this curse, his death will be on my head. I don't know if I can live with that knowledge."

"What of yourself? Do you carry the curse?"

"We don't know," he replied, his expression bleak. "Possibly. I am male; I am a Chattan. As for my sister, Margaret fears that even if she isn't a part of the curse, she could carry the legacy of it. She fears for any children she could have."

"She is married?"

"No, and she won't. She and I both agree that none of us should have married and certainly we should not fall in love. We want the curse to end here, with us. But Neal didn't agree. He wanted a son." The colonel sounded as if he was amazed by the thought. "Thea is a widow and has two sons by her previous marriage. Neal had told me they were enough for him, but Thea got with child almost immediately."

His brows came together. He looked up at her, and then away. "I am usually careful when I'm with a lover."

Portia felt heat flood her face. She clasped her hands in her lap, trying to be sensible about what they'd done.

"I don't want bastards," he said, "and I don't have any."

Well, there was comfort there . . . she thought.

"I haven't been so careful with you." Now he was the one with a bit of color to his face. It made him appear more masculine, if that was possible. "We shall hope for the best," he said. "However, I will meet my obligations."

Obligations . . . a baby.

For a second, Portia knew fear.

"Well, this isn't going to happen again," she said quickly. "I don't understand what comes over us, but it is out of my system."

"Mine as well," he assured her, then paused before adding, "but if it does happen again, I shall be more careful."

Portia wished the floor of the room would open up and swallow her whole. She didn't have conversations with many men, let alone conversations like this. She wasn't some sophisticated Londoner who dallied with lovers. She wasn't even certain how he could avoid getting her with child, and her naivete embarrassed her all the more.

He shut the book and glanced toward the door. "We'd best leave if I'm to have you home before dark." He stood and offered her his hand. "Thank you for this book and for hearing my story."

Rising, Portia said, "I hope it may help."

"I pray it does. My sister wrote and said that Neal is taking more and more to his bed. He grows weak quickly and so is trying to pace himself."

The thought went through Portia's mind that perhaps what he saw as a curse was merely a family disposition toward weak hearts or another malady. Perhaps the timing of all the deaths was coincidence?

She held her tongue.

He escorted her from the bothy and picked up the basket for her. "Hold the book for me," he said, and went to untie his horse.

The bay had a distinct personality and let him know with a butt of his head he'd not been pleased to be left standing for so long. "I'm sorry, Ajax," Colonel Chattan said, rubbing the animal's nose.

"I was preoccupied." He smiled and directed the last in Portia's direction.

She felt herself blush.

He mounted and came over to her, holding out a hand.

Portia had never mounted a horse this way. And the animal was big, larger than any horse she had ever seen or ridden. "I can walk," she murmured.

"Take my hand," he ordered in a tone that allowed for no disobedience.

She placed her hand in his. He'd put on his gloves. They were softer than his hands. He easily lifted her up to sit in front of him. His arm came around her waist. She had the book in the basket on her lap.

"Hold on," he said, his voice tickling her ear. With a kick, they were off.

Ajax was a mighty steed. A warrior's horse. He carried them at a fast clip through the woods toward Camber Hall.

Colonel Chattan had one arm around her waist. His other hand held the reins. As they rode, the masculinity of him seemed to circle around her, teasing her. He now smelled of sandalwood and the musk of their lovemaking.

They were close to Camber Hall when she felt his breath on her hair. He kissed her, once, twice, a third time, and then brought his lips down to gently kiss her temple. His hand came up to cup her breast. He kissed her neck.

Portia knew she should stop him. She could feel his hardness against her. She had a need as well.

He reined Ajax to a stop. He did not release his hold.

Pressing his head against hers, he said, "I want to see you again."

Portia started to shake her head. "I can't, Colonel—"

He hushed her. "Harry," he said, amusement in his voice. "My name is Harry, and after what we've been to each other, I believe we may be less formal."

"I can't meet you, *Colonel*," she answered.

His hold tightened. "I'm not letting you free until I hear you say my name."

She glanced at him to see if he was serious.

He was smiling but he didn't loosen his hold. "Har-reee," he said, drawing out the syllables. "Try it."

"I'm not that amenable, Colonel," she responded, proud of herself for standing up to him.

Her bravado earned a laugh from him. "I've known that." He turned serious. "Meet me again tomorrow."

The suggestion alone was enough to send the blood racing through her veins. "I shouldn't," she said, common sense warring with this newly discovered desire for sexual pleasure. It was wrong to want him. Wrong to be so willing.

"Meet me tomorrow," he repeated, his voice in her ear. "We need to make love naked, at least once."

Portia didn't dare speak. He was her weakness. He was a temptation, a *devil*.

"I'll be at the bothy around noon," he said. "I shall wait for you." He then let her down to the ground. Portia started walking toward the house, and then began running.

Minnie was in the sitting room darning socks when Portia came in the door. Her sister smiled at her and asked how Crazy Lizzy had been.

Portia stared at her, uncomprehending for a second, and then remembered her excuse for leaving the house. "She is the same as always." Portia put the basket down on a side table and began removing her cloak.

"You are such a good person," Minnie said. "Oliver has commented at how happy he is that our family is a far cry from the sort of man Father was. He confided in me today that there had been gossip in the valley when we'd first arrived. I don't know how they expected us to be. We wouldn't have carried on the way Father did. We may be Black Jack Maclean's children but we have the moral standards our father lacked."

Portia smiled, not trusting her voice to speak.

Minnie put down her piecework. "I'm so happy, Portia. So very happy. I hope someday you meet someone who makes you as happy. And I don't believe you are too old. I've never thought that."

"Thank you, dear." Portia started for the stairs. "I'm going to my room."

"Oh, Portia, there is something I should tell you. Mother and General Montheath had their heads together all afternoon. He came calling and she received him without one grumble. He's given her carte blanche to plan his soiree and she is reveling in it."

"Mother and General Montheath?"

"I know it is amazing, but you know how she likes to spend money. The soiree has turned into a grand Christmas Day dinner. Mr. Tolliver is going to ask his parents to join us. Mother wants to invite the Duke of Montcrieffe and his daughter, Lady Emma. I'm not very excited for that, but Mother feels we must extend the invitation."

"How interesting," Portia murmured. The last thing she wanted to do was spend her Christmas

Day with Lady Emma. But she didn't offer a pro-test. Instead, she escaped to her room, where she lay on her bed fully clothed as the room grew darker with the day's end.

What was she doing? She'd behaved today in a way contrary to her good breeding. She'd behaved as her *father* would have. She must not go to the bothy tomorrow. She had to resist temptation.

Then again, she *was* Black Jack Maclean's daugh-ter. He'd certainly enjoyed sensual pleasures—and she did wonder what it would be like to lie naked with Harry.

Harry. Colonel Chattan was a distant figure, a cold one. Harry was a man who whispered in her ear. A man whose touch ignited her senses.

The next day, Portia met Harry in the bothy.

He'd been right. Making love naked was truly remarkable.

And so she met him the following day as well.

Chapter Twelve

"I need your help," Harry said to Portia.

They had just enjoyed a very strenuous and very happy bout of lovemaking. She was exhausted and lay with her head on his chest, listening to his heartbeat.

Portia's excuse to leave the house for her trysts with Harry continued to be her need to help Crazy Lizzy, and she did not lie about the old woman. She *did* deliver the food.

But only after spending an hour, sometimes more, in Harry's arms. And he had been true to his word. They now took precautions to prevent a child.

Of course, her sister and mother didn't appear to care where Portia was. Minnie was caught up in planning her marriage to Mr. Tolliver. They would wed on January 2 of the new year. The banns had been posted twice now.

Surprisingly, Lady Maclean no longer spent her days in bed. She was up and ready for General Montheath's call. Any of her earlier complaints about him vanished as she almost gleefully spent his money. She still wouldn't let any of his many dogs into the house, but Portia had caught sight of her mother's hand reaching down to scratch Jasper's ear a time or two.

Therefore, Portia was able to do exactly as she pleased, with only a semblance of propriety. No one questioned her, not even Glennis was suspicious. So far their liaison was a secret, and Black Jack Maclean's older daughter liked it that way because she was proving to be his child.

They'd turned the bothy into their own paradise. Harry brought a stack of fur-lined blankets to keep them warm and they didn't need much else. The weather might be cold or windy or wet, but there in his arms, the world was perfect.

Her lover was a masterful teacher and Portia was an eager student. Nor did she weigh the rights and wrongs of what she was doing. She knew it would end someday, but for now, *this* was what she wanted.

Indeed, there was only one small matter that concerned Portia—she hadn't seen Owl since that day she'd first met Harry at the bothy. The cat seemed to have disappeared. Everyone told her cats did that from time to time, but that didn't stop Portia from worrying and calling for Owl to come home.

"What do you need help with?" she asked Harry, propping her head up on her hand resting on his chest.

"The book." He sat up, forcing her to move. She pulled the blanket up around her breasts. Heedless of his own nakedness, he rose from their makeshift bed and went over to where his saddlebags lay.

She liked his body. He was hard muscle. She imagined that the Spartan warriors of old must have looked like him. Not even the scar on his leg deterred from his masculine beauty.

"How did you receive that wound?" she asked.

A frown marred his brow as he pulled the book from his bags. "A French sword. It came at me and I forgot to move."

"The cut must have been deep." The scar was angry and occasionally she had noticed him favoring the leg. She remembered at the dance, when they'd been on the floor together, he hadn't hopped and skipped the way the other men had. She'd assumed his reserve was because of pride. Some men didn't like to dance. But now she understood.

"It was." His voice was curt. He returned to her just as she shivered in the cool air. He pulled the blankets over them.

"What battle were you in?" she asked, snuggling against him and running her hand along the scar.

"Vitoria. I don't like talking about it." He opened the book.

"Why not?"

Harry gave her his full attention, his expression somber. "Because I proved myself to be a vainglorious fool and cost many good men their lives."

"It was war, Harry. War always costs lives."

His lips twisted into a sardonic smile. "How callously they speak who don't witness the cost."

"I'm not trying to be callous," Portia said, a bit hurt by the label. She sat up.

For a second, he appeared ready to say something but shook his head and opened the book.

Portia wasn't ready to let it go. "You should say what you think instead of swallowing your words."

"No one cares what I think," he answered, turning a page.

"I do."

The word seemed to hover in the air. Harry looked to her. "You shouldn't, Portia."

Her throat tightened. "But I do."

"I'm not worth it." He slipped a hand around her neck and kissed her forehead as if ending the subject.

There was great sadness in him, a sadness that she had seen that moonlit night when he had been on his knees. She placed her hand on his chest, right over his heart. *His heart.* She loved the steady rhythm of it. When they made love, and his weight was on her, she relished its pounding beat as much as she did his heat and strength.

"Yes, you are," she said.

Again, he pressed a kiss against her brow. He did not believe her.

He held up the book. "I've read this from cover to cover three times," he said. "I can't find any clue as to what can be done to break the curse. I find nothing 'witchy.'"

"What are you looking for?" she asked. He'd changed the topic. He did not want to discuss the matter further and she knew he remained unconvinced of her belief in him. She reached for her spectacles on the stool and placed them on her nose.

"I don't know what I'm looking for," he admitted, stabbing his fingers through his hair in frustration. "I suppose something such as 'Eye of newt and toe of frog.'"

Portia smiled, recognizing the reference to *Macbeth*. "Another Scot with a witch problem," she murmured. She took the book from him and turned a few of the pages. "Why don't we read this aloud to each other? Sometimes, I miss details when reading silently. Hearing the words spoken makes them clearer to me."

"Capital idea. You start, my lady." He stretched out on their bed of furs.

She glanced at him, at his spent maleness, knowing that before she went home, he would please her again. He saw where she was looking and laughed. "Read," he ordered, slipping his hand beneath the covers and placing it possessively on her thigh, and so she obeyed.

It wasn't easy reading. Some of the recipes were in the old Gaelic and the ink of many of them had faded. He listened as she stumbled along, watching her intently.

Portia didn't read every recipe. She'd scan them for something of interest. There were hundreds of them. She'd barely had time to investigate the book at all before she'd given it to him.

"Here is something," she said. It was the last entry in a section. *"Reunioning a soul with an animal,"* she read. She looked to Harry. "What does that mean?"

"In the East there is the thought of reincarnation where the soul returns to live again. The Hindus believe all life, including animal life, reincarnates. Read on."

"Choose the animal you wish to live on in. Very old power. From Gypsy." Several of the recipes had given their source. *"Make an elixir of mugwort oil and powdered spruce needles. Mix with frankincense resin. Chew while repeating, 'Life come hither, Life is mine' until passing."*

Portia looked up in shock. "What does it mean by 'until passing.'"

Harry frowned. "Death, I suppose."

"How strange," Portia said, and made a face as she shivered in distaste. "I don't like this spell."

"It can't work," Harry assured her. "How many of us choose the hour of our death. How would one know when to start chewing the resin—" He broke off as if struck by a new thought. "Wait a moment, a suicide would know the hour of her death."

Portia looked down at the recipe and shook her head. "There is no way of knowing if this spell was used or not. I don't like thinking about it." She started to shut the book but Harry placed his hand on the page.

"How did you find this book? Has it been in your family?" he asked.

"No, I found it in the attic at Camber Hall."

"Was it in a trunk?"

"Actually," she said, a strange sense of foreboding rising within her, "Owl gave it to me."

"The cat?"

Portia nodded and told him of going up the attic to put a bucket under where the roof leaked.

"So the book was on top of something it could be knocked or pushed off of?" Harry asked.

"I assume that was the case," Portia answered. "I don't really know. There are stacks of wooden boxes and crates and trunks up there. I was weaving my way around them when the book dropped down in front of me. I didn't know why until I saw Owl peek around a corner. She could have jumped from the top of something and knocked the book off."

Harry sat up. "Where is the cat now?"

"I don't know," Portia admitted. "The last time I saw her was the first time we met here. She was waiting for me. I haven't seen her since."

He pushed the covers away and stood, pressing his brow with the fingers of one hand as if trying to answer a riddle. He looked to her. "I said to you once, I thought the cat was Fenella."

"And I thought the idea ridiculous. I still do."

"Fenella took her own life as well," he said,

ignoring her criticism. "She knew *when* she was going to die."

"Oh, not again. Why do you keep suggesting that Owl, a poor little cat with deformed ears, is a two-hundred-year-old witch? That's impossible."

He knelt beside her. "Not if she is reincarnating herself."

"Over and over again?" Portia let her doubts show. "Cats can't repeat chants."

"Portia, your cat came to me at General Montheath's house. I was going to leave Glenfinnan. I'd exhausted every resource in the surrounding area without success. I decided I must go to Edinburgh. There is a man there who specializes in country tales and traditions. Someone suggested he might know of Fenella's legend. I doubted it but I was on a cold trail. I didn't know what else to do. And then your cat woke me. I was asleep, in a deep dream, and I didn't know what it was waking me, and I threw her off the bed. She ran under the wardrobe to hide and I started thinking about how strange it was that a cat had managed to steal inside Monty's house. The place is a dog haven. They bark at everything. Monty has no control over any of them. And yet, not one of those hounds made a sound to alert us there was a cat on the premises. So I looked under the wardrobe and the cat wasn't there. I couldn't find her anywhere in the room."

"Perhaps you dreamed her," Portia suggested gently.

"You can't feel dreams. I heard the cat purr, felt the roughness of its tongue. Your cat was in the room and that is when I decided I needed to stay here."

Portia looked down at the words of the spell written in the book. Owl was an independent creature and she did have a habit of appearing without fanfare. "There must be a hidey-hole or some other opening for a cat to use to find her way into Montheath's house. Cats are very clever that way."

Harry shook his head. "I know to my bones, Portia, your cat is a part of this. I told you that once, and I feel it more certainly than before." He took the book from her. "But if your cat is Fenella, then why give us the book? Her hatred was so strong, she would never offer any clues to lifting the curse."

She didn't speak. What he was saying defied common sense.

"We need to find your cat," Harry said.

"Owl comes home when she feels like," Portia answered, a bit uncomfortable with the idea of him hunting her pet.

"I must find the cat." He came to his feet and started dressing.

Portia watched him a moment, disappointed that her afternoon with him would end so abruptly. "Where will you go?" she asked.

He looked at her, surprised. "With you, of course. The cat comes to you—"

His voice broke off as he realized the import of what he'd said. "The cat comes to *you*," he repeated softly. "*You* and *I* were meant to meet. That's why the cat didn't want me to leave Glenfinnan."

Now he sounded completely mad.

"That's nonsense," she snapped, strangely annoyed. She reached for her clothes and began dressing.

"Is it?" he asked, sitting on the stool and pulling on his boots. "Can you not imagine, just the smallest bit, that we were destined to meet?"

Portia pulled her dress over her head and stood a moment, wanting to reject his theory . . . and wanting to accept it.

Had they been destined to meet? It would seem that she was always in his path. He'd almost run over her that first day and then there was the connection of General Montheath and her mother. They could be coincidences, and she found she wanted to believe that they were.

"I can't accept that there are forces at work that we can't touch or feel," she confessed.

"Do we not pray to God?" he challenged.

"God is good. You are speaking of an evil."

"Or not. Rose wasn't evil. What if Rose was the one who had reincarnated herself? What if your cat is her?"

"What if you stopped speaking this insanity." Portia reached back and pulled the laces of her dress, quickly tying them into a bow. She grabbed her stockings and shoes. Her feet were cold now and she was out of sorts because the afternoon spent making love to him that she had looked forward to with sweet anticipation was destroyed. "I need to take that basket to Lizzy," she said, putting on her shoes.

"Good, I'll go with you," he answered, picking up the basket.

"No, put it down," she ordered sharply. She began folding the blankets. They left them in the bothy. It was easier than one of them carting them around, except now she wasn't so certain she should meet him on the morrow.

He noticed her change of mood. "What is it, Portia?" he asked. He stood five feet away from her. "I've spoken of the curse before," he said slowly. "I know it is hard for those who aren't affected to grasp the reality of it."

She nodded. "I don't think you are mad," she said. "Not truly." Or at least she didn't *want* to think he was. She wanted to believe in him. "But this talk of the cat being Rose or Fenella—" She faced him, her doubts clear. "It is not rational. And Lizzy truly is nothing more than a sad soul who dotes on herbs and flowers."

"Then she'll know about mugwort."

"But you want to know about reincarnation." And every ounce of good sense Portia had resisted his speaking to Lizzy about that spell. *Something bad would happen if he did.* The warning was very clear in her mind.

"I don't believe it wise we are seen together," she said, tying her cloak at her neck. "I thought we knew we must keep up an appearance."

"Why do you fear my going with you to Lizzy's?" he asked.

"I'm not afraid," she lied. "And Lizzy isn't the reason we shouldn't be seen together. It is Lady Emma. She will not take kindly to you and me keeping company." She took the basket from him.

Harry made a dismissive sound. "I don't care for her opinion."

"I do," Portia said. "She is my landlord's daughter, remember? I like Camber Hall. I like Glenfinnan. I want to keep my roof over my head. If she grows too jealous, she will make her father turn us out."

She went out the door. Harry followed, catching her arm and turning her to him. "I'm not worried about Lady Emma," he restated. "And if you want Camber Hall, I shall buy it for you. It is the least I should do for you."

"You should do nothing for me, especially buying my house for me. What will people think?"

"I don't care what they think," Harry answered. "I'm only concerned that you are free of the tyranny of Moncrieffe's pampered daughter."

"And I worry about my reputation." She looked around to assure herself they were alone. This sense of impending disaster was not comfortable. "I would be ruined completely if the valley knew."

"If the valley knew what? That you are my mistress?"

Mistress. It was such an ugly word.

It also was the truth. And this was not how her life was supposed to be. She'd prided herself on being circumspect and dutiful. She'd thought she would die a spinster, never knowing the touch of a man, and now, here he was. Harry had turned her life inside out. All he had to do was glance at her and she would toss aside all that she'd once held dear.

"I'm not your mistress," she said. "I come here of my own free will."

That didn't sound good, either.

"I didn't mean an insult," Harry said. "Please, Portia, I care for you. I only sought to help, not to insult you. But I'm a wealthy man. My brother saw to my investments, and I could make your life easier. I can buy whatever you want and would do so happily."

I care for you.

After all the passion they had expended on each other, all the energy, "I care for you" sounded like the milk toast one would feed a child. The words sounded trivial.

"I know you care for me, Harry," she responded in a surprisingly strong voice. "I just don't want you to ruin me."

"I already have," he replied, the words heavier than any physical blow. Immediately, he heard what he'd said and apologized. "I didn't mean that the way they sounded." He held out his hands as if begging her to understand. "I meant *no* offense. I *want* to be here with you. I think you want to be with me as well."

She did. But she also realized they couldn't go on forever like this. Something *would* change. It was inevitable.

He spoke, his jaw tightening with resolution. "I'm going with you to see Lizzy." He began saddling his horse.

Portia's response was to turn and start walking, her stomach feeling as if it was full of stones. She was being unwise. She should stop meeting him—

"Portia." He said her name before taking her arm and turning her around. His lips came down on hers. He held her, kissing her and saying with his touch what they were both afraid to speak aloud. In his kiss was an apology, a wish that all could be different, a promise that his feelings were honest.

She closed her eyes, giving herself over to him, not embracing him, but standing in his hold, Lizzy's basket still on one arm.

He broke the kiss, his eyes serious as he said, "You may not want to let me be your protector, but know I shall protect you all the same."

Their time together was passing—and she was afraid.

Could she return to the loneliness of her spinsterhood after knowing the joy of being in his arms? Or would life be even more unbearable than it had been before him?

She understood why Rose had jumped from her tower.

"You will go with me to Lizzy's no matter what I want, won't you?" she asked.

"Yes," he said. "I must."

Portia stepped back. His decision was made and her concerns were unimportant. "Let me visit her first. You can come later." She walked off without waiting for his response.

She'd gone no more than ten steps when she saw Owl. The cat was on the ground close to the tree line. Portia stopped, watching as the cat pounced on something only she could see, hustling with her paws to catch it.

"Portia?" Harry said behind her.

Owl looked up. Her large eyes met Portia's, and for a second, the animal appeared human. Then, with a flick of her tail, Owl bounded off into the woods in the direction of Lizzy's house.

Harry was coming up behind her. Portia could hear his booted steps. She turned, almost afraid he'd seen Owl.

And if he did, what would he do to the cat?

Instead, he was focused on her, his expression concerned. "Is something the matter?"

"Don't follow me," Portia heard herself say. "Don't follow me." She was backing away from him, watching him until she reached the tree line.

She plunged into the forest, but Owl was nowhere to be seen. Even when she called Owl's name, the cat did not answer.

Portia hurried to deliver her basket to Lizzy.

Harry *would* follow. He wasn't the sort of man to wait patiently.

Chapter Thirteen

Crazy Lizzy's hut was made of rock, mud, twigs, and straw. It was a strange, round, windowless building with only the doorway for light. The old lady kept a fire in her hearth at all times. Some days it would be of peat, the smoky scent of it filling the air; other days, her fire would be of wood, acrid and hot.

Lizzy claimed that her different fires served a purpose. Portia had assumed the choice had more to do with what was at hand and Lizzy's eccentricities. However, after Harry's talk of spells and reincarnations and curses, Portia feared she was ready to give anything Lizzy said more credit than what it deserved.

Portia knew from having been there that the walls inside the house were stacked with shelves and shelves of herbs. There was a humble table in the middle of the room and Lizzy's pallet on the floor to the side of the hearth.

As she entered the clearing surrounding the hut, she saw Lizzy sitting on a chair outside the door, eating a meal of cooked turnips. The crone's face split into a toothless smile of greeting. She was as round as she was high and wore a mob cap over her frizzy gray hair. Her cheeks were chubby and her eyes reminded Portia of two brown buttons. But she was also old and wrinkled, with a huge mole close to her left eye that gave her a sinister look.

She wore the castoffs given to her by members of the kirk. Most times, considering her size, the skirts were too long, but she wouldn't hem them. She'd wear them as they were, even if she continually tripped over them.

"I was hoping to see ye today, lass," Lizzy said in her thick brogue. She'd stood. "Would ye like a cup of mint tea?" She started for the door.

"I don't think I have time, Lizzy, but thank you," Portia said, aware that Harry was following. She held the basket out to her. "The bread is yesterday's but still fresh."

"I shall enjoy it," Lizzy said.

"Good. Well, then, I'll be on my way."

"Why are ye so anxious to run off? Let me show

ye my newest doll." Lizzy made dolls of scraps of materials and dried fruit and whatever she could find. The bodies were twigs she fastened together. They were truly very clever and Lizzy had gifted Portia with several.

"I wish I could, but I am needed at home." Portia took a step in the direction of Camber Hall, until a thought struck her. "Lizzy, by any chance did you see a small cat around here?"

"Oh, I see many cats. I don't like them. They make me sneeze."

"This would be an unusual one. She's white like a ghost and her ears are deformed. They fold over so her head is shaped like an owl's."

"I've not seen a cat like that."

So Owl had *not* come in this direction.

"Lizzy, why do people think you are a witch?" The question just popped out of Portia. She'd assumed all the whispers about Lizzy in the valley came from the superstitious and ill-informed.

But after her conversation with Harry, she was no longer convinced of what she thought.

She had expected Lizzy to deny the charge or to be offended. Instead, the woman cackled with delight. "They think that," she agreed.

"Is it true?"

Lizzy's smile grew larger. "What do ye think,

lass?" It was almost as if she was daring Portia to say she was.

"I don't know. Do you have special powers?"

Placing a knowing finger by the side of her nose, Lizzy said, "Why should I tell ye?"

"Because we are friends," Portia said, a bit annoyed. "I bring you food."

"Ye do, ye do." Lizzy patted the basket.

"Then answer my question, please. Are you a witch?"

"There was a man who came through these parts who asked the same thing," Lizzy said. "An Englishman. A Chattan. He wants one particular witch."

"But there is no such thing as witches, is there?" Portia pressed.

Lizzy reached up and scratched her head beneath her mob cap and pulled her skirt up over her belly before saying, "I don't know of any."

"Then why do they say you are a witch?" Portia repeated.

The crone took three steps toward her. Lizzy smelled of the herbs she treasured and the deepest part of the forest. "I have the gift of sight," she whispered.

"Sight? Such as you can tell the future?"

"I dinna like it," Lizzy said, placing a finger

of each hand together as if creating the sign of a cross. "I try to not do it, but sometimes it comes upon me. I hear the voices. Terrible voices."

"What do they say?" Portia asked.

Lizzy ignored her question. Instead, she said, "Rose of Loch Awe had the gift of sight. Hers was greater than mine and she was younger. I just see the edge of the future. Just a wee bit and not much more. Makes me useless. Makes me . . . afraid."

Portia felt the blood drain from her face. "Rose of Loch Awe? Rose of the Macnachtan?"

"Aye, one and the same. It's a story told to me by my mother. Rose's clan and mine were once the same. My mother told me not to be afraid of my gift. A wise woman knows how to use it. But the others"—she nodded her head toward the woods as if speaking of those in the valley—"they don't understand. They are afraid of me. When I told Nan Bellamy that her baby would be born dead, they were angry with me, even though he was. They thought I'd caused his death."

"It is not a good thing to say," Portia murmured.

"It is what I saw."

"Have you seen other things?"

"Oh, many." Lizzy walked over to where she'd set her bowl of turnips on the ground. "I saw when the old reverend's horse would die. I could tell that Jaimsie Macdonald would drown in the loch. I warned his mother not to let him out of her door. She laughed at me. No one wants to hear sad news. None of them paid me any heed."

"Has anyone listened to you?"

Lizzy's face lit up. "Ye know Robbie, the laird's gardener? I told him to stay off a boat crossing Loch Shiel ten years ago on All Hallows' Day. He listened. The boat sank." She pointed her finger down to the earth and gave a low whistle to illustrate her point. "Four good men died. Robbie lived." She leaned toward Portia as if having a great secret when she said, "We can all change our fate."

"And did Rose know her fate?" Portia asked softly.

Lizzy shrugged. "Who knows? No one can see everything. Not perfectly."

But what if Rose had?

"Do you know anything about reincarnation?" she asked Lizzy.

"Wot?" Lizzy cocked an ear as if not hearing her.

"Reincarnation," Portia repeated. "Coming to life after you are dead, in a new body."

Lizzy dropped the turnip bowl and the basket and whirled in a circle before coming to a stop and forming another cross in front of her. "That's blasphemy. Keep yer blasphemy away."

"I'm sorry, Lizzy," Portia hurried to say. "I didn't mean to upset you."

"Why are ye asking these questions?" Lizzy wondered, craning her neck and tilting her head. She was growing agitated. People had warned Portia that Lizzy could be set off.

"I was curious," Portia said. "Nothing more."

Lizzy jerked away, her brows coming together, her shoulders hunching. "There are things of which we should not speak, lass. Dark arts. I'm not of the dark arts. My herbs are of the earth."

But Portia had come too far to back away now. "Fenella knew dark arts, didn't she?"

"I don't know Fenella. I don't know Fenella," Lizzy began repeating the words over and over, her voice low as if she spoke to herself.

At that moment, Harry rode into the clearing. Portia had meant to be gone by the time he arrived.

Crazy Lizzy looked up at him and then jerked her head toward Portia, then back to him. "Nooooo," she keened in a low voice as she sank to her knees.

"Lizzy, what is it?" Portia demanded, hurrying to the small woman's side.

A hand gripped Portia's arm like a vise. Lizzy's nails were long and dirty. She held tight as she said to Portia, "You shall be the *death* of him."

It was a benediction that sent a chill to Portia's heart.

"His death. *You* will be *his* death," Lizzy repeated.

Harry had dismounted and come over to them, leaving Ajax to stand. He heard what Lizzy said. "*Why?*" he asked, kneeling beside her.

Lizzy started to speak, and then her eyes rolled to the back of her head and she collapsed. Portia held on to her. "She's swooned," Portia said in surprise.

"Here, let me have her," Harry said. He carried Lizzy into the hut, where he laid her on her pallet.

Having picked up the bowl and the basket where Lizzy had dropped them, Portia set them on the table. She found some strips of material that she made into a compress. She doused it with cool water and rested it against Lizzy's brow. Her hands shook as she worked. Lizzy's outburst had been unnerving. It had been frightening.

Harry seemed calm. "What was going on between you?" he asked. He was wandering around the hut, investigating the rows of herbs on the shelves. He had to stoop because the ceiling was low. The air was smoky and oppressive from the peat on the fire. He coughed.

Before Portia could answer, Lizzy moaned and

opened her eyes. "Hello, Miss Maclean," she said as if greeting Portia for the first time. "Good to see you today."

"It's good to see you," Portia said, uneasy. She glanced at Harry. He took a step forward so he would be in the woman's line of vision.

"Hello, Lizzy."

She smiled up to him as well, her earlier distress gone. "How did you come in here?" she asked the two of them.

"You invited us," Portia said.

"I forgot," Lizzy answered with her toothless grin. "Did I have a spell?"

"I believe so," Portia answered.

"I'm all right now," Lizzy assured her, and started to sit up to prove the truth of her words.

Portia came to her feet as well, taking the hand Harry offered.

"Ye are a couple, aren't ye now?" Lizzy said. She chuckled. "There will be an uproar in the valley about this. There are those who don't want ye together."

"Who?" Harry asked.

Lizzy became sly. "I'm not to be telling. I know better."

Portia placed a hand on Lizzy's arm. "You don't remember anything you said before you swooned?"

"I swooned?" Lizzy tilted her head in happy surprise. "Aren't I fancy now? Swooning!"

The light was growing dark outside. Portia knew she needed to leave. "I must return home. Will you be all right?"

"Let me escort you home," Harry said.

Portia shook her head. Lizzy might have forgotten what she'd said but Portia hadn't. She needed a moment to herself to clear her head and steady her nerves. "Perhaps if you would stay with Lizzy a moment until we are certain she is all right."

"I'd be happy to do. She can explain to me what all these herbs are for," he said.

"I will, if you wish," Lizzy answered.

"Then I'll go," Portia said, and went out the door. Harry followed.

"What do you think?" he asked.

"I don't know. She seems to have forgotten everything we had discussed."

"And what *were* you discussing?"

"Fenella," she said, knowing the impact of that one word on him. "But she doesn't seem to remember now."

"Or else she is pretending."

Portia glanced back at the hut. "If she is, hers is an excellent performance. I truly believe the conversation is gone from her mind."

"What did she mean that you would be my death?"

She drew a deep breath and released it. "She says she has the gift of sight . . . or the person she was at the time claimed to have it. Right now, she acts completely different. Harry, she referred to Rose as 'Rose of Loch Awe.' She told me her family was distant cousins of Rose, Fenella's daughter. Perhaps that is how Rose met Charles Chattan of Glenfinnan. She may have come to visit."

"What else did she tell you?"

"Not very much. I asked her if she was a witch." To his raised eyebrow, she explained, "Well, I never knew. Everyone in the valley claimed she is. I believed she wasn't but all this talk of strange things has made me curious. Perhaps *I* am the one who is wrong."

"And what did she say?"

"Lizzy said she isn't, but she has the gift of seeing the future. That's when she claimed I would cause your death, and then she swooned."

He made a scoffing sound. "How could you cause my death?"

"I don't know." She crossed her arms. "Aren't you worried?"

Harry shook his head. "No, are you?"

"I would not want your death on my conscience."

"Well, it won't be there," he answered. He walked over to Ajax and picked the reins up off the ground. Only then did the well-trained horse move. Harry tied the reins to a low-hanging tree branch.

He was so vital and alive, so self-confident. He was the warrior, the rebel, the man who feared nothing.

Yet there was a gentler side to him as well. He cared for his family enough that he would sacrifice his life for his brother's. She had come to know this side of him well. He was a man who understood her yearnings and pleased her in a way she knew no other could. He was a man who had regrets, who was vulnerable, who had fears but persevered anyway.

He was the man with whom she'd fallen in love.

Yes, she loved him.

She had not intended to do so, but perhaps she'd had no choice.

She'd started falling in love with him at the dance when he had pleaded General Montheath's case. Or had she felt the first inklings of love that night when he had knelt in front of her in the moonlight and begged for his brother's life?

Crazy Lizzy's warning now made sickening sense.

Portia knew Harry valued her, but did he love her?

No, not yet.

Could he? Was that what Lizzy had been warning her against? He was a Chattan male. Even as a second son, the curse could apply to him. If he loved her, he would die.

But that didn't mean she couldn't love him.

For a second, her world was transformed with the knowledge. The green of the firs around her was more green, more vibrant. The air was sweet with their scent. She'd not noticed before, but now, the world was perfect. *She loved.* Two words more powerful than any magic.

And that was why she'd grown so unreasonably annoyed with him earlier. *I care for you* wasn't enough. She wanted more.

And yet he couldn't return her love. Not without paying a price, and that price was too high.

"I don't think we should meet any longer," Portia heard herself say.

He frowned. He'd been walking toward her but stopped. "Portia, that is nonsense. Of course we should meet—"

"*No,*" she said cutting him off. "And I'm not saying this because of Lizzy. I don't *want* to see you any longer." *I don't want you to fall in love with me.* But she kept that to herself. "We're done."

He rocked back as if she'd physically hit him but Portia knew better than to linger. She loved him. And she could never let him love her in return.

In that moment, she felt her heart break.

He took a step toward her, his expression concerned. She couldn't let him touch her. She mustn't.

This time Portia didn't walk away from him, she ran, dashing headlong into the woods.

*H*arry started after Portia. He understood what was happening with her. Her responses, her behavior were like those of so many women who had thought they'd caught him. She was angry, disappointed.

He should let her go. The truth of their relationship would be easier for her this way, except Harry didn't want to just let her go.

Portia was more than some woman he bedded. He'd never slept with a woman longer than a day or two, and yet, for the past week and a half, he'd been meeting her in the bothy, and it hadn't all just been sex.

When he was around Portia, he relaxed. He valued her honesty, her wit, her view of life. She was a bit of a rebel like him, and yet traditional, and a survivor. Those were all qualities he would have used to describe himself.

Of course, Portia was more passionate about what she believed in than he was. Harry knew he was jaded. The world had made him that way, but Portia was still untouched and he found her refreshing.

Now, everything had changed, and he didn't understand why—no, that wasn't true. He understood.

He'd wager all he owned that Portia was still angry at him for referring to her as his mistress. He needed to explain more . . . although he'd already attempted to explain himself.

She would want an apology and Harry did not apologize. In his view of the world, a man didn't have regrets. He couldn't afford them. They would cripple him. He wouldn't be able to go on. He hadn't even apologized for that fateful day on the battlefield in Vitoria—

"Ye are wise to let her go," Crazy Lizzy's voice said from behind him.

She'd come out of her hut and sat on a stool by the door.

Harry faced her. "Because she will be my death?" he asked, repeating the accusation she'd flung at Portia before she'd collapsed.

The crone's smile grew crafty. She raised a finger of warning. "I saved your life. Leave her be, Chattan. Leave her be."

"What do you know of Fenella?" he demanded, walking toward her.

She stood up, her beady eyes alive with defiance. "I know there is nothing you can do. You are doomed, Englishman. *Doomed*." With those words, she ran inside her hut and slammed the door.

Harry walked right up to it. He would tear down her home if she pushed him too far. He grabbed the door and attempted to open it. The door was barred against him from the inside.

"I'm not finished with you yet," he said. "Open this door."

There was no response.

Harry put his shoulder to the door. Using all his strength, he shoved it open, breaking the wooden bar she'd used. He entered the hut, and then stopped.

Lizzy sat on a stool before her fire. She was staring into the flames and mumbling to herself. Her arms were full of the strangest dolls. They were made of twigs and nuts, stuffed cotton and scraps of whatever she could find. She was holding at least eight, her shoulders hunched protectively over them as if they were children.

"Leave me alone, leave me alone," she said repeatedly without looking at him standing there.

He started for her, and then he smelled the air. In the smoky haze hung the pungent incense of opium. She'd thrown it on the fire. The scent of it was filling every crevice of the hut.

He backed toward the door.

Crazy Lizzy turned to him, still holding her dolls, rocking on her stool. The pupils of her eyes were black pools.

And he longed to stay there with her.

Instead, he turned on his heel and threw himself out the door. Outside, he grabbed huge gasps of air, trying to clear his lungs. His nerves were stretched thin. He wanted to return to that hut. He wanted to disappear in it.

Ajax nickered as if understanding that something was afoot. Harry moved to the horse. He had trouble mounting. His head spun and he had started to shake.

A month ago, he had taken a cure, sweating out the need for drink and opium, fighting his demons alone. And there wasn't a day that passed that he didn't think of returning to them—that is, until he'd met Portia.

Her sweet body and her quick mind staved off evil desires. She'd kept him strong.

But she had run away from him, and he suddenly realized he didn't know if she would come back. Never before had he given a care whether a woman stayed or whether she went. But Portia was different.

Harry threw himself over the horse. A black despair threatened to engulf him. Fenella knew his weaknesses. She was using every power at her disposal to stop him from breaking the curse— including taking Portia away from him.

"Walk on, boy," he whispered to Ajax.

The horse began moving, and Harry felt his strength start to return.

He'd been right to come to Glenfinnan. Fenella *was* here. He imagined her presence in the shadows. She was watching, waiting. He prayed he had the courage to battle her. He'd never met an enemy who knew him better than he knew himself.

As he regained his senses, he directed Ajax away from the road leading to Monty's estate. Instead, he rode to Camber Hall. The house was dark. It appeared deserted. They'd probably all gone to bed.

Could Portia have dismissed him so easily?

Harry did not know the answer but he had an uneasy sense that all was not as it should be this night.

Portia had been an innocent in this venture. And because of him, she was now a part of it. He trusted his instincts. There was danger.

Fog drifted across Camber Hall's drive, hovering in its woods. Clouds covered the light of the waning moon.

It was the winter solstice, he realized with a start. December 22, his sister Margaret's birthday. She'd been pleased that it was to fall on such an auspicious day. Christmas was three days away . . . and suddenly, Harry *knew* that he was supposed to be here at this place and at this moment. He wasn't certain what it all meant, but he *was* to be here.

In that moment, he felt the presence of his ancestors, of all those good men who'd had their lives destroyed by a witch. The battle lines were drawn. He could feel it in the air.

He pulled Fenella's book and his pistol from his saddlebags. He checked the weapon. It was loaded and ready.

He moved to the tree line bordering Camber Hall's lawn and took his post in the shadows. The book in one arm and the pistol in his other hand, he stood guard over Portia.

Chapter Fourteen

The wind had kicked up a pace. It rattled Portia's window and seemed to creep in from every nook and corner of her room.

She had returned to the house distraught and frightened, but if Minnie or Lady Maclean had noticed anything amiss, they didn't say a word. They were both involved in their own affairs, both happy with life. There had been no questions about her ventures through the day. They'd sought their beds after a day full of plans and with anticipation for what the morrow would bring.

Portia had never felt such discontent.

She had walked away from Harry. No, she had *run* from him, and at a time when he might need her.

Lizzy's prediction frightened her, and yet, the crone was a poor, mad soul. She wasn't right in the head, and Portia knew it. Since when had she given credence to the woman's rantings? Why now?

There was no answer to those questions save for her sense that something was amiss.

Portia had no appetite for the dinner Glennis had left for her. She went to her room, curled up in a ball on her bed and wept, so miserable she'd not bothered to build a fire in the hearth or light a candle by her bed. She cried until the pillow was soaked and she didn't have the strength to shed another tear.

She loved Harry and he would not, could not love her.

However, he had offered for her to be his mistress.

The pain of that proposal, the humiliation of it, still resided in her. It was easier to focus on that dishonor rather than how she could never have him for her own.

What if he had offered to make her his wife? Then what?

And of course that he had made the suggestion of his keeping her was her own fault. She had done nothing to make him believe she wouldn't entertain such a position. She'd thrown herself into his arms and, in defiance of convention and propriety, had sneaked away every afternoon to meet him like some shepherd's daughter. And she hadn't held back in her affections. She had not been decorous and proper but had initiated their lovemaking, had even been at the bothy waiting for him impatiently on many an afternoon.

Even now her traitorous body yearned for him, but the truth was, the game had changed. She'd discovered she wanted what he was not willing to give.

There had been a time when Portia had wondered if the sameness of her life was to continue on forever without any variation. She'd wanted *more* in those days without knowing what "more" was.

Now she wished she could return to where she'd once been—a time when she'd not risked anything of herself.

Harry would never love her. The curse had seen to that. He avoided love, and if he hadn't, someone more beautiful and more clever than Portia would have caught him long before now.

And then there was Crazy Lizzy's warning. Portia didn't know what the woman meant with her prediction of Harry's death. However, the threat gave Portia one more reason to stay away from him. To protect her own heart, to protect *him*, she must stay away from Harry.

Portia heard a soft feline growl from Owl before the cat jumped up on the bed. Until now, she hadn't known the cat was present in her room.

Owl stalked the length of the bed before reaching Portia's arm and rubbing her face against it. Portia reached over and scratched Owl's ears.

"*Now* you show up," she whispered to the cat. "Where were you earlier when I needed you?"

Owl rolled onto her back and playfully batted at Portia's fingers before reaching up to nudge her hand for another pet. Portia obliged, laying her head on the mattress so that she was practically nose-to-nose with the cat. Even in the dark, Owl's eyes appeared large and human in their understanding.

"*Are* you a reincarnated soul?"

The cat began purring.

"Is that a yes or a no?" Portia whispered.

The purring didn't stop or change.

"I see," Portia said. "It is for me to decide." She lightly touched one of Owl's folded-over ears with one finger.

Owl grabbed her finger with both paws, as playful as a kitten.

"What shall I do, Owl? I love him. Yes, I've been foolish. I didn't think of anything beyond the moment when I let him make love to me. It was so wonderful," she confided to the cat. "Every moment in his arms has been heaven. Except now I want what I cannot have. He's too above my touch, Owl. I'm like Icarus whose father made him wings out of wax and he thought he could fly. But he went too close to the sun, and fell to earth. I thought . . ." She paused, her heart as heavy as a stone in her chest. "I thought I could fly. Now I realize I'm probably like every woman Harry Chattan has ever met. I'm just one more. I had thought I'd be the exception or, at least, able to control my emotions. My father's callousness did not rub off on me and I suppose I should be glad, but it just hurts so much—*ow*."

Owl had bitten her finger.

The cat jumped to its feet and then leaped off the bed. She padded to the closed bedroom door and meowed.

The bite had hurt. Portia couldn't tell in the moonlight if there was blood. Sitting up, she sucked the hurt away, frowning at the cat. "Why should I do anything for you?" she asked, and then was struck by the obvious realization the door was shut and had been ever since she'd gone to bed. Owl had not been in the room, or had she? Harry had her imagining Owl had ghostly powers as well.

Owl meowed at the door, impatient, insistent, sounding very much like what she was, a spoiled cat.

If Portia didn't do as Owl wished, then the cat could yowl at the door all night.

Portia rose from the bed. She still wore her evergreen cambric day dress with its long sleeves. She pushed her hair back from her face. Her curls were going every which way. She should take a brush to it after she changed into a nightdress. She was exhausted but it wasn't the tiredness that led to sleep. No, she felt spent, defeated, and overwhelmingly sad.

She opened the door. Owl went out, then stopped in the dark hallway, a silver shadow. Portia started to close the door, and the cat slipped back in.

Frowning, Portia said, "I'm not playing this game with you." She started to shut the door, but the cat boldly put herself in the doorway. "Move on," she ordered. "Make a choice. In or out."

Owl grabbed the hem of her dress with her teeth and pulled.

It was a strange action for a cat.

For a second, Portia stood in indecision. The cat wanted her to follow.

Owl turned to go out the door.

Portia was tempted to shut the door, but then a new apprehension reared its ugly head. Her first thought was Harry.

"Is he all right, Owl?"

The cat came back into the room and circled around Portia's feet before starting out the door again.

Portia knelt and held out a hand. Owl bit the tip of her finger. The cat was urging her to follow.

Fear, Portia discovered, was a contrary emotion. She feared following; she feared not following.

But what if Owl was merely a cat wishing Portia to chase mice with her?

Or what if Harry's suspicions were right and there was more to Owl than met the eye?

"Rose?" Portia asked. Again, Owl circled around her.

"*Fenella,*" she said, as if challenging the cat.

Owl came up on her hind legs, placing her paws on Portia's arm and kneaded. Was that a sign that Portia had chosen the right name?

"Why can't you speak?" Portia said, rubbing the cat's head. "If you were reincarnated, why couldn't you have chosen a talking parrot?"

A purr was the only answer she received. And perhaps she was being silly. She was placing human characteristics to an animal. If her mother or Minnie overheard her, they would think her ridiculous.

With a sigh, Portia rose, but before she could take a step away, the cat ran in front of her path. Owl looked up at her expectantly as if to say, *I thought you were coming with me.*

"I need to put on my shoes and my spectacles."

The cat made a low, throaty trill and went to the door.

"This is too strange," Portia said, and yet Owl was very clear in what she expected. Portia picked up her spectacles from the bedside table, adjusting them on her nose, before pulling on her walking boots. She followed Owl out the door.

All was quiet in the hallway save for the faintest sound of Lady Maclean's snoring. Portia went down the steps, Owl right at her side. She took her cloak off the peg by the door and threw it around her shoulders.

The last time she had gone out into the night had been to pretend to be Fenella. Now, Portia might very well be letting Fenella herself in the guise of a cat lead her to who knew where.

On the front step, Owl looked back to see if Portia was behind her. The moon had come out behind the clouds and the cat's coat had a ghostly hue.

"Yes, I'm coming," Portia said, and closed the door.

*F*rom his post in the shelter of the tree line, Harry thought he saw movement on the front step—and then he did see Portia standing there. She pulled the hood of her cloak up around her head and took off with great purpose across the yard, disappearing behind the house.

Harry reached for Ajax's reins. The horse had been sleeping. He'd actually been snoring, a sound that Harry found annoying since it made him tired.

"Come on, my friend," Harry said, putting Fenella's book in his saddlebags and tucking the pistol in his waistband. He lifted the reins over Ajax's head and put a foot in the stirrup. "We are on the chase."

Mounted, Harry trotted around the side of the house. Portia was just disappearing in the woods. To his surprise, he realized she was heading in the direction of the bothy.

Harry kicked the horse forward, giving Portia plenty of room to walk ahead of him.

Through the woods midnight-quiet, he could hear her voice. She was talking to someone—and then he realized she was talking to the cat. Was she following the cat to the bothy?

Nothing made sense in this day. Nothing.

When he was close to the clearing where the bothy was located, Harry hung back. He dismounted and tied Ajax to a tree. The horse knew he was close to the cottage where he'd spent agreeable hours grazing while Harry had been taking his pleasure with Portia. He rumbled his protest.

"I'm sorry, old friend, but you are best tied up right now."

With a pat on his horse's neck, Harry went out into the clearing. He didn't see anything amiss. He also didn't see Portia, and he grew afraid.

What was the matter with her? She should have more common sense than to traipse around the countryside in the dark.

By the light of the solstice moon, all appeared calm and serene, and yet Harry's instincts warned him to be prepared for anything.

He walked toward the bothy, pushing aside his coat and reaching for his pistol. He moved slowly, stealthily. "Portia?" he said, daring to call her name.

A woman gasped her surprise, the sound coming from inside the bothy. Harry rushed forward, just as Portia started to run out of the cottage.

They collided in each other's arms. He had cocked the hammer. He now pointed the pistol in the air as his other arm came around her.

"*H*arry," Portia said, startled to find him right outside the cottage's door. "What are you doing here?"

"I could ask the same of you," he said. He had a hold around her waist as strong as a vise. "Why are you going prowling around in the dark? Don't you have more sense than to go out alone?"

The criticism stung. "I could ask the same of you."

"I was watching over you," he said.

"Watching?" She frowned. "Whatever for?"

"You were upset when you left that madwoman's hut. I wanted to be certain you were safe." He had not let go of her.

"I'm safe," she said, not really wanting him to let go. An hour before, she'd been weeping over never feeling his arms around her and now she had him.

"What are you doing here?" he asked.

"Owl wanted me to come here," she confessed. "And I don't know why I did. I suppose it was all that talk of reincarnation and the incident with

Lizzy today . . . I, well, the cat acted as if I should follow and she led me here."

"Where is she now?" Harry asked. He released his hold around her waist to go into the cottage, his hand reaching for and finding her hand. He laced her fingers with his. He held his pistol up and ready.

The moon through the open window cast a ray of light upon the floor. "I don't know," Portia said as he looked around the room. "She came in here and I followed and then I lost track of her. It was as if she disappeared into the corners. But it doesn't mean anything, Harry. She's a cat. Cats have the ability to vanish when they wish."

"As effectively as this cat seems to do so?" Harry asked, his skepticism clear.

"I don't know. It doesn't make sense."

"No, it doesn't," he agreed, turning to her, and she was aware of how close they stood to each other.

She didn't dare look up at his face. He was her weakness. She should step away now, but she didn't.

"Why are you here?" she asked.

He uncocked the pistol. "I was worried about you. This afternoon you were upset."

"I see."

"I stood guard."

"Over what?" she asked.

"Over you."

She stood silent, suddenly aware of the racing beat of her own heart, feeling his pulse as well, even through his gloved hand. He didn't speak, either. She knew she should leave. She didn't want to.

"Portia," he said, her name barely a whisper, and that was all it took. With a shuddering breath, she looked up at him, and she was lost.

There was so much concern in his expression, it was the excuse she needed to rise on her tiptoes and plant a kiss on his lips.

Foolish, foolish Portia, she thought, a sentiment that was wiped from her mind when he set his pistol on the window ledge, put his arms around her, and kissed her back.

They knew what each other liked. Their lips always fit together perfectly and this moment was no exception.

His hand smoothed the curve of her hip. He held her tight, possessively against him. He was ready to make love. He wanted her, and that she could evoke such strong passion in her lover filled Portia with joy.

He might never be hers completely. He would

leave. But for tonight, she could pretend that all was how she wanted it in the world. His arms were around her and that was all that mattered.

Their kiss deepened. Their tongues met and teased each other. Their hands began pulling at laces and buttons.

Why was it that whenever she was with him, she was so needy for his touch? He had set his brand upon her.

Harry spread out the fur blankets. The patch of moonlight from the window fell upon them as he brought her down to lie beside him. Their fingers intertwined; he covered her with his body. His weight felt good upon her. She cradled him with her legs. He positioned himself, kissed her cheeks, her nose, her ears, her mouth . . . and slid into her.

The first moments of their joining were always overpowering to Portia. She adored the feel of him, the connection. It was as if their souls were mating and not just their bodies.

Harry began moving in her. He whispered in her ear, telling her how lovely she was, how desirable, how perfect.

Didn't he understand? Her love for him transformed her from plain, sensible Portia to a creature of light and being. She offered herself wholly and without reservation.

She took from him in the same manner. She circled his waist with her legs, bringing him deeper.

They were moving harder, faster. He held himself up over her. Sweat formed on their bodies. He held nothing back. Portia would not have it any other way. She strove with him, a spiral sensation beginning to form within her. It began where they were joined, growing tighter and tighter until she could take it no more.

Portia cried out his name, pulling him even closer to her. The sense of completeness overwhelmed her. She felt as if she'd reached the highest heights in the heavens and had then shattered into a shower of stars; glorious, bold, sparkling stars.

She was not alone. Harry came with her. She felt him stiffen, felt his release. They'd been so careful, but they were not this night. This night, they were both caught up, and to have cut any of this short would have been unthinkable.

His seed was a wondrous thing. And Portia knew in this moment that they truly had become one. She would bear his child, but she was not afraid. Suddenly, her life made sense. Creation made sense. She'd found her destiny.

Harry held her fast. He rolled over onto his back, carrying her with him. His whiskered jaw felt good against her fevered cheek.

The air smelled of the fragrant night and their bodies.

She kissed his lips, the underside of his chin, his neck. His lips curved into a smile. "You are magic," he whispered.

No hosanna could ring louder than this praise from her lover.

He brought the blankets up around them. The air might be cold, but snuggled close to him, she was warmer than she would have been in her own bed. "I swear, if I had the finest sheets, they would never feel as good as your skin against mine," she whispered.

Harry kissed the top of her head. His arms held her as if he would not let her go and that was completely fine with Portia. She couldn't have gone anywhere. She was spent, pleasurably exhausted.

His hand stroked and played with her curls.

No matter what would come their way, she knew she was his. It was her choice . . . or perhaps not. Perhaps they had been destined to be together.

"Harry, have you ever been afraid?" she asked.

"Many times," he answered.

"Are you afraid now?"

The movement of his hand paused. "No. This feels right. It *is* right."

She smiled and held him tighter. She knew she

should move. She needed to return home before she was discovered missing.

But being with him like this, being in the moonlight and the night air, felt too good for her to move.

And then he was making love to her again. He lifted her up, placing her astride him. He knew she liked this. Watching the changing expression on his face as he lost himself in her made her feel bold, pagan, all-powerful.

He was her man, and she loved him.

When they were done, Portia fell upon his chest, her spent body as languid as a cat. His arms around her, she fell asleep, but not before she murmured the words upon her heart, "I love you."

He did not respond. She had assumed he was asleep and would not know. But she had to speak them aloud. Their truth could not be denied.

At first, Portia thought it was the sunlight that woke her. She thought she was in her bedroom at Camber Hall and was so disoriented, she thought she was falling out of her bed—and then she realized it wasn't the bed moving, but Harry.

She'd fallen asleep in his arms and the day,

judging by the brightness in the bothy, was well into the morning.

He brought the covers around her to hide their nakedness, and that was when she realized they were not alone.

They were surrounded by a pack of dogs, their tails wagging even as they began barking and baying to signal they had found their quarry.

Chapter Fifteen

A cold nose had nudged Harry's neck. Annoyed, he'd pushed the nose away only to discover it was attached to a hairy muzzle with bad breath.

Jasper.

Years in the military had taught Harry to always be on guard. He was a light sleeper and he had anticipated that he would wake before dawn and see Portia safely home. He should have escorted her home after they'd made love the fourth time that night. But she had felt so good in his arms, he'd wanted to hold her a little longer, which was unusual for him. He did not sleep with the women he bedded. He preferred to keep a distance. Sex was uncomplicated, easy. Sleeping was intimate.

Last night, all barriers had come down.

Portia had been magic in his arms. For the

first time, he'd understood what it truly meant to "make love." Nor was it just her innocence that touched him. Portia always gave the best of herself, but he had held back. He knew what women wanted. He knew how to please them, but he'd never pleased himself . . . not until Portia.

He'd worshipped her, adored her. His body, even now, wanted more of her.

Harry would not see her hurt in any fashion. And he knew if Jasper and the pack were here, then Monty was not far behind.

Sitting up, holding Portia with one arm, Harry reached for the dog, but he was too late. The hound lifted its snout and began baying, a signal they had found their quarry. His fellows joined him.

"Shut up," he growled at the dogs, striking out at the one nearest him.

The beast's response was to grin happily, his tongue hanging out. They knew Harry and apparently liked him, even though he wasn't overfond of the whole pack of them.

And then Harry heard Monty's voice. "The hounds are over here," Monty called. The voice was not far from the bothy. "They've found something. I think they've found her! Tally-ho!"

"We must dress," Harry said, reaching for Portia's gown. The clothes were all over the bothy's hard dirt floor. He tossed the dress at her and went to grab her shoes and stockings. The dogs, seeing what he was about, decided to play. Jasper snatched the end of the stocking and pulled. Tug-of-war was one of his favorite games.

The other dogs joined in. The din of barking, growling, and howling reverberated around the bothy's stone walls.

"Don't worry about the stockings," Portia whispered frantically, putting her arms in her dress and then realizing she had it backward.

Harry knew good advice when he heard it. He let go, and Jasper went running off through the door, several of his pack chasing him, each wanting its chance to play. Harry jumped up and scrambled for his breeches on the floor by the stool.

He had just snatched them up, bending over to pull them on, when he heard a horse's hooves and Monty's voice. "Here now, here now, Jasper? Where is she—?" There was a beat of silence. "Ajax? What are you doing here?"

Harry knew he would not be dressed before Monty appeared in the doorway. He was right. A shadow blocked the doorway light. Harry turned to face his friend, holding his breeches in a strategic place in front of him.

Monty stuck his head inside the bothy. "*Oh God*, Chattan."

"Hello, Monty," Harry said as if they had just met on the street. "Brisk morning."

Harry had never seen Monty stunned speechless. He looked Harry up and down from his naked feet to his unshaven growth of beard and his mussed hair, and then slowly turned his head toward the mound of fur-lined blankets. Portia was hidden beneath them. Considering the amount of movement, she was apparently still trying to dress. The dogs thought it a sport to root around with their noses and climb on top of her. After all, it was her scent they had been ordered to follow.

In the distance, Harry heard Lady Maclean shouting, "That's her shoe. That dog has my Portia's shoe. Oh where is she? Where is she?"

"Over here, ma'am," a male voice called.

"You have a party of people coming," Harry said to Monty, but more as a warning for Portia. "Here, let my pull on my breeches and I'll join you outside."

"That would be fine, Chattan," Monty said stiffly. He turned, blocking the door with his back.

Harry hurriedly put on his breeches. He'd just started buttoning them when the bothy was surrounded by people. Monty had organized a huge search party.

"Where is she? You said the dogs have found her," Lady Maclean demanded anxiously. "Is she all right?"

Her voice sounded as if she was hurrying as fast as she could toward the bothy's door. The heads of two of Monty's stable lads appeared in the windows along with the curious faces of others whom Harry recognized from the village. They craned their necks, anxious to see all—and immediately, given the scattered clothing and Harry's state of undress, jumped to conclusions.

Poor Portia. This was not going to be good.

The dogs were overjoyed with so much attention and very proud of themselves. They kept leaping at the windows or nudging Monty.

"Stay here," Harry warned Portia, hoping she would listen. After all, she rarely did as he suggested.

Outside, Lady Maclean was asking more questions, this time directly of Monty. "Is she in there? Why can't I see her? Portia? Are you there?"

His friend stood stoic in the face of his lady's concerns, and Harry knew he was asking a great deal of his former general.

He picked up his shirt and pulled it over his

head before saying to the grinning faces in the windows, "Begone, lads." They responded to the command in his voice and stepped away, but he knew by their smirks they would have a field day with this later. He picked up his pistol and her spectacles from the window ledge and tapped Monty on the shoulder to step away.

Harry went outside. The day was a good one for late December. The sun shone and the air was crisp.

Lady Maclean appeared overwrought. Her eyes were red as if she had been crying. Portia's sister, Minnie, was also among the search party, along with Mr. Oliver Tolliver and about everyone else from Glenfinnan. Lady Maclean's questions came to a halt when she saw Harry.

She took in his bare feet and disheveled appearance. Her mouth opened. No words came out. Harry ran a self-conscious hand through his hair.

Grim-faced, Monty did not meet Harry's eye.

Knowing there was only one way to salvage Portia's reputation, Harry said, "Good morning, Lady Maclean. May I ask for your daughter's hand in marriage?"

Her ladyship reacted as if she had not heard him. "Colonel Chattan?" she answered, a question in her greeting as if she couldn't believe he was here.

But someone inside the bothy *had* heard. "*No,*" Portia cried.

Harry ignored the protest, moving so he blocked the door.

"I would be honored to have your daughter for my wife." Funny but he'd never thought he would say these words. However, now, asking for Portia's hand, they seemed like a logical step.

Sounding slightly dazed, Lady Maclean said, "Is she all right?"

"She enjoys excellent health," Harry responded.

The stable lads snickered. Harry would "discuss" the matter with them later. He'd allow no one to mock the woman who would become his wife—and then he received a great thump in the back as Portia literally ran into him.

Harry was not expecting an attack from the rear. He lost his balance and there was enough space for Portia to squeeze her way between.

She was a mess. Her dress was sloppily laced and her curls sprang in every direction around her head, wild and carefree. She had one shoe on her stockingless feet and the other foot was bare.

When she realized how large the gathering was, her eyes widened. She gathered her cloak around her and lifted her chin.

"Hello, Mother."

A frown etched itself on Her Ladyship's features. For a moment she appeared ready to fly off in hysteria, and then she glanced at Monty and seemed to gain courage. "Put your spectacles on, Portia," she said.

Whatever Portia had been expecting her mother to say, it was not that. She appeared confused and then turned to Harry, who held out his hand holding her eyeglasses. Her eyes not meeting his, she put them on, curving the wire temples around her ears.

"I'm ready to go home, Mother."

"Yes, I imagine you are. However, Colonel Chattan has asked me for your hand and I am going to give my blessing."

Everyone nodded. It was what was expected.

Portia shook their complacency when she squared her shoulders and announced, "Well, I will not marry him. Your blessing or no."

Harry made an exasperated sound. He turned to her. "Portia, don't be obstinate. Of course we must marry."

"There is no 'of course' about it," she said. "I do not wish to marry you."

That set tongues wagging. Many a Scot was grinning at Harry's comeuppance, and he realized she was on her way to becoming a local hero.

He knew they had not liked him because he was the "English" Chattan, but he thought them silly.

Monty jumped into the fray, taking charge. "You men, we are done here. We've found her. Thank you, thank you. A good day's work," he said. "Now off you go. There's no more to see here."

By the expressions on everyone's faces, they disagreed with him. But he was waving his hands, moving them on and clearing a space around Portia, Harry, her mother, her sister, and Mr. Oliver Tolliver.

Portia said to her sister, "I'm sorry, Minnie, I would not wish to embarrass you with such a scandal."

"I'm not worried for myself, dear—" her sister said.

"And there is no reason to do so," Lady Maclean said, interrupting. "You shall marry Colonel Chattan."

"I shall not," Portia answered.

"You *shall*."

"Shall *not*."

"One moment," Harry said, pulling Portia aside without waiting for permission.

Her expression was tight with anger. She crossed her arms as if not wanting to touch him at all.

Was this the woman who had so sweetly given all that she had to him?

Her attitude puzzled him.

He placed his hands on her shoulders. She flinched. He refused to back away.

"We have no choice," he said. "If we do not marry, you are ruined, and I will not let that happen."

She studied the ground. "I will not marry you."

He leaned down, attempting to make her look at him. "Perhaps I'm not the man you would wish," he said, "but we haven't fared too badly these weeks together, have we?"

She didn't answer. His sweet Portia had gone mute.

"And this is perfect," he continued, realizing he was going to have to convince her to save herself. "You won't ever have to worry about money again. I can take care of your mother and set a dowry for your sister." He wondered why he hadn't thought of doing that already. In fact, he was eager to make Portia's life easier.

"You didn't want to be my mistress, and I would never have expected that of you," he hastened to add. "But as my wife, Portia, I can offer you so much. You have merely to ask and I will give."

Still, she said nothing.

But he was warming to the idea. What had started off as a matter of honor was taking hold as a very sound, likable plan. He wanted to care for Portia. He wanted to keep her—forever, if need be.

"There is a good side to all this," he said. "With you as my wife, I won't have to worry about falling in love. You understand the curse. You know I could never love you. And we won't be disagreeable the way our parents were. We're friends, companions, and will be watchful so that we'll never love each other. You will never be a danger to me."

She raised her head then. Silent tears streamed down her face. "It's too late, Harry. I already love you."

Her declaration bowled him over.

He didn't know what to answer.

She knew what he was thinking because she nodded her head as if confirming she understood the dangers. And with that, she left him, crossing to her sister's horse. She put her foot in the stirrup and heaved herself up to sit behind Minnie. She said something to her sister, and Minnie kicked the horse in the direction of home. They rode away.

Portia did not look back.

Lady Maclean heaved a sigh filled with regret.

"I suppose we are done here," she said, breaking the silence.

"I'm not done," Harry vowed. "She needs to listen to reason."

She'd left him. She'd confessed that she loved him and then left. No woman had ever just walked away. Or if she had, Harry hadn't given a care because he couldn't remember.

"If you can reason with one of my daughters, please help yourself," Lady Maclean answered. "I fear she's made her choice. She would rather be ruined and the talk of the valley than with you, Colonel Chattan."

With those words, she took Monty's arm and together they returned to their horses. The dogs went charging after Monty.

The others walked or rode off as well.

And Harry was alone.

Chapter Sixteen

"I'm sorry," Portia said after she and Minnie had dismounted in front of Camber Hall. Mr. Tolliver—Ollie—had taken their horses with the intention of returning them to General Montheath.

"For what?" her sister asked.

"For everything," Portia whispered. She'd thought she'd cried enough over Harry the night before, but now she realized she had fresh tears to shed. "This will cast a terrible shadow over your wedding."

Minnie put her arms around her sister. "I'm more worried about you. This has been a frightening morning."

"What do you mean?" Portia asked as they climbed the front steps.

"Mother was beside herself when we realized

you were missing. We searched everywhere and then when we couldn't find you, we panicked. Mother sent for General Montheath and he organized the search party." Minnie placed a hand on Portia's arm. "I wish I had known what you were about. If I had, we would never have alerted everyone. I fear we have not done you any favors."

Portia shook her head. "It is fine, Minnie. I kept it secret. Having clandestine meetings with one of the most notorious rakes in all England is not something one shares with her mother and sister." She didn't wait for Minnie's response but ran inside the house and up the stairs.

She shut herself in her bedroom. The bed, the draperies, the two chairs by the window near her desk looked the same but now everything was different. She placed her hand on her belly. Yes, very different. She should never have left this room. Being publicly humiliated was what she'd deserved . . . but what of the future? What of the child she was certain they had created?

Need for Harry stabbed through her. They had been apart from each other not even an hour and already she missed him. Was this what the rest of her life would be like? She couldn't imagine ever forgetting him. He was a part of her.

She'd turned down his offer of marriage.

The realization robbed her of breath . . . and then she remembered the happy way in which he'd told her that they would never love each other.

There might have been a time when Portia would have claimed she could love him enough for both of them . . . but then she thought of her father, of her mother, whose disappointment in her marriage was so very clear.

No, Portia was better off alone.

Sitting on the bed, Portia was overwhelmed with fear. She looked around the room, wishing Owl was there. The cat was nowhere to be seen. She was alone. Completely alone.

Portia lay down and surprised herself by falling asleep almost before her head hit the pillow.

A light knock on the door woke Portia. She sat up and looked around the room. She'd not closed the curtains, and the weak morning light filled the room. She must have slept all day and all night. She felt good—until she remembered all that had happened the day before.

The knock sounded again.

"Come in," Portia said, expecting her visitor to be Minnie. She reached for her spectacles on the bedside table and was surprised when the door opened and her mother entered the room.

Lady Maclean was dressed for the day, something she'd only recently started. Always before, she'd lie abed until the evening hours, and by then, why change? She'd have Portia bring up a tray and that would be that. However, lately, her mother had been joining them for dinner as well.

"How are you feeling?" her mother asked, closing the door behind her, a sign that they were going to "talk."

Portia was not ready to talk. "I've been better." She put her legs over the side of the bed and stood. The world seemed to spin a moment. She crossed over to the washbasin and poured cold water into the bowl. She splashed it on her face.

Her mother was watching her with great concern in her eyes.

This was not what Portia wanted or needed. She faced her mother. "I know you believe it would be wiser if I accept Colonel Chattan's offer of marriage. I will not."

"I realize that," Lady Maclean said. She walked over to one of the two chairs by the window and took a seat. "Come sit."

"Why?"

Her mother smiled. It appeared genuine. "I've already told you—we must talk."

Portia considered her mother a moment. She'd changed. Certainly, she was calmer than Portia would have imagined under the circumstances. Her guard still up, Portia crossed to the empty chair beside her mother's. She sat.

"General Montheath has asked for my hand in marriage and I said yes," her mother said.

For a second, Portia wasn't certain she'd heard her correctly. She waited, expecting some excuse or complaint to follow. She had assumed this conversation would be about *her*. It wasn't.

"Aren't you going to wish us happy?" her mother asked.

"Oh, yes," Portia said, still thrown off balance by this conversation. "I am happy for you."

"I shall expect both of my daughters to stand as witnesses for us."

"I will be honored," Portia murmured, and then realized she had a new concern. What would become of her? "When did he ask?"

"Yesterday evening. You seemed to need your sleep or else I would have woken you."

Portia pressed her lips together, feeling the worst daughter. Then again, since when had her mother become so independent? "You were set against him," she said. "What happened?"

"Actually, it was something you said. I realized I'd mourned your father long enough. Indeed, I mourned for him when he was alive. I wanted him to be the sort of man I thought he should be. You accused me of not seeing Black Jack Maclean clearly. You were right."

Leaning back in her chair, Portia saw her mother with new eyes, and was a bit embarrassed by her own callousness that evening after the dance. "I was a bit harsh."

"Sometimes harshness is what one needs to make a change."

There was a beat of silence.

"Do you not think it wise to consider marriage to Colonel Chattan?" her mother suggested.

Portia hardened her jaw. *This* was the conversation she'd expected.

Before she could answer, her mother said, "I understand you are upset with him, although I don't comprehend why. If I think back on your activities over the past two weeks, you have been seeing him, have you not? Alastair suspects the two of you have been together."

"Alastair?"

"General Montheath. Monty." Her mother blushed with fondness as she said the names.

And Portia had a sense that she herself had been absent while the rest of the world had changed.

"Being Colonel Chattan's wife would not be such a bad thing," Lady Maclean continued. "He's wealthy, well connected, very easy on the eyes—"

"And cursed."

"What?" Her mother frowned as if she hadn't heard correctly.

"He's cursed, Mother." Portia crossed her arms. "You haven't heard of the Chattan Curse? All the locals know it. When a Chattan male falls in love, then he will die."

"I doubt if such a thing is true. You know how these country folk are—full of superstitions."

"It's true, Mother."

Lady Maclean lifted a brow at the conviction in Portia's voice and then reconsidered. "Is he in love with you?"

The question lingered in the air a moment.

I won't have to worry about falling in love. That was what he'd said yesterday.

Portia wished she could go back to bed, pull the covers over her head, and forget those words.

"No, he isn't," she said to her mother.

"Interesting. He's called on you several times since yesterday. He's been most anxious to see you."

"He has?" Portia said, her traitorous heart almost singing with the possibility that Harry cared.

Or was he calling because of guilt?

For all his faults, he was an honorable man. He certainly felt duty bound to marry her, but Portia didn't want to be a duty. Her love for him was such that she'd rather live without him than be a mere obligation.

Or be the cause of his death.

"Does that not move you?" her mother asked.

Portia shook her head as she studied the grain of the wood on the floor.

"People here have long memories. They will not forget," her mother warned.

She was saying that Portia was ruined. Forevermore when they talked of her, they would bring up the story of her foolish affair with a man most definitely above her touch.

Her mother sighed. "Well, so be it. Alastair has assured me you will always have a place under his roof."

Now she had Portia's attention. "You are moving?"

"I must if I marry him."

"Why can't we all live here?" Camber Hall was home to her.

"I don't like this drafty place overmuch," Lady Maclean said. "The house Alastair is living in is better suited to servants and the stable is larger."

"You never cared about the stable before," Portia said.

"Oh yes, I did. I want a coach and team. Alastair has promised to give them to me as a wedding present."

And her mother would be the grand lady she'd always wished to be. "Are you just marrying him for security?" Portia asked.

"A bit." Her mother smiled at her. "It will be nice. But I've grown fond of Alastair. He's not handsome. And certainly he is not as dashing as your father was. However, I find his looks are growing on me. Furthermore, it is nice to be adored."

Yes, it would be. "I'm so happy for you, Mother." Portia meant those words. "You are going to be at peace with all of his dogs?"

"Alastair and I will reach a compromise. I told him no dogs in the dining room and the bedroom and he thought that acceptable. To be honest, that beast Jasper is rather sweet. The wedding will be in February. I thought it best we settle Minerva and Oliver first."

"That's wise." And Portia would be alone.

Portia shook her head to clear it. She was sinking into self-pity, a trait she did not admire. She must be practical. Soon, she would be thinking for a child as well.

"I don't know how Owl will like living with all those dogs."

Her mother's brows came together. "Owl?"

"She's a cat I found, Mother," Portia confessed. "I've been hiding her from you."

Lady Maclean started to speak and then stopped as if she thought better of it before plowing ahead. "Portia, Minnie told me about your 'cat' many weeks ago. Please, you must no longer talk about Owl."

"Is she all right?"

Her mother looked away.

"*Tell me*," Portia ordered.

Lady Maclean swung around to face Portia, taking her hand. "You truly believe there is a cat, don't you?"

"I know there is a cat."

Her expression concerned, her mother slowly shook her head no. She went to the door and called for Minnie.

After a few minutes, Minnie came to the room. Her face broke out into a smile when she saw Portia sitting by the window. "Are you feeling better? We were all so worried. Ollie debated whether or not he should examine you. He believed we should wait and see how you felt when you woke. You are all right, aren't you, Portia?"

"I'm fine," she answered. "But Mother insists I am imagining my cat Owl."

The smile died on Minnie's face. She looked to their mother, who nodded as if urging her to admit what she knew. "You are," she told Portia. "There is no cat."

Portia came to her feet. "*There is a cat*. Her name is Owl. You were in the sitting room the day I found her in the attic."

Minnie had clasped her hands in front of her. She appeared ready to cry.

"We set out a bowl of cream for her every night," Portia said. "You do it for me when I am busy."

"I do it to help you," Minnie said.

"Because we have *a cat*," Portia was close to shouting.

Minnie shook her head. "No, dear, we don't. You imagine the cat."

If she had said the sky was as green as grass, Portia could not be more surprised. "Minnie, are you daft? Of course we have a cat. Why, the cream is gone from the bowl every evening."

"Because I pour it out," Minnie answered. "I understand why you would imagine a pet that you could confide in. I've explained to Ollie that you've carried the weight of this family on your shoulders. It has been challenging."

Portia took a step away from her mother and her sister. Were they trying to tell her that Owl didn't exist? How could that be true when she'd held that cat and petted her? She'd felt Owl's weight, slight as she was, in her arms.

Their mother spoke. "We would have been fine letting you pretend. However, our family's circumstances are about to change. I haven't said a word about your pet to Alastair."

"Ollie understands your need for an imaginary pet," Minnie chimed in. "He's had patients who have imagined all sorts of things in order to manage their lives. Such as Crazy Lizzy and those dolls she calls babies."

"However," Lady Maclean continued, "if you are going to live under my roof, you can't keep carrying on about the cat. You must give the cat up."

For a moment, Portia doubted her own sanity. And then she thought of Harry. "Colonel Chattan has seen the cat. He knows Owl exists."

"Alastair told me that the colonel claimed to have seen a cat, but there are so many about," her mother said, "who is to say if it is your cat or not? And, Portia, if you wish to secretly pretend you still have the cat, then that is fine. Just please be prudent. Not everyone will understand you the way your sister and I do."

"I even put the cream out last night," Minnie said proudly.

Portia had witnessed Owl drinking the cream . . . or had she?

"No cat?" she said, looking to these two people who loved her more than anyone else in the world.

They both shook their heads.

"May I have a moment alone?" Portia said. "I need to polish my teeth—" She was going to cry, and here she had not thought she had tears left.

"Of course," her mother said, heading toward the door as if relieved an unpleasant interview was over.

Minnie was right behind her. "Glennis has fresh buns for breakfast. Shall I bring up a tray? Or will you come downstairs?"

"I'll be down."

"It's going to be fine," Minnie said as if to reassure herself. "In fact, Mother and I were talking about a pet for you. A real cat."

Portia didn't want a real cat. She wanted Owl.

When she didn't answer, Minnie excused herself and left. Portia's first action was to get down on her hands and knees to search for Fenella's book and then remembered it wasn't there, and hadn't been for almost two weeks. Harry had it. How could she have forgotten?

She pressed her palms against her temples. She mustn't think this way.

The book existed. Owl existed. *The curse was real.*

She knew of only one person besides Harry who could tell her if she was mad or not. She climbed to her feet and flew through her toilette. She dared not tell her mother and Minnie where she was going. After the disastrous escapades of the past weeks, she didn't think it wise to tell them she was going out again.

And they would certainly believe her a lunatic if she told them why she needed to see Lizzy. The crone might be able to help her make sense of all this. Lizzy had known of Fenella. And Lizzy had predicted Portia would be the source of Harry's death.

So Portia stole out of the house one more time.

*C*razy Lizzy was sitting on her stool beside her door when Portia arrived.

"Why, Miss Maclean, what a pleasure. Did you bring some treats for me?" She spoke as if there had not been a scene days before. As if all was well.

Portia approached and went down on one knee

so that they were eye level. "No, Lizzy, I didn't. I shall remember you tomorrow."

"Christmas Day," Lizzy said as if pleased with herself for remembering.

Her reminder surprised Portia. Her world had been spinning like a top and she'd not stopped to realize the passage of time. Her mother and General Montheath were to have a dinner. "I'll bring a basket of something special."

Lizzy smiled her approval.

"Do you remember my being here?" Portia asked.

"I do. You had the Chattan with you."

This was a good sign. Portia leaned toward the crone. "You spoke of Fenella."

Again, Lizzy nodded.

"I'm so grateful you remember. I feared I was going mad."

"You made a wise decision, Miss Maclean," Lizzy whispered. "Stay away from the Chattan."

"And what if I can't?" Portia asked, thinking of the child she knew she carried.

"Then Fenella will have her way. Much power she has, does Fenella."

"Is there any way to stop her?"

"None that I know."

Portia closed her eyes and realized that a part

of her had hoped that if she had imagined Owl, then she had imagined all the rest.

"The Chattan shall die," Lizzy said, reading her mind.

"He can't, Lizzy. He mustn't." She couldn't bear thinking of him dying. She would rather give him up.

"It's too late," was the whispered reply. "You were meant to be here."

Meant to be here.

Portia came to her feet. She backed away from Lizzy as if putting more distance between them would serve to weaken her words. "Are you saying there is no way to change what is to be?"

"Is there ever?" Lizzy asked, her smile as innocent as a child's.

Portia would not accept that prediction. She couldn't. Just the thought of it sent the pain of despair ripping through her—and then she realized, this was some of what Rose had felt.

Rose, who had stood on her tower, knowing her love was lost to her.

Just as Harry was lost to Portia. And her son growing within her would bear this curse as well.

She had to believe there was a way out of this madness. There must be. "What part do I play, Lizzy?"

"How should I know, mum?" was the reply.

Frustrated, Portia walked back to Camber Hall, her mind working furiously. She'd been destined to play a part in this. Hadn't Lizzy said she was to be here? But how did one escape her fate?

She kept her eye out for Owl . . . but she did not see her. The cat had disappeared.

Or perhaps she had never existed.

Portia managed to sneak into the house without her mother or Minnie being the wiser.

For the rest of the day, she stayed in her room. She read her Bible. She opened and shut one book after another in her meager library, searching for anything that could free Harry of this curse, and she found nothing. If she was supposed to be here for Harry, then what role did she play? Why was she not here to save him?

He called. He sat in the sitting room for hours waiting for her. She did not go down to meet him. Instead, she pushed herself into a corner of her room, sitting with her knees up and her head down, aching to run to him and knowing she couldn't.

Minnie came several times to her room, begging her to see him. "He's remorseful," she said. "I've never seen a man of his stature struck so low."

Portia would huddle deeper in her corner and refuse to go. No good could come of it.

And then Minnie informed her that he had left the house. "He is gone. You are free." Her words were etched in bitterness.

Portia ran to a window overlooking the front drive then and watched him ride away. She pressed her hand against the glass as if she could pull him back.

But she must not.

Nor did she halt her quest to find some hope for both him and herself.

It wasn't until midnight that she finally gave up. That's when she found herself on her knees praying. "Dear God, please help Harry. Please keep him safe. Know that I love him."

She studied her clasped hands a bit and then added, "I once wished for something more in my life without knowing for what I was asking. I now know what was missing was love, and I thank you for sending Harry if you are the one who brought him to me. Now protect him. *Please.* And please, give Rose peace. I understand now why she felt as if her world had come to an end. I shall not take my life, Lord, but please help me be brave enough to continue living without him."

As is too often the case, the response was Divine silence.

Portia climbed into bed, exhausted, knowing she had done all she could.

*C*hristmas dawned on what promised to be an excellent day. It was also Sunday and services were definitely in order.

"You don't have to go, if you wish to stay home," Lady Maclean offered.

"Do you wish me to stay home?" Portia asked. She was wearing the dress she'd worn to the Christmas Assembly. She'd combed her hair out and wore it curling and loose.

"I wish you to do what makes you comfortable," her mother answered, taking a moment to straighten Portia's spectacles on her nose.

"I won't be comfortable until I go out in society the first time. I must be done with it. At least in church, Reverend Ogilvy can remind the others that gossip is a sin."

"Is it?" her mother asked, and then reached for her hand. "You are very strong."

"I'm only doing what must be done," Portia said. "Besides, I plan on being a guest at your dinner."

Her mother smiled, tucking her hand in her arm. "And so you shall."

Portia hooked up the pony cart and drove them to the chapel. She squared her shoulders as she caught sight of the crowd gathered there. Since it was Christmas morning, well, of course more people than usual would be in attendance.

She noticed that her mother and Minnie squared their shoulders as well. The Maclean women were not short on pride and they held hands as they went forward.

Their appearance created a bit of a stir, a sign that they were the topic of discussion. People tried not to stare and smiles grew forced.

One person who avoided Portia's eyes was Mr. Buchanan. He stood beside the Duke of Montcrieffe and Lady Emma, whose open hostility in her expression would undoubtedly fuel more gossip. The duke's man would probably be paying them a visit sooner or later to evict them because Lady Emma would want Portia gone. Her pride would demand it.

Of course, that no longer mattered, not now that her mother and her sister would be married women. Both General Montheath and Mr. Oliver Tolliver had been anticipating their arrival. The two gentlemen fell into step beside them, flanking them as if to gallantly ward off any attacks.

And then Mrs. Macdonald and Robbie, the gardener, joined them. "Good Christmas to you," Mrs. Macdonald said.

Her words were echoed from all around the Maclean women, the greetings coming from even the Scots who had usually kept their distance. "Good Christmas," they said in greeting. "Happy Christmas."

They gathered around the women to escort them to the chapel doors, and Portia realized they were protecting her. Was she still considered English? Yes, probably, but she was also one of them and they were letting her know it.

Still, Portia was relieved when they'd taken their seats in the pews. General Montheath sat at the end of the pew, her mother beside him, then Portia, Minnie, and Mr. Tolliver.

Portia bowed her head, letting the opening words of the service flow over her. She studied her hands folded in her lap and remembered her midnight prayer—

"Stop this service."

Harry's voice rang out over the congregation, interrupting Reverend Ogilvy's reading from the Gospel.

Harry. Portia closed her eyes. He could not be here. She was too fragile to resist him. Too emotionally drained.

Heads turned to the back of the church. Minnie reached over and squeezed Portia's gloved hand.

"I beg your pardon, sir," Reverend Ogilvy said, "but this is a place of worship. You are welcome to sit and join us but your outburst is not acceptable."

"Yes, I know," Harry said. He'd been in the back of the church. He now marched forward. "And I apologize, but what I have to say can't wait."

He stopped when he reached Portia's pew. She could feel him, smell him, almost hear the wild beating of his heart.

"Portia Maclean, I love you."

Chapter Seventeen

*T*ime seemed to stop.

No one moved, made a sound, or even seemed to breathe in the close confines of the chapel. They were all waiting for Portia's response.

She released her hand from Minnie's and crossed her arms as if she could protect herself from his words. Love was so wrong, so dangerous for them both.

"You can't *not* hear me," Harry said to her. "You know I love you as well as I know how deeply you care for me."

She *did* know his feelings. That was what she'd been hiding from. He had pretended a distance, but she'd known in her woman's soul that he loved her. She could see all of that clearly now.

"Say something," he ordered. "Call me every vile name, deny me, refuse me—but *say* something."

Portia stood, faced him. She was taken aback at how reckless he appeared. A day's growth of beard darkened his jaw. The intensity in his eyes almost broke her resolve.

"We *can't*," she said. "We mustn't."

"We already have," he answered. "I love you. I thought never to say those words to anyone. And yet, from the moment we met, there was something about you that was different from anyone else I'd ever known."

"It's the curse, Harry. The curse is doing this. The witch wants you."

Was everyone in the church listening? Did it matter?

"She can have me," Harry answered, "because my life is not worth living without you. I realized that from almost the moment you walked away from me."

His words filled her with both joy and fear. "Oh, Harry, don't say that."

"I plan on shouting it from the rooftops. I tried to pretend you didn't matter, that you were just another bed partner. That I didn't need you in my life. I was wrong. When you refused to let me pretend I was doing what was noble, I was forced to question my motives. And I realized I could no longer hide from what I felt. I love you. Please, Portia, be my wife."

It was so tempting. And then she remembered Lizzy's warning. "I can't. I don't want to watch you die."

His eyes took on sympathy. "I know, my love, but the truth is that not one of us will go on forever. And I want to make the days of my life meaningful. I'm a flawed man, Portia. I've made many mistakes and usually from my own hubris. You prod me to be better than what I am. You bring me peace. You've taught me to accept not only myself, but my fate."

"I don't want that fate for you," Portia said, imploring him to understand. "I don't want Fenella to win."

"She won't win," Harry said, "not as long as we love. I now understand my brother, Neal. I understand why he has embraced loving Thea. While those on the outside of our family feel we Chattans are being punished for love, we know in our hearts we are the victors. We *choose* to love, and that will always be more powerful than Fenella's evil." He held out his hand. "Come to me, *my* love."

Still, she didn't move. "If you die, I die. I love you that much. The pain would kill me. I must protect you."

"It's too late," he said. He'd offered her his left hand. He now bent the fingers. "Do you think that marriage is necessary for love? I felt the first pain last week. Then the other night, it was stronger. The curse knew what was in my heart even as I was denying my feelings for you. I will deny them no longer, Portia. You can go your way, but I will not stop loving you. Come, *be with me* for the time we have together. Live in the moment."

Live in the moment. Fear left her. She reached for his hand, the fear left her. Yes, this was where she belonged.

With a triumphant laugh of joy, Harry brought her out into the aisle and lifted her up as if she weighed nothing. He swung her round and kissed her, right there in the church in front of everyone.

A burst of applause surrounded them.

Even the Scots had been moved by Harry's declaration to her.

Portia kissed him back, realizing in his arms was where she was meant to be. She never wanted to spend another day as miserable as she had been without Harry.

Their kiss was more than a kiss—this was a welcoming, a promise, a commitment.

And when they were done, they could only stare in each other's eyes, grinning like two happy fools.

It was the Reverend Ogilvy who brought them

back to the moment. "May we continue with the Christmas service now?"

Harry bowed, directing Portia back into the pew and, squeezing his way into a seat beside her, almost dumping the general onto the floor. He held her hand as if he would never let it go—and he didn't. Not through the service, or the Christmas dinner afterward hosted by General Montheath with her mother as hostess, or through the evening.

For Portia, it was enough to be with him. Her fevered anguish of the past days had evaporated, replaced by more happiness than she had ever known.

While the other guests and her family visited, she and Harry sat quiet and alone, just pleased to be in each other's company.

But there was one question Portia had to ask. "Did you really see my cat, Owl?"

Harry appeared surprised. "The cat with the deformed ears? Yes, several times. I told you she came to me one night. Why are you asking?"

For a second, Portia was tempted to tell him that they were the only ones who could see Owl, and then decided against it. Whether Owl existed or not no longer mattered.

There was one piece of information she needed

to share with him. Portia whispered in his ear that she believed she was with child. Perhaps she was being overanxious. It was too soon to tell, but she knew.

Instead of being alarmed, Harry hugged her, and she could see she'd pleased him greatly.

The curse would have to be brought to an end, but it would not be done so by them. They understood that now.

They had made their decision.

They would love and love well.

They were married by special license the day after Christmas, St. Stephen's Feast Day.

Harry had not been certain Portia would marry him. After all, she was a headstrong bit of muslin. However, he'd hoped for the best and had sent his man Rowan off to make the arrangements. It had not taken much effort. Scotland was more lax in its marriage laws than England, and Harry had seen to it that the bishop was well compensated for his assistance.

The Duke of Moncrieffe, in defiance of his daughter's pouting, had offered the chapel. The wedding breakfast would be hosted by General Montheath and Lady Maclean. Lady Maclean had come alive at the prospect of another dinner to plan. Poor Monty was going to have a future of entertaining, but he didn't seem to mind.

Once Portia had told him he was to be a father, Harry had been happy he'd made the arrangements he had. He did not want to delay the marriage any longer than necessary.

He'd even spoken a word with the duke over Christmas dinner, and a tentative agreement had been reached between them for the purchase of Camber Hall. Harry knew how much the house meant to Portia. He also wanted to see his son raised in a place that would support his child. The people of Glenfinnan, while not having been particularly welcoming to him, had demonstrated their care and concern for Portia. They would see her well after Harry was gone. He also liked the idea of his son being in touch with his Scottish roots. It seemed a good thing.

The morning of their wedding was one of clear skies and a cold wind. Winter was arriving in the Highlands.

Harry and Monty made their way early to church, and Harry was not surprised that Portia and her family were already there.

She was wearing her best dress, the one she'd worn to the dance, the one she'd worn when he'd declared himself to her. Her hair had been carefully styled high on top of her head, but the Scottish wind had already freed her curls from pins and put roses in her cheeks.

He thought she had never looked more beautiful.

The service was short and to the point. For that, Harry was grateful to Reverend Ogilvy. The best moment for him was when he put his signet ring on his wife's hand.

His wife.

Harry had thought never to have one. Now, he was so proud of Portia, he could not imagine his life without her. He'd been a shell of a man until he'd met her.

And no woman could have been as perfect for him. He adored everything about her, including her stubbornness. He liked her spectacles, her curls that defied any taming, her nose, her mouth, and her delicious body.

But what he loved the most was her mind. His Portia had courage. She had wisdom. She would see his son safe. His generations might not destroy the curse, but he believed a future one would. He had no fear for his son.

They adjourned to Monty's house, and the whisky poured freely. For the first time, Harry felt no pangs of desire for spirits. No yearnings. Instead, he felt whole and complete as a sober man.

They were just sitting down to the wedding breakfast when a new visitor arrived, one Harry had not anticipated—his sister, Margaret.

The company had been so involved in the celebration they had not noticed the arrival of her coach. Margaret entered the dining room unannounced, moving as if the wind had blown her in.

She was a tall woman with curling black hair and the Chattan's shrewd blue eyes. She had been a celebrated beauty when she'd made her comeout. Everyone had expected a brilliant match, everyone, that is, save her brothers. They knew the burden of the curse and were not surprised when Margaret had withdrawn from social circles.

Margaret was dressed in the height of fashion. She wore an apple green velvet coat, and a velvet cap of the same stuff upon her head. Lady Emma would have been jealous, Harry thought as he stood and rushed over to welcome his sister. She held him at arm's length, fire in her eyes. "What is going on here?"

Instead of answering her question directly, he called to his wife, "Portia, please come here and meet my sister."

Portia pushed self-consciously on the nose of

her spectacles, a gesture he knew she made when she was nervous. She did as bid.

"Margaret, this is my wife, Portia."

"It is a pleasure to have you here, my lady," Portia said.

Margaret made no move toward Portia at all. "You married?" There was a wealth of unspoken disappointment, anger, and fear in those two words.

"Yes, and happily so," Harry answered, placing his hand on the small of Portia's back. Margaret noticed the gesture. She also glanced around the room as if just realizing they had an audience. "Come and eat with us, Margaret, and then we shall talk."

The lines of Margaret's face tightened. "I can't," she said. "I can't smile and pretend I am happy with this. You sent a letter saying you had found information that could help our brother and then I don't hear from you for weeks?" She'd lowered her voice as if not wanting the others in the room to hear.

"This is Glenfinnan, Margaret. They know about the curse." He was tired of secrets. Done with them. "Now come, sit and eat. You must be tired after such a long journey."

"Are you interested that our brother Neal is

failing rapidly? Or do you care? Perhaps neither of my brothers care whether they live or die," she said, answering her own question. She frowned at Portia. "You will be the death of him."

To her credit, Portia did not flinch. "I consider myself the *life* of him."

If she had punched Margaret in the nose, his sister's reaction could not have been any different. Margaret took a step back, her brows coming together. Her gloved hands doubled into fists. "I will not sit at the table for this celebration," she said. "I won't. Harry, please see me in the other room. I believe we must speak alone."

"*After* I have celebrated," Harry said.

Margaret's reaction was to flounce out of the room.

Harry gave his wife's waist a reassuring squeeze and turned to the guests. "You can see I've had great experience with strong-willed women."

The comment relieved the tension in the room, as he'd hoped it would. But he was conscious all the while through the meal that Margaret waited.

And wait she must . . . because the Scots were not going anywhere quickly when there was celebrating to do. The afternoon was late before Harry could finally turn his attention to his sister.

"I shall let the two of you have a moment alone," Portia said.

"No, I'd like for you to be there," he answered.

She frowned, and he understood why. She'd already recognized that Margaret was going to blame her for this marriage, and to his thinking, that was all the more reason she must be there. Harry wanted Portia to hear him defend her. He did not want his wife to have any doubts as to where his allegiance lay.

He fetched Fenella's book and entered the drawing room where Margaret had been sitting stiff and unyielding most of the day. She'd refused several of Monty's offers of hospitality although she had accepted it for her drivers and her abigail. Margaret had wished to make her displeasure with Harry known, and she had.

"Are you in the mood to talk, sister?" he asked, directing Portia to a chair. He remained standing.

Margaret's hard gaze flicked over Portia and dismissed her. "How could you, Harry? How could you give in to the curse?" She had taken off her coat to reveal a lovely dress of the whitest gauze muslin. Harry thought she had to be chilled wearing it in Scotland's damp weather

"Because I fell in love," he answered.

His sister practically shouted her frustration.

She came to her feet. "You and I had a pact. It was to stop with *us*. With *our* generation. You've broken my trust."

Harry knew she was right. He also knew she would not understand. Someone who had never known the power of love could not comprehend the courage he had gained from it.

He offered Fenella's book to her.

"What is this?" she asked, looking down at the leather-bound tome, its cover cracked with age.

"A book of spells that Fenella used. Portia found it in the house where she was living."

Margaret moved toward the book as if it was the Holy Grail.

"Fenella wrote her name on the inside," Harry said as she took it from him. "There is a spell to reclaim a lost love with the name 'Charles' written in the margin."

"Can it help us break the curse?" Margaret asked.

Portia answered. "We don't know, but Harry and I are aware that *we* do not have the power to do so."

"The power?" Margaret echoed. At last she looked at Portia with something other than contempt. His wife was being *very* patient.

"We suspect we have taken this matter as far as

it can go," Harry said. "Portia and I sense we have discovered the root of Fenella's curse. I believe she is on the run."

"What makes you say so?" Margaret asked.

"Because she's attacking me so virulently." He held up his left arm. "The curse is reacting in me even quicker than it has with Neal. I believe she is afraid."

"You sound as if she is in the next room," Margaret said.

"She could be," Harry answered. "One of those spells is for reincarnation. I have a theory, and it is more of a guess, that Fenella has reincarnated herself over the centuries so that she can keep the curse alive."

Margaret went pale. "This is madness."

"Aye," Harry agreed. He placed his hand on Portia's shoulder. "I don't want to go further with this, Margaret. I don't know how much time I have left, and I want to spend it with my wife."

"But what of defeating it?" Margaret demanded. "If you know so much, why stop now?"

"I can't go on," he answered. "She knows my weaknesses. I'm not strong enough," he said, and told her of his meeting with Lizzy.

"*I* can't give up," Margaret said. "I won't. You and Neal are all I have."

"Then pursue," Harry said. "But a soldier knows when he is facing an overwhelming force."

"Then I am fortunate to *not* be a soldier," his sister responded.

"We also know more about Rose," Portia said. "She was originally from Loch Awe."

"Where is that?" Margaret asked.

"South and east of here," Harry said. "I give you the book, Margaret, because you may be the one to see us free. The curse was placed upon us by a woman and done so to honor the spirit of a woman. Perhaps the reason we Chattan males have not been able to break it is that we are the wrong sex. We may be the weaker sex in this case."

Margaret considered the book in her hand. "I don't know," she whispered. "I've never done anything like this. I'm not strong like you and Neal."

"If anything, Margaret, you are the strongest of the three of us. Do not be afraid of your destiny."

The moment he spoke those words, it seemed as if the very air in the room changed.

Margaret held the book to the window's fading light. Tears welled in her eyes, but his sister was not one to cry. True to character, she angrily wiped them away.

"I accept the challenge, she said, her voice barely a whisper. "I shall leave now—"

"No," Harry said. "You must rest. You must let

your servants rest. Tomorrow will be time enough to begin the journey."

Margaret hesitated as if ready to argue. She was willful. But then her shoulders slumped and Harry recognized that he had been right, his sister was exhausted.

"I fear for you and Neal. What if I fail?" she whispered.

"You won't fail."

His sister seemed to draw courage from his conviction. She straightened. "I will not. I will travel to Loch Awe on the morrow, and Fenella of the Macnachtan had best beware."

For the briefest moment, the book seemed to glow in her hands. Uncertainty unsettled him.

"Perhaps I will go with you," he said.

"No, you are correct. I must go alone," she answered, staring at the book.

"Margaret," he said in protest, but she shook her head.

"We are both safer with you here, Harry. Think, the curse is having its effect on you quicker than it has on Neal. Why? Is it because you are close to Loch Awe and the Macnachtans? Right now, Neal is far too weak to travel. If the same happens to you, Harry, you will become a disadvantage to me because I will worry about you."

"True," he admitted. A warrior had to have

focus to go into battle and right now, he realized, his sister was a warrior.

She looked to Portia. "Keep him with you."

"I will."

"At least take my man Rowan," Harry protested. "He is as close as I can come to being with you myself."

She nodded and then took her first step toward Harry since she'd arrived. He put his arms around her and hugged her close. "God be with you, Margaret," he whispered.

"I will succeed," she promised. "And I'm not about to fall in love. I'm sorry to say such on your wedding day, but, for me, it is a foolish emotion. Look at what it has cost so many who are close to me." With that declaration, Margaret left the room.

Portia leaned against Harry. "Do you believe her safe?"

"I hope so," he said. "I pray so." He brushed his lips across her hair and held her close. "The one thing I know is that I do love you. And no witch may take that away from me."

Margaret

Of course Margaret could not sleep.

She spent a good portion of the night going over Fenella's book, trying to read the faded handwriting and make sense of words in the old Gaelic she didn't understand. She wanted answers, solutions, and she wanted them now. That she could lose both her brothers was a horrific thought. They were all the family she had left—save for Neal's unborn baby. And, if the curse went true to form, her new sister-in-marriage, Portia, was probably breeding as well.

Margaret could not stand aside and let those children be tainted with this curse.

The next morning, she was up early and ready to travel, anxious to be on her way to Loch Awe. She thanked General Montheath for the hospitality.

Harry and Portia managed to see her off. They both looked as if they hadn't slept a wink the night before and were none the worse for wear. Margaret could only sigh. Love had made her brothers addle-brained. Here she was so worried . . . and they were contentedly in love.

She did notice that Harry favored his left arm even more this day than he had the day before. He handed her his pistol and his ammunition bag.

"You know how to use this," he said. "I taught you. Guard yourself well."

"I shall," she answered.

Margaret then hugged her brother, gave a perfunctory kiss on the cheek to her new sister-in-marriage, and climbed into her coach.

She traveled with a retinue. Her abigail Smith accompanied her inside the coach. Smith was new to the staff. Margaret's longtime abigail, Rogers, had married one of the Lyon household footmen and had begged to stay in London. Margaret debated whether or not Smith would be with her long. The maid had very little personality and would never become the close confidant Rogers had been.

Four armed outriders, insisted upon by Neal, provided for Margaret's protection. There were also her driver, Thomas, a coachman, Balfour, and now Rowan, Harry's quiet Indian valet.

She wasn't overly fond of Rowan. His loyalty to Harry was unquestionable, and yet there was something Margaret didn't trust about him.

Thomas estimated they would reach Loch Awe in three, maybe six days' time, depending on the weather. "There is no direct line from here to there," he had informed Margaret. "Let us hope the weather is in our favor."

No matter how long the trip took, it would be *too* long for Margaret. She sat on the tufted velvet coach seat with her fists clenched, anxious to arrive at their destination—and uncertain of what to expect. Fenella's book was on the seat beside her. Her brother's gun was in a traveling bag at her feet.

A gentle mist had started outside. They'd had to close the windows against it. Margaret hoped it didn't turn into a rain or, worse, sleet. She'd heard traveling in the highlands in winter could be treacherous.

"You should relax, my lady," Smith advised. She was in the seat across from Margaret and was doing a bit of needlework to while away the time. Margaret didn't know how she concentrated on the stitches without feeling slightly ill, especially in such poor light. Margaret couldn't even read when she traveled.

"I'll relax when we arrive at Loch Awe," Margaret said. She'd not told the servants why they were making this trip. Balfour and Thomas, long-time retainers, were probably aware of the curse, but not the others. Well, save for Rowan.

And then she heard the meowing.

She frowned. "Smith, do you hear something?"

The maid scrunched her face and cocked an ear. "I don't hear anything out of the ordinary, my lady." She returned to her embroidery.

They traveled on and Margaret heard the sound again, loud and distinct this time. She scooted around on her seat. "I hear a cat. The sound is coming from the boot. No, it is coming from *beneath* the coach."

"I've not heard a sound other than the coach wheels and the horses," Smith replied. "Well, except for the arguing of the men in the box."

"Then something is wrong with your ears," Margaret answered. She knocked on the roof. There was a panel there that could be slid back and forth to allow her to speak to the coachman.

"Yes, my lady?" Balfour said. The misty rain splashed in through the door.

"There is a cat beneath the coach somewhere. Let us stop and rescue it."

"Now, my lady?"

"Of course," Margaret said, suddenly anxious

for the diversion. It helped to have another concern other than the curse. "I would feel sad if something happened to the cat and we had done nothing to help."

"A cat," Balfour repeated as if mystified.

"Yes, *a cat*," Margaret insisted.

The door was slid shut and within minutes the coach stopped.

The vehicle leaned as Balfour climbed down from the box. Margaret opened the door slightly. "Do you see the cat?"

"I beg your pardon, but I do not, my lady," Balfour said.

Margaret heard the meow again. "Oh for pity's sake," she said, pulling the hood of her cloak over her head and opening the door wider so she could step out of the coach.

Rowan and the driver had climbed down from the box as well. Thomas took this opportunity to check on the horses. The outriders also gave their horses a rest.

The road was muddy. Margaret lifted her skirts to protect the hem. She wore her walking boots, good, sensible shoes for the weather.

Balfour looked very aggrieved. "There is no cat, my lady."

Margaret had to see for herself. She bent down

to look at the undercarriage and there, clinging for her life, was a small, mud-covered cat.

"Poor kitty," she said, offering a hand.

The cat let go of her precarious perch and raced to Margaret's arms. Picking up the cat without a care to her gloves, Margaret said to Balfour, "See, there was a cat." She didn't wait for his response but cooed, "You poor muddy thing. Smith, hand me that shawl in the corner of the seat."

Silently, her face puckered with suspicion, Smith did as ordered.

Balfour said nothing, other than raising his eyebrows.

Margaret dismissed the servants' reactions. She was quite pleased with herself for saving the cat. Here was a project to help her pass the time.

She climbed back into the coach.

"Are we free to leave, my lady?" Thomas asked.

"Yes, of course," Margaret responded. She was busy using her shawl to wipe away the mud. Kitty did not like these ministrations but tolerated them.

Balfour shut the door.

"Oh, look, Smith, this cat is white beneath all this mud. And she has a funny head." Margaret held up the cat for her abigail to see. "Her ears are folded over. Poor thing to have deformed ears and yet how precious you look."

The cat purred and rubbed her cheek against Margaret's thumb, and Margaret was charmed.

Smith did not answer. Instead, she huddled into her corner of the coach with a look of grave concern on her face. Margaret tired of her sullenness. Some people just didn't like cats.

Obviously, Balfour and Smith were two of them.

The cat meowed.

Margaret smiled. "You are the sweetest thing. And what big eyes you have for a kitty. What is your name?"

Of course the cat didn't answer other than to continue its contented purring.

"Owl," Margaret said, the name coming to her, and it seemed to fit. "I shall call you Owl because you remind me of one with your funny ears and large eyes. Are you as wise as an owl?" she asked.

The cat meowed an answer and Margaret laughed. "We have a new travel companion, Smith. One that will keep us entertained on the way to Loch Awe. Owl. Such a precious little cat."

With a snap of the whip, the coach continued on its way.

Don't miss the next
romantic adventure in
Cathy Maxwell's
Chattan Curse series

The Devil's Heart

Coming 2013

Margaret Chattan knows that in 1814 no one should believe in curses, but she's convinced that her family is . . . and that it all began in 1632 . . .

London, 1632

"*R*ose can't have died. Not at her own hand," Charles Chattan said, repeating the words his clansman had just spoken to him.

"I'm sorry, Charlie, but she has," his cousin Drummond said in his clipped Highland brogue while reaching for another piece of beefsteak from a plate on the table before them. They sat in the kitchen before the fire. Drummond appeared worn to fatigue. It was a hard ride from Scotland to London and he had apparently not wasted any time in making it.

They were alone. Drummond had arrived only an hour earlier with "important news." The servants had woken Charles. He'd told them not to disturb his father and mother-in-law, Lord and

Lady Lyon or his wife, Patience. He wanted to speak to Drummond freely. He had assumed a messenger from Scotland would not be carrying good news, but he was unprepared for what Drummond had to say.

Charles's hands began to shake. He reached for the goblet in front of him. He downed the wine, wishing it was something stronger . . . and still his mind could not accept that his willful, vibrant Rose was no more.

"That's why the clan sent me here," Drummond said, hacking at his meat with his knife and shoving it in his mouth like a wolf. "The mood is ugly. Most blame you for her death."

"I blame myself." Charles pushed his chair away from the heavy table. He stood. "She should not have taken her own life."

"Aye."

"How did it happen?" Charles had to ask. He feared the answer.

"She jumped from the tower wall of her family's keep."

Apprehension hollowed Charles's stomach. "On what day?"

Drummond reached for his wine goblet and drank it down before answering, "Your wedding day."

A knife to the heart could not inflict more pain. Charles wanted to double over, to scream in horror, to rant and rave.

But he would not do that, not here in front of his clansman. Not here in the home of his English wife.

"I did not mean to harm her." Charles had to force the words past the tightness in his throat.

Drummond met his eye and then looked away, a muscle working in his jaw. For a second, Charles thought his cousin would not speak, but then he said, his voice low, "You handfasted her. Did you believe the lass had no pride?"

Guilt threatened to overwhelm Charles. It was staved off by the worm of resentment. "Handfasting is not marriage. The church frowns upon it. You know that. So did Rose. She understood I had to marry in the church."

Drummond pushed his plate aside as if he'd lost his appetite. He stared at some point at the far wall, his censure clear.

"I—" Charles started, wanting to defend himself, and realizing he couldn't. A long silence between them. Charles stared at the pattern of the kitchen's stone floor. *Rose. Dead.*

She'd been so vibrant, so beautiful, it was hard for him to imagine her not in this life.

"There's more," Drummond said, breaking the silence. "'Tis why my father sent me. Rose's mother, Fenella, has cursed you."

"Cursed me?" Charles raised a distracted hand to his head, combing his hair back with his fingers. "Yes, she should." His voice almost broke. He could not cry, not here in front of Drummond.

Not in front of anyone.

He would have to mourn Rose with his silence. There was too much at stake. His English father-in-law would not want his daughter's husband weeping for another woman.

Charles had loved Rose with all his being. He'd meant those handfasted vows they'd spoken between them. But there had been no formality, no witnesses. They'd been words shared between two lovers who had believed the world encompassed each other and nothing else.

He was wiser now. His parents had never liked Rose. They thought the Macnachtan a rebellious, coarse lot. They did not want their son and heir breeding with her.

When the very wealthy, very powerful English Earl of Lyon had approached Laird Chattan about matching Charles to his daughter, the answer had been yes.

These were uncertain times in the English court. Buckingham had been assassinated and the king was at odds with Parliament over the levying of taxes on the nobility. There was fear of a Catholic uprising.

Lyon had decided Scottish ties could protect his legacy by giving him an escape if England turned to civil war. He'd remembered Charles when he and his father had been presented at court. It was not vanity for Charles to admit he was a handsome young man. Lyon's daughter Patience was not attractive. She had buck teeth and weak eyes but Charles was confident his line would breed strength, and looks, into her.

In return for the marriage, Lyon offered a generous dowry that would add greatly to the Chattan coffers and, more importantly, the opportunity of a title. Procured for a very large sum of money was a royal prerogative granting the rights of Lyon's title to be passed down to Charles and Patience's firstborn son, a son yet to be conceived. Charles's parents urged him to waste no time in seeing that matter done. They liked England and enjoyed the delights of the city. They wished to remain there . . . something Charles knew his cousin Drummond and his clansmen would not admire.

He looked to Drummond now. "If I know Fenella, she'll curse me every day of her life."

"No, she'll not be able to do that, Charlie. The witch died by her own hand as well."

"*What?*"

"Rose couldn't be buried on holy ground, so Fenella had a funeral pyre built along Loch Awe's shore."

"She *burned* her daughter?"

" 'Tis the old way."

" 'Tis the *devil*'s way," Charles shot back.

"Aye, well, you won't like the rest of it then."

Charles sat in his chair. "Tell me."

"While her daughter's body burned, Fenella placed a curse upon you, Charlie, and upon your line. She then threw herself upon the fire and left this world burning with her daughter. They say her scream still echoes in the air."

The horror robbed Charles of breath. "How could she do that?"

"Rose was her favorite."

"But it's madness."

Drummond faced him, his expression bleak. "No madness is the curse, Charlie. Fenella's words damned you."

"She would." Charles reached for the wine bottle and drank from it.

"She had a power, one that seemed stronger than most."

"I don't know that I believe in witches," Charles said. *God, Rose dead. Why?*

"Her curse was that if you fall in love, *you* will die."

Drummond looked so concerned, Charles said, "You needn't worry there. My marriage is one of advantage. I have no love for my wife although she receives my high regard."

"The curse isn't just on you, Charlie, but on your line as well. Be wary."

Charles shook his head, suddenly overcome with grief. He could not stay here a moment longer lest he shame himself as a man. He needed to be alone. This was all too much to absorb. He didn't know what to think, what to believe. He stood. "The night porter will see to your bed, Drummond. Thank you for coming." It hurt his chest to speak. He didn't wait for an answer but stumbled toward the door.

It took all his strength to hold himself together until he reached the sanctuary of his bedroom. All was quiet, the fire in the hearth the only light. He fell onto his knees on the patch of rug in front of it—and the tears came. Big, choking sobs. He could not control them. They racked his body, releasing his grief to the world.

His Rose, his beautiful Rose. How could he have betrayed her love?

He'd meant those vows he'd made when they handfasted to each other. She was the only one who held his heart and now she was gone from him forever.

'Twas his father's doing that Charles hadn't married her. He'd swayed Charles by telling him the oldest had responsibilities. And it had been Charles's own vanity. He'd sold his soul for a title for his sons, and Rose had paid the price—

"Charles, what is it?"

Patience's sweet voice made him realize he was not alone. She must have heard his grieving from her room that adjoined his.

Hurriedly, he tried to gather himself up. He swiped his shirtsleeve across his ravaged face. "Nothing."

He felt Patience kneel on the floor behind him. He pressed his lips together, willing himself not to break.

She placed her arms around his shoulders, leaning her head next to his. "What is it, Charles?" she asked in her soft, gentle voice. "What grieves you so?"

He knew he shouldn't tell her. It would not be wise. A man didn't speak of past loves to his wife, and yet he could not help himself. He told her of Rose. He babbled of her, anguished tears breaking him down.

And Patience, dear, plain, sweet Patience, held him in her arms and listened.

She listened. Nothing more, nothing less.

But it was what Charles needed.

And when he was done, when his grief had its run, she told him it was all right. "She knows you love her, Charles. She knows that now."

"Her soul cannot be in heaven—"

Patience shushed his fear. They lay beside each other on the rug before the hearth, her arms still around him. "I cannot believe God would not forgive her. Her heart was broken, Charles, and no woman can bear a broken heart."

"*I* did that to her."

"You did," his wife agreed, "but you did it innocently. She was very lovely?"

He nodded.

"Then you may have assumed that someday she would find another to love. It would have been expected."

"Yes, that *is* what I thought, what I hoped," Charles whispered.

"Then it is not your fault she made a different choice," his wife said, soothing him. "It is not your fault." She kissed him then, a kiss that grew heated until they began making love right there on the floor.

His body responded. He grew hard and needy. He was young and strong and very male. A woman mourns a death, a man must replace. It was the way God made them.

As he entered his wife, it was as if Charles was coming home. Patience was kind. She was good. She was willing. She would never cause him the pain Rose had.

And in the moment when he watched his wife's plain face grow beautiful in the ecstasy of desire, Charles felt in himself the first stirrings of love. It was that easy.

His father had been right to steer him toward the Lyon heiress. She was good for him. He would be good for her.

He would love her.

Six months to the date after his wedding, Charles Chattan died. His heart stopped. He was sitting at his table, accepting congratulations from his dinner guests over the news his wife was breeding, when he fell facedown onto his plate.

The news of his death shocked many. He had been a vital, handsome man with much to live for. Had he not recently declared to many of his friends that he'd fallen in love with his new wife? How could God cut short his life, especially when he was so happy?

The only clue to his being unwell was that he had complained of a burning sensation in his left arm. It had been uncomfortable but his physician could find nothing wrong with him.

However, Chattan's marriage was not in vain. Seven months after his death, his wife bore a son to carry on the Chattan name . . . a son who also bore a curse.

And so it continued. They tried to stop the curse. Generation after generation attempted to break the witch's spell, and did not succeed.

Such was the power of Fenella.

The last days of December
1814

Margaret Chattan knew she was going to die.

She closed her eyes, pain searing through her body. Bones were broken. Her head hurt. Sleet fell down upon her but its coldness was no match for the numb certainty inside her that this was the end of her life.

The violence of the storm had caught them unawares. She'd been on her way to Loch Awe with coach, servants, and outriders. She'd felt completely safe in spite of undertaking this journey to battle a witch. Her brothers' lives were at stake and she'd stop at nothing to save them.

The road had been a good one through the mountains. Her drivers had not been worried even when the storm's winds had increased. The outriders, of course, traveled with the coach. They were all safer together.

And then, it was as if the storm had formed a huge hand and swept Margaret's coach and all the horses and all the men off the road. They'd gone tumbling down a granite slope. Margaret could still hear the screams of the horses, the shouts of the others, the breaking of wood as her coach had fallen apart.

She and her abigail, Smith, had been trapped in the coach. They'd been tossed over and over with the crashing wood until there came a moment when Margaret felt as if she'd been flung into the air.

How long she'd been unconscious, she did not know. When she'd regained her senses, it was to see Smith's face not far from her own, the maid's lifeless eyes wide with terror.

Here and there was a moan, or was that the wind through the trees? There was no stirring, no movement of life.

Her coach had been pushed off the road in a manner that defied any explanation devised by men—and Margaret knew it was Fenella.

The witch meant to claim them all.

The curse would live on.

Margaret had done nothing to stop it. She'd been prevented before she could try. She began to cry, silent tears that felt hot against her cold cheeks. She didn't cry for herself. No, she wept for her brothers' wives and the sons they would bear who would be marked with the curse.

And she would die here at the base of this mountain, alone.

A purring caught her attention.

Owl, the little cat that had stowed away in her coach. The cat with the funny, deformed ears and large, sad eyes. She'd forgotten about the animal.

The cat nudged her cheek, and then gave it a lick as if to wipe away the tears. Margaret yearned to touch Owl's soft fur and gather her up, but she could not move. Her arms were broken.

She felt Owl's breath upon her skin. The cat nestled itself into the space between Margaret's chin and shoulder. The purring grew louder and Margaret found herself thanking God she would not die alone.

Warmth replaced coldness. The purring vibrated through Margaret's being as she blissfully slipped from consciousness, her last thought being that she did not want to die . . .

You also won't want to miss

Lyon's Bride,

the first installment in
Cathy Maxwell's
Chattan Curse series.